ERIC JEROME DICKEY

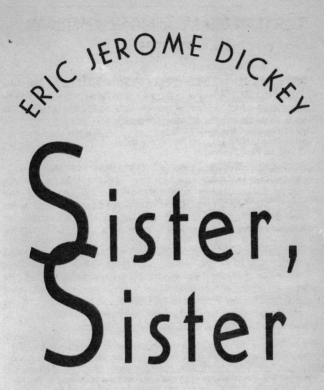

Sister, Sister

A SIGNET BOOK

SIGNET
Published by the Penguin Group
Penguin Putnam Inc., 375 Hudson Street,
New York, New York 10014, U.S.A.
Penguin Books Ltd, 27 Wrights Lane,
London W8 5TZ, England
Penguin Books Australia Ltd, Ringwood,
Victoria, Australia
Penguin Books Canada Ltd, 10 Alcorn Avenue,
Toronto, Ontario, Canada M4V 3B2
Penguin Books (N.Z.) Ltd, 182–190 Wairau Road,
Auckland 10, New Zealand

Penguin Books Ltd, Registered Offices:
Harmondsworth, Middlesex, England

First published by Signet, an imprint of Dutton Signet,
a member of Penguin Putnam Inc.

First Signet Printing, December, 1997
10 9 8 7 6 5 4 3 2 1

REGISTERED TRADEMARK—MARCA REGISTRADA

Printed in the United States of America

PUBLISHER'S NOTE
This is a work of fiction. Names, characters, places, and incidents either are
the product of the author's imagination or are used fictitiously, and any
resemblance to actual persons, living or dead, events, or locales is entirely
coincidental.

1 / **VALERIE**

Valerie knew Walter wasn't impotent. Not by a long shot. So, she figured it must be something about herself, something that she'd perhaps neglected, or maybe she wasn't trying hard enough.

During her married years, her stomach had softened and she'd grown vague love handles. Her body was no longer that of a firm collegiate cheerleader from UCLA. That figure she believed would live forever had gradually changed. Now she was at her heaviest, up to almost one-thirty-five, twenty aggravating pounds more than she carried in college. But still, not bad for being five-seven. Besides, like her mother, her top stayed slim and she carried most of her new weight in her hips and thighs.

And even though he was still his manly, handsome self and still wore his broad-shouldered, football-thick build, Walter had gradually gained almost forty unflattering pounds himself. Now at six feet, he weighed almost two-forty. Since he'd stopped working out, Walter had gotten lethargic and grown a noticeable gut. After college, despite his popularity, he didn't make the football draft and didn't make it as a walk-on. Over the last few years, he hadn't gotten much aerobic activity selling exotic cars.

After Valerie showered and powdered, she dropped her hooded housecoat and looked at herself in the full-length mirror, touching her skin and breasts almost as if she was getting to know herself, making sure she was as perfect as she could be. Other than her butt not being as ethnically shaped as she wished—sometimes she'd joke with her mother that her backside was a result of being the product of an interracial marriage—she was a far, far cry from a woman with an undesirable figure. Occasional comments from youthful studs who thought she was as young as they reassured her. She used to love the way men of most races avidly flattered her. Now she hungered for her husband's attention.

Her thick calves and small waist, her "happy tits," the things Walter used to rave about, never seemed to interest him anymore. The dry heat of September had come, reminding her that months had passed without him looking into her light green eyes. Now he looked away on the rare occasions he spoke to her and assumed she heard. He no longer pawed at her. The most affection she'd get would be when they bumped each other in the hall. Even then, she'd have to do it on purpose just so she could feel him and know he wasn't an apparition. At times she was afraid to touch him because he'd twitch and look at her like she'd committed a heinous wrong.

Before he came home from work, Valerie prepared. She put a Vanessa Williams CD in the player that her mother had given her and cleaned the house from top to bottom. Even though it was still fresh, she changed the linen in both of the other upstairs bedrooms. In the master bedroom, she made sure the chest of drawers was dust-free, that no spots or stains marred the vanity mirrors, that everything in the walk-in closet was organized. After she took all the dirty clothes to the laundry room, she wiped down the burgundy leather furniture in the den, then fluffed the plush pillows on the pure white living room sofa and love seat. Next, she took Windex and Soft Scrub to both the upstairs and the downstairs bathrooms, then the kitchen counters. By noon, everything sparkled with devotion.

She nervously smiled at the fresh new sheets on her king-size bed. Valerie had covered the love nest with a new soft paisley comforter that would glow amour under the dimmed lights. As sandalwood incense burned, she opened her cookbook and threw together Walter's favorite meal—Cajun-style chicken, red beans and rice, and a three-layer pineapple cake.

After her labor of love, she napped to make sure she would be rested. Then she thoroughly bathed, douched the cobwebs from her overly neglected womanhood, and put on a very sweet, lusty, rosy fragranced toilet water that she paid too much for. She'd bought the best, the most potent, negligee she could find—one with a beautiful, crotchless entry to add to her burning naughtiness. She bought red because of the way it complemented her fair skin.

She sat in the den and fidgeted, kept fixing herself up, then double-, triple-, quadruple-checked on all the already-perfect preparations. Still, after six years of marriage, she was as nervous as on the night she'd given him her virginity. He'd been her one and only.

But time had done something to their union. Either he'd become a stranger, or she'd become a stranger—which one she didn't know. But she wanted her old love back.

She did something else, something bold that she'd never done before. She put on a baseball cap, stuck on dark glasses, and drove from their middle-class tract located up in the safe Chino Hills down to the Pomona Indian Hill Swap Meet, waited until she thought no one was looking, at least no African-Americans, then slid into a video booth and bought two African-American XXX-rated movies—*Boomerwang* and *Baby Got Back*—for educational reasons. She wanted to see what the sisters were doing, how they did it, what the brothers expected, and maybe find out if there was something she didn't do right or needed to learn how to do—sort of size up the competition. All she managed to get was horny because she got caught up in watching explicit things that hadn't happened to her in too long.

Maybe she needed to change her look. *Try something fresh*, Valerie thought.

When he was on the phone, she'd overheard Walter raving to his brothers about how good actress Halle Berry looked with her contemporary, short hair style. He said when Halle was Miss Ohio, her hair was much longer, and now she looked even better, "like a woman."

So to please, to add to the spicing, to mold herself into something acceptable and attractive, she went to the beauty shop carrying a picture of Halle she'd cut off the cover of *Ebony* and had her back-length auburn hair mimicked down close and lightened.

Hair that she'd lived with all of her twenty-nine years, the one thing she swore she'd never let go of, was gone in a flash. With each opening and closing of the scissors, her heart bled. With her hands balled tightly in her lap, she cringed and fought back a few tears with every strand that was abandoned. When the ecstatic hairdresser turned Valerie around to see the result, she only looked down at the floor and stared in disbelief at her pride, which had recklessly fallen to the ground. Fallen for him. Even when the other ladies in the shop told her that the "fresh cut" and new color seriously complemented her youthful, round face, she found no room in her heart to smile under her mourning. Sixty dollars and two hours of self-destruction.

Walter came home an hour later than usual and noticed nothing. At least he said nothing about what he noticed before he showered, fumbled with the alarm clock, crawled under the covers, and made his camp on the far side of the bed. This Friday night she didn't want to give up that easy.

In the middle of the night, she woke up and watched him sleep. Too much on her mind, too many wanting sensations running crazed in her body. Her urges needed to be baptized. As he slept, she slowly and gently began masturbating him. When it stood at a groggy attention, she eased the covers back and stared at it, eyes to eye.

"Hello, stranger. Nice to see you."

He hardly shifted when she began kissing and licking his manhood. When she put him inside her mouth, he lengthened, he moaned, he wiggled. She felt herself getting excited when his hips started to gyrate. She knew she was going to have her way.

But then he suddenly woke up, looked down at her, and asked a disgusted, "W-W-What are you doing?"

She continued savoring as she smiled up at him. He gently put his hands down on the side of her face. She thought he was going to help in the overdue therapy, to re-consummate the marriage, but he pushed her head back, pulled himself out of her mouth, and yanked the covers back on top of himself.

"Can I get on top? Walter, let me get on top. Baby, I know you've had a long day. I'll do all the work. It won't take me but a minute to please both of us, then we can cuddle up and go back to sleep. Walter? I need you, baby."

He said a curt, "Shhh, Valerie. Tired."

"Will you just touch me then? Let me put my head on your should—"

"SHHHHHH!"

She bit her lip, held her tongue, lay back wide-eyed, stared at the ceiling and made herself not cry. Fighting the tears made her head ache. A few minutes later, he pushed the covers back and stormed into the bathroom. She habitually moved closer to his side so he'd have to touch her when he got back into the bed. He closed the door and it was quiet, too quiet. No sounds of fluids breaking fluids. No water running. Silent. A minute later, she heard him let out a rude, muffled groan. The bathroom door unlocked and opened. When Walter walked back out, he didn't flush the toilet or wash his hands. When he crawled back under the covers, she waited to feel him bump her before scooting back to her side. His body temperature was up. His penis, a self-satisfied limp. She moved to the far side of the bed. All of her urges to touch him or be touched by him had died. Two minutes later, he was sound asleep.

She mumbled, "I should've bit that fucker off."

2 / **CHIQUITA**

He kept hollering my doggone name. Yelling like it was going out of style, "Chiquita!"

My body was hot and upset from anger. There was sweat all up and down my arms. Across my breasts and down my legs too. Over and over, I kept pulling at my natural. Then stomping my feet on the round tan rug and repeating, "Go away."

"Open the damn bathroom door."

"So you can hit me again?"

I was trying to clear my head and figure out how I ended up in the middle of this tragedy. It was one of those days when a sistah stared into the mirror of life and said to her teary-eyed reflection, 'This bullstuff couldn't be happening to me *again*,' because this was the kinda crap that happened to other folks.

"I'm sorry." He was pouting like that was going to make me feel better about the vulgar phone call. "It was an accident."

"Accident, my ass." That *accident* made me think about when I saw my own momma get beat. A woman never forgot bullstuff like that. After I'd witnessed that with my own five-year-old eyes, I'd sworn that no lover man would ever touch me and live to tell about it. But I'd run away from my man as soon as I felt the pain. I snapped, "What if you had knocked my teeth out?"

"Chiquita, listen. You were tripping and I was just trying to get my phone back from you and you slipped."

"I slipped into your fist and damn near split my lip?"

"Hey, I didn't hit you."

"Yeah, right. Any-who. So what's up with your ex?"

"You already knew about her."

"But evidently she didn't know about me and you."

"She was lying. Don't get played like that."

"You just bought the c-phone, how'd she get your number?"

"For the last time, I don't know."

"That's a convenient memory lapse. Especially since you can't remember to give me the doggone cellular number."

Arrrgh! First off, I wanted to know how I ended up here. Mentally. What the hell was I doing wrong? I dropped my ten percent in the tithe plate whenever my work schedule let me get enough rest to go to church. Plus I had my application in to Big Brothers and Big Sisters down here in San Diego so I could help pull a sistah over the wall. But right now I was wondering how I was going to help somebody else if I couldn't help my doggone self.

My eyes looked deep into my empty, damp hands. Searched like I was looking for the answer to my future through my past. And my hands seemed so small. Like a weak future. And I felt like I was my grandmother's baby, Big Momma's child again. Then a knock on the door broke my trance.

I said, "I ought to call the police."

"For what? Chiquita." I heard his sigh. "You're tired and overreacting to nothing. Don't let her mess up our weekend."

"Don't try to reverse-psychology me. I don't appreciate you grabbing my wrists and manhandling me over some stupid phone."

"If you had've let it go," he grunted. "Hey, I'm sorry."

"Sorry?" I was hollering so loud I didn't recognize my own voice. "You body-slammed me on the bed. What kinda shit is that for a grown-ass man to do to a woman, huh?"

"We got out of hand for a minute."

"We? You had some heifer calling my house talking smack."

"Want me to get her on the phone so we can talk?"

"Get the hell out of my place."

"I was on the road in traffic for two hours, then up half the night, and you kicking me out? You serious?"

"Do I sound serious?"

Why was I locked inside my own damn bathroom like a prisoner of love? Naked. Sitting on the edge

14

of the cold bathtub. Shivering like I had the fever of death. Crying like it was my last cry. Holding my throbbing lip that felt like it had been stung by a bee. All while my so-called lover man of the last few months stood on the other side of the door, shaking on the handle and banging on the wood like he wanted to break it down. Why?

Well he had left his c-phone on my nightstand when he came in from Los Angeles last night. I guess he forgot it was turned on. It rang at six a.m. Why did I answer it when I knew the call couldn't possibly be for me? Plain and simple. Because I wanted to know who the hell was calling him at six a.m. Now it could've been his j-o-b, but something in my gut—call it a woman's intuition—didn't think so. Last time when I saw she'd left something behind at his place, he said it was there because she'd dropped by to get the last of her things. And she'd probably left it in the bathroom on purpose to start something. That *it* was an un-new tampon. He told me to think about it. If she was on her period, then obviously nothing happened when she came by and she had to do it on purpose. That was what he said.

My lover had taken a three-day weekend and come down to take me back up to his place. That way we could ride the coast highway with the cool air and ocean on our sides and spend some quality time. We hadn't seen each other in almost two weeks. Not since he'd helped me find a jamming car at the Rancho Cucamonga Auto Auction. That lapse in the relationship was because of my coast-to-coast flight schedule, so when we laid eyes on each other a few hours ago our hormones took over and took us straight to bed. Well, almost to bed. We didn't make it out of the living room. I still had on my blue flight attendant uniform. He was still draped in his olive suit that he'd worn to work.

——And like I said, when he woke up from his love slumber and went to get his clothes out of his car, the c-phone rang. So I pulled the pillow off my head and answered. And of course it was a sistah who was trying to figure out where *her* man had gone. Why he wasn't at home when she went by his place last night. And wanted to know why I was answering his c-phone "at six in the goddamn morning." My voice was still love hungover and groggy. Almost like I was dreaming. I told her who I was, because honestly I knew my sistah had the wrong number.

I sat up, clicked on the brass light on my oak nightstand, and said to her, "I'm sorry, but I didn't catch your name."

"I didn't throw it, hoe," she snapped. "Bitch, get off his dime and put the nigger on the phone."

"Excuse me?" That was when I snapped, threw my peach comforter off me and started hollering like a fool. Right about that time he walked back in with his overnight bag and tried to wrestle his c-phone back. But I had a grip on it because I had a few four-letter, one-syllable things to say. Bastard threw me down on the bed. But I didn't let go of the phone.

Next thing I knew my damn lip had been hit some kind of way.

He knocked on the bathroom door again. "I took a day off work to be with you and this is what I get? You're always complaining about me working so much, you know how many sales I'm passing up to spend time with you? And you want me to leave?"

"Damn right."

"Call me when you calm down and come to your senses. I'm gone." I heard him pick up his bags. Keys jingled. A moment later my front door opened and closed. I exhaled. Hard.

Then I really cried. For me, I cried. My tears wouldn't stop. Unlike most brothers, my lover hadn't ever done anything to make me think he wasn't trustworthy. For anything that was uncertain, he had a quick and easy explanation for it. Real quick. Real easy. But at this time of morning, the sistah's words sounded so angry and believable. But she could've been lying for GP, general purpose. Sistahs were devious and would do worse. I know because I'd done things worse than that myself.

My lip throbbed. Each pulse made me think about my mother under that table. When I closed my eyes I saw her face cringe when she was struck down by a pissed-off lover man. It scared me more because she looked just like me.

And of course this was my fault. Because I answered the phone. Because he said the other heifer meant nothing to him. That he loved me and she was just an immature sistah he used to date way back when. A silly woman who was playing mind games at the crack of dawn. He was willing to call her back to prove his point. And he had already given me keys to his apartment up in LA County months ago. That gesture felt like an open invitation to his heart, because him handing me those two shiny pieces of metal sure opened mine. Softened me up with hope. And he reminded me that he was here with me, had loved me with a passion last night and had made plans for us to enjoy the weekend.

I wiped my eyes and looked in the mirror. There wasn't anything wrong with my lip that a couple of minutes of ice couldn't fix. But I was irate because he had touched my doggone face. Had gotten hostile. Accidentally or on purpose, that pissed me the hell off. A harsh touch could turn into a vicious slap. A slap into a fist. A fist into a kick. A kick into a stomp while I cringed under a table. Then the next thing I know I'd be taking Polaroids of my swollen face and locking them in a safety deposit box in case the fool tried to kill me.

Not only that but my panties were in a serious bunch because of the six a.m. wake-up call. Plus I was mad at him because he left. Now I was alone. Damn. I had wanted to get out of San Diego. I didn't want to spend my three days off by myself. All my girlfriends were either on flights, personal trips, married, with their lover men, or lived in Atlanta.

And I'd have to admit I was sprung on my lover

and really looked forward to being with him, undisturbed.

Maybe I was wrong about what I did. Maybe not what I did, but the way I did it. My nose should've stayed in my business and let that call come and go. Then opened my eyes a little wider and kept my ears to the ground. I mean, off and on, I've had a few ex's call me to touch base at weird hours for no reason. Just to say hi.

Even with an innocent hi, ten minutes into the conversation their words would drift to talking about yesterdays. Their voices would dip an octave or two and I knew what they really wanted.

But my lover man didn't sound like the girl meant anything to him.

So I told myself that I didn't have a reason to be upset.

3 / **VALERIE**

Valerie woke the next morning to the sounds of a football game and Walter's scream-cheers migrating up from the den. She didn't know when she had finally dozed off. Didn't know when Friday gave way to another Saturday. The last thing she remembered hearing was what sounded like the paperboy throwing the *Daily Bulletin* against the front door. She remembered it was getting light out before her eyes closed. Walter's navy pinstripe suit and vivid red tie from the night before were still draped across his wooden valet. His starched white shirt had fallen onto the floor. Cuff links and pocket change were scattered on his nightstand in front of his golden "Salesman-of-the-Year" statuette. His cellular phone was next to that.

She ran her fingers through her hair and freaked because she'd already forgotten that she'd butchered herself.

"Gone," she mumbled, then moved her jewelry box and Bible to the side so she could get a good look at their wedding picture on her nightstand. Him in a coal-black tuxedo and aqua cummerbund. Her in a stunning Victorian lace wedding gown and veil. Both smiling. Both touching. Both younger.

Funny, but she didn't realize how long her hair was until she cut it off. Now her head felt funny. The cool breeze from the ceiling fan that ran across her neck and scalp was a new, awkward sensation. As she twisted her head, her neck felt too light, strong without all the hair.

She pulled her gown down over both shoulders and went through her ritual of using the tips of her fingers to massage circles in her breasts, checking to make sure she wasn't getting any of the lumps that stole her mother's mother from them last year.

When she finished, Valerie looked down at her wasted negligee, covered it with her green hooded housecoat, meandered down the stairs, and walked across the shiny parquet floors into the carpeted den. Walter was dressed in jean shorts and a Howard T-shirt, sitting in his favorite big leather chair with both feet propped up on the ottoman, arguing with the referee inside the television set. As she strummed her fingernails along the doorframe, Valerie cleared her throat. Walter glanced at her, stroked his pencil-thin moustache, then put his eyes deeper into the entertainment center. She stood there for a few seconds, debating if she should say anything.

"You okay?" she asked as she put her backside against the doorframe. "What was wrong with you last night?"

He didn't look her way. "Morning."

"What's up, Walt? Why you keep pushing me

away? Have I done something to offend you? If I have then—"

"Shhh. I'm watching the game."

"You still too tired to come back to bed?"

"I just took a shower."

"We've got plenty soap and water."

"Valerie, do you mind? The game. Redskins and Cowboys."

"Wouldn't you rather talk to me? I cut and styled my hair. What do you think?"

No look, no answer.

"You want to go out to dinner tonight? My treat."

No look, no answer. She stood in the door and watched him watch the game. So much passion, so much intensity. So much attention. Again, she stood neglected and jealous.

"You can remember the name of every damn player in the NFL. Every last one of 'em, even the ones who don't play in the damn game, and you've never met any of 'em. Not a one. You've known my family for damn near nine years and can't get their names right."

Walter turned up the volume. She thought about walking over and slapping the remote out of his hand, but reneged when the phone rang. If it was for her—maybe her early-bird mother, maybe her bitchy sister or roughneck younger brother, maybe somebody calling from the temp agency—she wouldn't want the noises from an argument transmitted over the phone. In her anguish, she wanted to exercise tact and keep her personal business in check. Especially from her "friends" at work. As long as everybody at the agency assumed she was happy, they wouldn't be concerned.

Between the first and second ring, tired-ass Walter sprung past her to the wall phone in the kitchen and answered it with enthusiasm. It was for him. He lit up, laughed, and had plenty to say to whoever called. Whoever it was had to be damn important because he turned his back on the game and ignored the Redskins and Cowboys for them.

This morning, she felt like an old twenty-nine. When there was nothing to look forward to, a twenty-four-hour day seemed to last more than forty-eight. Her last nine months felt like they had lasted about twelve dog-years.

Valerie threw on a golden Kente-patterned sweatsuit and stormed out the door without washing her face or brushing her teeth. When she drove up the street, she slowed as she passed by one of the newer neighbors who was out running. Even though she'd seen him several times over the last few months, she didn't have the slightest idea who he was or where he lived. Short stylish hair with light sideburns. He was a clean-cut, pretty man. Maybe thirty. He always ran in different pastel-colored jogging shorts and no top, the few hairs on his chest holding his sweat. About five-nine, maybe five-ten, with caramel-flavored skin and an agile distance-runner's build. He always moved forward with a strong, even pace. When he saw her car, he smiled, made eye contact and waved. She blew her horn, shyly smiled at her unknown friend and finger-waved back. As she drove off in the opposite direction, she watched him in the rearview mirror. When he faded over the hill, she touched the ring on her left hand, then frowned and whispered to herself, "I'm married."

4 / CHIQUITA

The sun was up. The morning air was cool. Low clouds were moving away. Dew was on the copper plants, pine trees, and abelias outside of my first-floor window. I even thought the birds were chirping for once. San Diego was coming alive. And I was bored.

After I read a few pages of Susan Taylor's *In the Spirit* and tried to get my mind going on a more upbeat note, I took a long warm shower and oiled my skin. Then I washed and conditioned my hair with some KEMI I'd bought when I had a flight to Miami. It hit me that I was tired, had a touch of jet lag, but couldn't sleep. The bullstuff I had gone through at the crack of dawn left me too high-strung. To top that off, the Mexicans who landscaped the grounds were right under my bedroom window. Both of them had those Ghostbuster-looking blower thingamajigs on their backs. Each engine was humming loud as hell. All that noise just to rearrange dirt.

There wasn't much to do so far as cleaning up my apartment. Just mop the tile in the kitchen and bathroom, vacuum from the bedroom to the living room, unpack the garments I'd taken on my two-day trip, and put my scattered clothes where they belonged. The bathroom's shower wall needed a once-over because I hated that gritty feeling the cleanser left behind. My Rollerblades and racquet-balls were in the hallway, but I didn't move them.

Since I hadn't committed myself to the city, outside of my kitchen being packed with cooking utensils, my apartment didn't have much furniture. It made it easy for me to leave. My so-called bed was really a queen-size futon with a soft beige mattress, red comforter, set off by flowers and many rainbow-colored pillows. With the white walls, the sunlight kept it looking like a happy room. The closet had built-in drawers inside, so that was where I kept all of my personals and lingerie. I liked the open space. And I did what I wanted. I'd never had parents so there was no parental pressure. My uncle was never concerned with the who's and what's of my life. We basically had shallow five-minute conversations a few times a year and sent preprinted cards for the heavy holidays. He never talked about my past and neither did I. Our own denial. I loved the freedom. Enjoyed my own place and things. But independence could wreak havoc on a sistah's pocketbook. And a past made relationships hard.

My living room had a few jazzy pictures on the wall, enough to make the place look lived in, plus I'd bought about ten black-and-white postcards with artists like Louis Armstrong and Ella Fitzgerald pictured and had framed them. My creative side expressed. Pictures of my grandparents, Big Momma and Big Daddy, were on top of my speakers. The only thing in the living room was my stereo, CD player, television, and more plants and pillows.

After I realized my lover man wasn't just going to drive around and think of a bulletproof lie before coming back, I had thrown on some beat-up dark green sweatpants and green T-shirt and started working out to my Donna Richardson tape. I'd mess up my shower, but that way I could keep my thighs toned and burn off some frustration at the same time. Maybe later I'd pamper myself and get my nails done. Maybe even bust my budget and go for a full-body massage. But I needed to just lay out on the beach and get some free sun. Or throw on my jean shorts and go skate on the boardwalk. I had a girlfriend who used to live down here, an attendant named Shelby, who I used to hang out with. Her man wanted her by his side in LA and moved her up, lock, stock, and barrel. If she wasn't tied to his side she could hop on a flight and be here in thirty minutes. Or vice versa. Maybe I'd call her later and see what her weekend looked like.

Just as I got into my sit-ups, the phone rang. That was the first time I had looked at my watch. It was right before ten. I had been exercising for over an hour and a half, actually if I included warm-up and stretching, closer to two. I was soaked.

When I caught my breath and answered, it was a

male flight attendant from work. He'd gotten my number off the board and wanted to know if I wanted to pick up a two-day trip. And since I was free for the weekend, it sounded like something to do.

"Yeah, I've got time." I got a pen and paper. "Where to?"

"A turnaround to Memphis."

I paused. "I don't do Memphis."

"Oh. The board said you wanted to pick up some extra hours."

"To anywhere but Memphis."

He sounded put off. "Mind if I ask why?"

"Yes. I mind if you ask why."

"Well, thanks anyway."

I'd hung up before he finished his good-bye. Before I could clear my head from the past and get back to my workout, the phone rang again. This time it was my current lover man. My one and only. The first thing he said was, "I'm trying to make this the best relationship that I can."

I tisked then took a long swallow of Evian.

"I love you."

I wiped my sweaty upper lip then said my driest, "Uh huh."

"You're pushing me away and can't even see it, can you?"

His loving tone scared me in a good way but I didn't say anything. Sometimes a woman needed more than words.

"Chiquita?"

I said, "Where are you?"

"Back home."

"You made it to LA that quick?"

"No traffic."

"Forget something?"

"I wanted to make sure your face was okay."

"Thanks for caring after the fact."

"You know I didn't hit you on purpose."

"I don't know. You could've at least offered to get me some ice."

"You were acting so indignant . . . I didn't want your neighbors to hear us screaming like a pack of heathens."

"I don't care what they heard. I don't say a dog-gone thing when they play that rock music loud as hell." I exhaled. "Tell me, why did you rush out after she called?"

"You put me out."

"You didn't hesitate to rush out of here."

"Don't start. Think about it. You think I'd give you keys to my place and be messing around?"

"Where are you?"

"Home."

"If you're at home now, why are you on that c-phone?"

"It's a cheaper rate than AT&T."

"That don't sound right. It doesn't *ring* true."

"Don't start with that, okay?"

We got into the same old discussion. The other

open issue. Since we'd been seeing each other long enough and he kept saying he loved me so much, I wanted to know why he hadn't at least bought me a ring. Especially since when we first started dating, he told me that I was the type of woman he wanted to marry. I didn't bring it up—he did and planted the seed, so I'm not the one tripping. So where's the ring? Not an engagement ring or nothing like that, because I'm not interested in touring bridal registries or shopping at Robinson's for housewares, just a little something-something that was a token of how he felt about me, about us with a chance at a future. Since he was a thirty-two-year-old man, seven years older than me, had never been married, no children, still living in an apartment, I'd think he'd start thinking about moving to the next level.

What pissed me off, other than him teasing my emotions with a fake promise of matrimony, was that he already knew that something serious was what I wanted and how I felt. He'd been hollering that he'd think about a ring, but in the meantime he was so doggone broke. So I let it be. Then he ran out and bought a brand-new palm-size video camera and equipment. Over a thousand dollars for some bull-stuff that would be passé in less than six months. Which was a slap in my face. I told him that camera would last a few years, but my love would last a lifetime.

"Oh," he said, "now we're getting to what the real problem is. Your expectations."

"No, your promises," I said. "All I'm stressing is if I'm not the one and can't be the one, let me know so we can part as friends and see other people. It won't be anybody's fault."

"What's up? You don't like what we got? Why you want to see somebody else when you know what I feel for you?"

"I don't want to but I will. I'm not moving to LA because of a man, and you're not moving to San Diego because you said you can't find a sales job this way, plus I'd rather be in a relationship with some- body who is accessible and a local call."

I already knew that brothers had two types of women in their lives—the group they fucked and the ones they married. And the way he hopped my crav- ing bones as soon as he got here last night left me wondering. Before I kept on wasting my time and money on a long-distance-bill relationship, I wanted to know what category I fell into.

I said, "If I'm good enough to screw and not good enough to marry, let me know so I can decide if I want this to go on."

Then he started reminding me of the things he'd done for me, like last month he drove down and picked me up, then took me back up to the LA car auction and helped me find a slamming Mazda. Based on what the people at the used car lot told me, I only had enough money for a Hyundai, but my lover man knew about the car market and did get me a deal and a half. I'd have to admit that he wasn't a good boyfriend, he was a great boyfriend, and that made the whole situation worse. Especially since I knew I felt as much for him as he claimed he did for me.

At times I'd felt like I was the luckiest woman alive to have a chocolate-coated angel like him, somebody who had patience to put up with a bugged-out girlfriend like me. A great *boy*friend. But sometimes a fully developed woman wanted to know she had more than just a boy in her life. More than just a friend.

"First off," he said, "why do you think I'm always messing with somebody? What have you seen?"

"Nothing."

"Then you must be guilty and projecting it back at me."

"Really? I guess you forgot about the wake-up call."

"That was about nothing."

"Nothing? It was enough to make me want to get tested again."

Another thing that disturbed me was whenever I went to his place it was clean. Too clean. All the trash was taken out before I got there. No dishes in the sink. Bathroom still smelled like Soft Scrub. Toilet seat up. Not a crumb on the carpet. And he wasn't an obsessive-compulsive, because after I got there he didn't clean up a doggone thing until after I left. It was more like he was hiding something. Especially since anything I left behind was neatly put away inside his hall closet. Too neat to not be suspicious. Plus he was never at home. Most of his messages rolled over to a service. Which made me wonder if he lived there, or was married and had that place on the side.

And I thought all of that just because he was tidy. But I guess that's better than being with a nasty man, especially since cleanliness was next to godliness.

He said, "You could put in for a transfer and move to LA when it came through."

"You asking me to move in with you?"

"I could help you find your own place closer to LAX."

"You mean in a separate part of town?"

"Yeah."

That was when I said good-bye and hung up. One of us was missing the point. I still wouldn't have packed up my life and moved to LA and shacked with him. I needed my own space. The point was he didn't even offer.

5 / **VALERIE**

Fifteen minutes after she left home, Valerie had driven down the 71 expressway and was in Diamond Bar at her sister's spacious one-bedroom apartment, over-ringing the bell. Inda opened the door, dressed in a big Pocahontas T-shirt, Dumbo slippers, and a much too nasty frown on her face. Inda looked like she still had a little makeup on from the night before. Her untamed, thick, straight black hair made her look wild and uncivilized.

Inda was dark like their father, and Valerie had most of her mother's features—the oval face, full bottom lip, and especially the green eyes—so they didn't look like true sisters. Even their brown-skinned, wavy-haired, 27-year-old brother looked like a distant cousin. Thaddeus's complexion fell somewhere in between theirs. Thaddeus and Inda had light brown eyes like their father.

Inda snatched the door open and walked off. "Who the fuck died and why the hell you have to come tell me this early? If it's a damn emergency, go dial 911."

"Black, shut up."

Inda growled more obscenities as she stepped over

34

her lethargic gray attack-cat, Carlton. She scratched her backside, staggered back over and crashed on the couch. "It's not even nine. Damn, Red. Between your ass popping up and ringing my doorbell like you gone crazy, and Moms calling so fucking early for no damn reason, y'all won't let a sistuh get no sleep."

Valerie opened the patio door to let some of the stale, cat-smelling air out. "We don't sleep, you don't sleep."

"Don't make me put you out."

Valerie peeped toward the bedroom and saw the door was closed. "Company?"

"Nope." Inda scratched her nose, then scrunched her face. "Raymond's tripping and hasn't called me since Tuesday. He's playing that mad role so he can get his weekend and go mess off. I bet he got some tickets to Def Comedy Jam at the Celebrity and took somebody else. They had an all-woman show with big-mouth Adell what's-her-face and that sistuh Edwonda White."

"Edwonda's hysterical." Valerie walked over and sat on Inda. "What'd you do last night?"

"Move before you make me mad," Inda said and pushed Valerie down onto the Oriental rug. "Went by Main Street."

"How was it?" she asked. Paperwork from when Inda had to write reports for the courts was stacked neatly on the table. Valerie moved a couple of psychology books and picked up her hardback *Waiting to Exhale* off the stained-glass coffee table. The bookmark showed that Inda was only about halfway finished. She'd borrowed it over six months ago. Valerie looked at the back cover and smiled at Terry McMillan's confident, stunning picture and wondered what she was like. "How was Main Street?"

"Tired. Wasted ten dollars, stayed forty minutes. Wasn't a good twenty people up there. Met a guy named Tyrone Bynum, but I threw away his number as soon as he walked off because he was wearing a tired-ass pinkie ring. Left there and drove out to Santa Monica and kicked it at Tilly's Terrace. Fifteen more dollars. But, Red, it was live. Got me three solid numbers."

As Inda turned her back and forced her face deep into one of the fat pillows on the soft, beige-colored sofa, Valerie restlessly walked around and fooled with the plants. Inda had so many houseplants the apartment looked like a small forest. Big ones, little ones. Tall, tree-ish ones stood in opposing corners. Inda had a talent and could make any plant grow forever, but could make a relationship die quickly. Valerie sat on the arm of the sofa and tickled Inda's very sensitive feet.

"STOP-IT-RED-DAMMIT-YOU-MAKING-ME-MAD!"

"Wake up."

"RED!" Inda whined, kicked her feet and started beating her hand into the sofa. "Pleeeease take your ass back home."

"Throw on some clothes. I need to talk to some-body and big sister, you're it."

"You must be crazy. I'm out of it. I don't want to hear nothing but me snoring."

"I ain't had no sleep, either. I was up all night."

Inda stretched as she yawned and smiled. "Heeeyy! Walter finally come through?"

"Hell no. I'll drive. Sleep in the car."

"Where you going this time of morning?"

"Venice."

Inda finally opened her eyes. "WHAT THE HELL YOU DO TO YOUR HAIR??!!"

6 / **VALERIE**

Ten-thirty.

They found plenty of parking on the streets and only had to walk a half-mile to the Muscle Beach section. The waterfront was just coming alive. Crowds of multiethnic people were taking advantage of the roomy boardwalk and jogging before the strip got its typical weekend crowd. Rollerbladers, bikers, and the more serious runners whizzed up and down the bike trail. A few thick men and a couple of too-solid women were out lifting weights. Right next to them, the concrete bleachers and several basketball courts were getting crowded with people who came to watch an all-day full-court tournament. East of that, some women were doing Olympic-caliber gymnastics on the metal parallel bars.

Valerie sprung for brunch at the Sidewalk Cafe. After they ate, they strolled down the breezy promenade into one of the shops and bought some lighter clothing, T-shirts and boxer shorts, changed clothes, then got a cheap made-in-Mexico blanket from a boardwalk vendor and went barefoot out to the sand.

After she got the sand from in between her toes, Inda lay on her back and mumbled, "Like I need a tan. Red, save me a corner of that soda, okay? We should've got some suntan lotion. I don't want to get burned and peel. If I get skin cancer, that's your ass. Scratch my booty."

"Excuse me?"

"I just wanted to see if you were listening."

Valerie took a quick swallow and handed Inda the rest of the grape Snapple before she lay down on her stomach. Inda downed the last half in one long swallow. "Ahhhh. Good. Wake me in fifteen. And make sure don't no perverts sneak by and snapshot my ass."

Valerie flipped over on her back and turned her head away from the hard-breathing Inda. Valerie closed her eyes and let her senses flow. The sun was out, but it didn't feel hot. The slightly cool wind from the ocean felt good on her as it graced her skin. The way it gently ran up her back, the way it breezed through her legs and over her chest, how it lightly kissed across her face made her wish for what she was trying to forget. With her eyes closed, she reached out to touch her secret, elusive lover, but felt nothing. Still, every few seconds an experienced gust would fondle her, then rush away. The air finished its molesting and calmed thirty minutes later.

Then she sat up and thought about her choices.

She'd quit college in her senior year to follow Walter back East when he thought he had a shot at the NFL. Over the years, he'd failed to make two teams on the East Coast, two teams on the West Coast. But she never threw it in his face. She'd given him one hundred percent of herself. Love made her do that.

She looked at Inda, a moving target who had always been hard to pin down. Thirty-two and more culturally hip than her younger sister. Her smart ass had walked through Atlanta's Clark University in three and a half years. She got her MBA from Stanford a little over two years after that. Now she was a hardcore, no-nonsense social worker. Her coworkers respected her because of her commitment. Clients hated her because she "don't take no shit." She worked ten-hour days, four days a week, and had her Mondays to herself.

"Black? Sleep?"

"Almost." Inda moaned, rolled over, then folded her arms under her head as if she was preparing for a serious nap.

"I'm going to do it with somebody else," Valerie said.

Inda waved her off. "Anyway . . ."

"Serious."

"You know you're not going to get a boyfriend. Even though I think you should've a long time ago."

"Serious."

"You know you don't have it in you to mess around. You make Mother Teresa look like a hoochie mama."

"I was just thinking of how Walter used to be. We'd drive into LA to hang out. Out by the airport at the Golden Tail. He'd dance with me on every slow song. He'd always pull me into him and grind. A nice, slow grind. Two, three records in a row. Sometimes when the record switched to a fast song, we'd keep on slow dancing. When the song went off, I'd always stand close to the front of him so nobody could see he had a hard-on. Couple of times we got so hot for each other, we left and got a room."

"Used-to-be's don't count for today. It's always like that. Andre was like that. Next thing I knew, I couldn't even get him to get up and go get me a towel when we got through getting busy."

"What's the big deal about a towel?"

"It's not the towel. It's the consideration."

"Oh."

"Or lack of consideration. That's when our marriage went downhill. That wasn't *the* reason, but it was definitely a sign. They stop touching you as much. One day they don't kiss you while you're making love, don't hold you after, start acting like they're doing it to a hoe or something. Screwing out of obligation or something. Then they stop doing that. Sex is communication, and when his dick stops talking to you, you'd best believe it's starting to talk to somebody else. Having *loooong* conversations. The next thing you know, both of you in front of the judge trying to take as much from the other and keep as much you can. Irreconcilable differences."

Valerie's voice was soft. "You right."

"What happened?"

Valerie exhaled, "Don't know. Don't even fucking

know. It's hard loving somebody when they don't love you. Especially when you in the same house, in the same bed."

"Harder when you married. Been there, done that. Leave him. If he wants you back, he'll come looking for you. If he don't, move on and file the paperwork for an Uncontested. Show him you're for real. You can stay with me a while. You'll just have to sleep on the sofa when I got company."

"Can't. I love him. Wish I didn't."

"You think he's got somebody on the side?"

"Hadn't really thought about that."

"Lying heifer. You did."

"Hadn't."

"You should rent a car and follow him for a few days."

"I don't think so."

"Umm, huh. You just didn't want to think about it. Look, every nigger I know is either screwing somebody or trying to screw somebody. Men get the same urges we get, only worse because they try to do something about it, with or without you. Half the brothers I saw last night had on the ring and were still out on a mission."

"He's always at home or work."

"Maybe it's somebody down at the car lot. Lot of empty rooms down there with sturdy tables. Probably that room where that mysterious manager they always have to check with before they make a deal sits in."

"Get real. At the car lot?"

"It don't have to be a romantic getaway or nothing. Five minutes in the break room and, *bam-BAM-bam*, it's on. It don't have to be love, just a quickie booty-call in the back of one of them Lexuses. How long you think it takes to get some?"

"He comes home right after work."

"Don't take all night. I used to sneak and get busy when you, Moms, and Pops were in the kitchen watching TV. Five minutes, if that long. One of the best orgasms I ever had was when Moms and Pops were in the den eating dinner. I was out on the front porch with Danté. That's who I should've married. Instead of getting hooked up with Andre."

"What really went down between you two?"

"Don't want to talk about it."

"Never have."

"Never will."

Valerie thought about the porno movie she watched and remembered how they did it practically everywhere; nowhere was sacred. Doctor's office, massage parlor. In one, they did it in the front office where one of the guys worked. She exhaled a depressing, "Maybe I should go to counseling."

"Don't waste your money. It didn't work for me. I got a better therapy."

"What?"

"Meet somebody new."

"You trying to get me divorced, too? First Moms, then you, now me, huh?"

"Moms don't count because her and Pops got back together."

"They're separated again."

"But they're still married."

"Still, why you want me to have the same track record?"

"I'm trying to get you happy so you can stop banging on my door so early in the morning. I'm thinking about me. I don't give a shit about you."

"I don't know." Valerie laughed. "Black, I haven't been out in so long, my socializing skills are null and void. I wouldn't even know what to say other than my name and I'm a Cancer."

"Don't matter. They'll come to you and talk. Brothas are always yacking off. All you have to do is look cute and listen. You don't like what he's about, hey, you're married. Flash that ring and tell him to have a nice day."

"It ain't that easy."

"Brothas are always flocking over you, Red. Let's go out tonight. You need some fresh air. You ain't been out since my birthday back on Valentine's Day. You came by yourself and only stayed an hour. Over seven months ago."

"Has it been that long already?"

"Pick me up tonight."

"Maybe."

"You just said you were going to start seeing somebody else. Go for it. You start not being so available, his ass'll perk up and come around."

"That's right," Valerie sang and looked out into the Pacific Ocean at the people boogie-boarding. She thought about her beautiful neighbor who jogged every morning. "First one can't, second one can. A man is a man is a man is a man."

Valerie jumped up and ran out into the cool ocean. After going out far enough to tread around, she swam back, borrowed a big plastic bucket from one of the Latino kids making a sandcastle, filled it with water, then ran back and dumped it on Inda's head. Inda gagged-choked-screamed obscenities as she fought to get up and shook her hair. Valerie cackled, dropped the bucket and ran. Inda chased her across scorching hot sands, over and through the laughing and cheering spectators, about a hundred yards down the beach. When Valerie got out of breath and stopped running, Inda grabbed her arms, drug her out to the water and started dunking her. Valerie wasn't as strong as Inda, but she only went under when they both went under.

"Red, I'm kicking your Baldi-locks, high-yellow ass!"

"All right!" Valerie scream-gag-choked on the water. She twisted and squealed as she got away from Inda's grip.

"Stop! You're going to mark up my arms! You're scratching me!"

"So."

"I'm sorry, Black!"

"You better wash and curl my hair for me too, you dog-heifer."

"Scratch my booty."

They swam out a little, then came back and stood with the water right below their chins, each wave pushing them closer to shore. Minutes later, they had a water fight. After Inda lost, they headed back to the car. Inda slept all the way back.

7 / **VALERIE**

Valerie made it back home a little after five. It was still the same dry, stuffy September heat it'd been all day. San Bernardino County and the Inland Empire were fifteen degrees hotter than the beach cities and the smog layer twice as thick, so heavy it looked like low yucky-gray clouds.

When the garage whirred opened, she saw Walter's BMW was gone. She parked her turquoise Paseo on her side in front of the underused Lifecycle, weights, and other boxed workout equipment. Things she'd bought so they could start working out together. As she opened the side door and walked into the house, the first thing she noticed was the new potpourri smell from the carpet. She knew Walter'd vacuumed to kill the incense aroma from last night. Everything was clean, except for the dust on the furniture. She could see the thin layer of dirt on the full-screen TV and the glass top on the coffee table was spotty. Walter hated dusting, but he had straightened out all the gossip and African-American magazines she'd left out.

Walter's depilatory shaving powder was left out on the bathroom counter next to his saline solution and empty contact lens case. His cologne fragrance permeated the bedroom. The bathroom was humid. The tub was still wet. The mirror held a trace of dampness. He hadn't been gone long, which meant he probably wouldn't be back soon. She wondered where he was.

After taking a nap she woke up around nine-ish, showered again, then called Inda. Big sister still hadn't heard from Raymond and wasn't going to sit around and wait.

"Come pick me up, Red."

"Okay, Black."

She left Walter a short note letting him know where she was going because she didn't want to reciprocate his rudeness. Even though she was damn near spent by his mismanagement of their relationship, she still had a small trace of hope. Love makes you do that.

By ten-thirty, she was driving forty miles deeper into the now-cool desert. Inda bitched about Raymond and put on her makeup as they rode east to San Bernardino to watch a jazz band at the Radisson. Friday nights were usually packed with an adult crowd, twenty-five and over.

Before they got a good foot in the door, Valerie had turned down several dances. She felt awkward because she hadn't danced in months. For some reason, she felt rhythmless and didn't want to make herself look foolish with outdated dance steps. The only moves that clouded her head were old cheer-leader routines.

"Shit. I should've watched *Soul Train* this morning."

She watched Inda's wide-legged, open-shouldered pantsuit flow with her fashionable rhythms. The black fabric looked good against her dark skin. It enhanced her jet-black straight hair and gave her a mysterious appeal. Valerie felt awkward because she was dressed in a gray pinstriped business suit and sheer white blouse. When she looked at the other women, Valerie thought she should've worn something more hip or defiant, maybe like the tall sister in the miniskirt who was laughing as she smoked a More cigarette and sipped wine. Maybe something more leggy or breasty to show off her finer points. Something with an after-five flair. After all, it was a nightclub and not a work event. But she hardly ever wore anything too daring.

She sat alone at a table in a musically enchanted room, filled with people who were living for the weekend, and nursed her watered-down soft drink while she bopped her head with the beat and pretended she wasn't bored. She occasionally snapped her fingers and tried to give the appearance of being occupied with herself. She successfully fought off the urges to look at her watch, but she still wondered about Walter.

She became entranced watching her cocky, confident, big sister on the floor. Inda always looked like such a joy when she danced, smiling with every move.

As the record changed, and Inda flowed right with it, Valerie felt a soft, polite tap on her shoulder. She was prepared to give a plastic smile and respectfully turn down another dance, but when she looked up, her unknown friend was standing over her, smiling. The jogger who ran in her neighborhood, the man who ran past her house almost every day was now close to her. She'd only seen him in jogging shorts, but she definitely recognized him in the dapper black pants and collarless shirt covered by a trendy reddish-brown sports coat. His hair looked a little shorter and lined, a fresh haircut from this morning. What she saw face-to-face wasn't a disappointment at all.

Such a pretty man, she thought.

And now, he wasn't sweaty. She could smell his soft Drakkar fragrance as he leaned in.

Again she thought, *I'm married.*

She knew he didn't remember her. There would be no way he could. He'd never seen her outside of her car, never seen her when he wasn't moving at a swift pace. Valerie thought he was going to ask her to dance, but when he stooped close to her, he grinned like he'd known her all of his life.

"I like what you did to your hair." He smiled. "The color's nice. You complement that style better than most women I've seen with it."

She smiled and uttered a surprised "Thank you."

"I liked it long, too. Especially that time a few months ago when you pulled it back in a braid. Either way, this cut makes it easier to see your features. You have a nice face. I wouldn't hide it."

"Thank you."

"How are you doing this evening?"

Valerie smiled. "Fine."

"Would you mind dancing with me? I know you just got here and I saw you turn down a few other guys, so I figured I'd go ahead and get my rejection slip so I could move on."

Before she could even think of an excuse, she'd blushed and graciously taken his hand, weaved through the crowd onto the packed dance floor. She found a nice corner spot that had more people, less room, so she'd have an excuse to not try any complicated maneuvers. Instead of making herself look foolish by trying to emulate the trendy steps, she settled for a basic, more generic choreography. By the way he moved, she could tell he was a pretty good dancer. But he didn't try to outdance her, keeping his groove commensurate with hers. A couple of songs later, Valerie began to let herself go to the music. She loosened up and tried more daring, Reggae-inspired moves. The years of dancing, having to pick up a routine in a heartbeat, had paid off. When she got bold and spun around, she saw Inda back at the table with some guy, tall and dark with a goatee, just like her boyfriend Raymond. Inda playfully bucked her eyes, sent Valerie a surprised smile, then a thumbs-up and mouthed, "You go, Red." Valerie stuck her tongue out at her and continued her groove.

When the record changed to a slow song, Valerie started to walk away, but he gently took her hand and she freely walked back into his arms. She kept a little space between them for safety. They were the first couple to start dancing, but seconds later others joined in. She was sweating a little; so was he. Valerie looked away as they danced because she didn't want her buck-eyed expression to show her nervousness at being this close to someone other than her husband. She wanted to change her heart, but her mind had already committed to the dance. Walter was the only man she'd slow-danced with since she married; she'd saved that for him.

The second slow song the band sang was Earth, Wind & Fire's "Reasons." Her partner eased a little closer and whispered in her ear a very polite, "My name's Daniel Madison."

She covered her mouth, cleared her throat, and whispered, "Valerie Sinclair."

Daniel kept his distance, but Valerie was bumped closer to him by a couple dancing next to them. When they shifted over a step or two to get more space, he kept her close, touching. She closed her eyes and enjoyed his masculine feel against her femininity. When he held her hand, his fingers stroked across the reality of her wedding ring.

"Married?" he whispered, then added a playful, "Just my luck. Too bad."

She felt guilty, muddled with uncivilized thoughts of her lifelong obligation. As she loosened her hand from his waist, she bit her top lip and again a nervous smile came over her face. She looked at him and slowly backed away, wanting to go ahead and end the dance and deal with her personal frustration at having disappointed Daniel. He smiled and kindly pulled her back. She sighed, releasing her intruding thoughts, then cradled her head against his shoulder as he put his hand in the small of her back, pulling her into him. When she felt him grinding against her, she reciprocated and ran her hand up his back and across his neck. His breath felt warm on her skin. Tingly.

He said, "You smell sweet."

"Thank you."

"How long have you been living in Chino?"

"Six long years."

Just as she lost herself in the moment, the song ended. Everybody stopped dancing and applauded the band. Valerie and Daniel didn't clap because they were still holding hands, waiting for another song. As the lead singer took a moment to introduce everybody in the band, Daniel leaned in and kissed her on the cheek. "Thanks for the dance."

"You're welcome. Thanks for asking."

She slowly let go of his hand, and he slowly slid his fingers across hers. When he released her, she felt trapped. Since he was walking toward her table, she slowly followed, then slyly watched as he continued right past it. At first she thought he was heading toward the bar behind them, but he walked out the front door. She wondered where he was going, then remembered that the bathrooms were in the lobby. She waited a few minutes, blew time by standing near the front door and rejecting dances. If her curiosity walked back in, she'd be the first person he'd see, and this time she'd ask him to dance. Inda made her way through the shoulder-to-shoulder crowd and walked over, a drink in each hand. "Here, Red."

"What's this?"

Inda gave a broad smile and said, "Something you deserve."

Valerie raised a brow and smirked. "Sex on the Beach?"

Inda shook her head. "Screaming Orgasm. Take it one step at a time."

Valerie smiled. "Thanks, Black."

"What'cha doing," Inda teased. "Waiting on somebody?"

Valerie blushed. "Yeah. Now go away."

"Well, scratch my booty." Inda winked. "Break a leg."

Before she could make it three steps, Inda was drafted out to the dance floor by the husky brother sitting at the table behind them. When his smiling friend waved at Valerie to get her attention, then pointed at the dance floor, she shook her head *no* before she turned around and looked back toward the door.

Twenty minutes later, the band went on break and a tape of preprogrammed oldies came on, a well-done George Clinton mix leading the way. Five minutes after that, Daniel still hadn't come back. After a little more thought, Valerie walked out into the hall, figuring she'd pretend she was walking to the ladies' room. No sign of Daniel in the hall or by the pay phone. Gone.

Valerie made her way over to their table and sat, rocking her head to the music as she occasionally looked over her shoulder and checked the door. After dancing a couple of times with faceless men, she meandered back to her seat and didn't budge from her chair the rest of the night. Around one-thirty, the band played the last song. Sweat-faced, Inda finished her dance. Then they left.

As the crowd headed through the hotel lobby, Inda lagged behind, talking to a friend of her ex-husband's. Valerie walked ahead to get the car. When she started the engine, she saw a folded sheet of paper slid under her windshield wiper. Daniel had left his phone number.

8 / VALERIE

"Call him when we get in."

"No. It's too late."

"That ain't your problem. He left his number late."

"It's almost two."

"Two-fifteen. Anyhow, the later the better. This way you can see who's over. If he acts like he's sleepy, that means he's got company and is playing it off. If he talks to you, it's on."

"I'm married."

"Anyway."

The loving slow dance with Daniel kept rerunning itself in Valerie's mind; the sensation of him was still with her. It felt stupid, but she missed his foreign touch. As soon as they walked into Inda's place, Valerie hurried to use the bathroom, then rushed and picked up the phone.

"You go, Red!" Inda smiled. "I thought you weren't going to call."

"Not. I'm calling Walter."

The answering machine clicked on, but before the machine beeped, Walter picked up the phone. When she spoke, the liveliness in his voice went dry, flattened. That harsh, what-do-you-want-and-hurry-up-

and-get-to-the-point sound was in his voice and bumped with every brief syllable he spoke. The television was loud in the background, along with other laughing voices.

Valerie asked, "What'cha doing?"

"Nothing."

"Who's over?"

"My brother and Joe."

"Who, Jonathan?"

"Karl."

"What're you guys doing?"

"Nothing. Where you at?"

"I'm at Inda's."

"All right. Anybody calls, I'll send your calls over there."

Walter hung up. Valerie was left holding the phone. She was out, for the first time in months, and he was unconcerned. The note she left was a subtle invitation for him to join her. Even though she was glad he didn't, she wished he had. Maybe seeing her enjoying herself would've struck a jealous note and made him talk to her. Any kind of affection, even envious, angry affection, would've been appreciated. It would've shown he cared.

Valerie stood with her arms insecurely folded, silently pouting. Inda reached into Valerie's suit pocket, took out Daniel's number, dialed, and handed her the phone. Before it rang, Valerie started fidgeting with her hair, again reminding herself she'd cut it off for no reason. Then she started rubbing her stomach and tried to massage out the nervous feeling that was rapidly swelling up inside her.

"Hello."

"Eh, hello. May I speak—"

"Hi, Valerie."

"Hi. Daniel?"

"Yep. You have a good time tonight?"

"How did you know it was me?"

"I'd recognize your voice anywhere." His voice smiled. "I stayed up and waited."

"Oh," Valerie said. She was caught off guard, not by him, but by the fact that she was talking to a man in this way. Flirting. "Why'd you leave so soon?"

"I don't know," he said, then chuckled. "I thought I'd made a fool of myself. After I went to the men's room, I decided it'd be best I left. Then I saw I was parked right next to you."

"No, you didn't make a fool of yourself. I felt like *I* was foolish."

"I guess you made me nervous. I'd been watching you so long."

"When?"

"I live a couple of miles from you. I used to run up Chino Hills Parkway back toward Pomona, but one day I was bored, so I changed route and ran back your way. Kind of wanted to see the rest of the area. I saw you standing out in front of your house. So every now and then, I deliberately jog through your neighborhood so I can maybe get a peep at you."

"Why?"

"So, I guess, well, I don't know. Something about you caught my attention. I've had this sort of a schoolboy crush on you. When I saw you walk in I wasn't going to say anything. Then I finally coughed up enough nerve to ask you to dance, which was really, *really* hard for me to do because I wanted to meet you."

"Why did you want to meet me?"

"I've seen your face quite a few times and I wanted to hear what your voice sounded like, so when I thought about you I'd have a complete picture. Plus, if you saw me first, I'd look like a jerk for not at least speaking."

"Why did you leave your number on my car instead of giving it to me? You were right in my face, all you had to do was write it down."

"Saved me getting a rejection slip. I didn't want you to think the wrong thing. You know, a brother slipping you his number in a club, well, you know how that makes most women think."

"What wrong thing would I think?"

"I left you my number because, well, I wanted to sort of apologize for being so, eh, for being, you know, disrespectful to you and your marriage by coming on to you like that."

"Are you married?"

"Nope. Divorced almost two years ago."

"Girlfriend?"

"Nobody special. I haven't even been on a decent

date since I got divorced. I sort of threw myself into my career."

She looked over at Inda, who was grinning and snooping in on every one of her words. Inda mouthed for her to ask him to breakfast.

"Aren't you getting sleepy? It's late." Valerie said that to Inda, but Daniel thought she was talking to him.

"Nope," he reassured. "Actually, I'm wide awake."

Inda kept instigating, whispering what to say, coaching.

While Valerie held the phone at her left ear, Inda continuously whispered in her right, "Ask him if he's got any kids. Find out what kind of car he drives. See if he lives in a house or an apartment. Ask him if he has a single brother or a cousin or something."

Valerie wanted a little privacy away from Miss Nosey. It was late and she felt comfortable talking to Daniel.

"Do you know where the Denny's is in Diamond Bar?"

"Yeah."

She hesitated, then asked, "Can you be there in twenty minutes?"

"I can be there in fifteen."

When Valerie hung up the phone, Inda started screaming and jumped up and down. Valerie was still in disbelief at what she'd just done. Before Valerie could get her purse, Inda ran into her bedroom

and came back with a dozen-pack of Magnum condoms, tore two off and tossed them to her. Inda said,
"Cross your toes and hope they fit."

Valerie shook her head and softball threw them
back. "I'm just going for coffee."

"You need to go for what you can go for."

"I don't even know Daniel."

"I'm not saying you gotta fall in love with him,
just fall out of love with that piece of whatever you
got laying up over there at your house."

"Look, I'm just going to talk for a few minutes."

"And *don't* talk about your husband, not one
word."

"Should I change into one of your sweatsuits or
jeans or something?"

"No. And NO WALTER. Ain't nothing worse than
somebody who keeps bringing up her tired-ass old
relationships, her ex-this and that. It turns men off
just like *that*." Inda snapped her fingers.

"Okay," Valerie said as she straightened her
clothes.

"Want me to go with you? I could happen to show
up and get a table across the room and act like I
don't know you."

"Yeah." Valerie laughed nervously. "But I can handle it. Some things I have to do on my own. I should
be back in about an hour."

"Don't rush on my behalf," Inda said as she
started taking off her blouse. "I'll be asleep *loooong*

before then. Take the extra key off the rack in the kitchen. I got your back if Walter calls."

Valerie jetted into the bathroom, checked her makeup, poked around in her hair, checked for panty lines, changed into one of Inda's blouses, brushed and flossed her teeth, put on more lipstick, picked at her teeth, gargled, practiced smiling, practiced talking, checked her cleavage, put on more lipstick, and reluctantly headed out the door. She was already ten minutes late.

9 / VALERIE

Only two other people were in Denny's, both eating separately at the counter. When she walked in, Daniel was sitting patiently in a back booth, looking over a menu and sipping on a large orange juice. He'd changed into a more casual faded jeans and white embroidered sweatshirt ensemble. Again, she felt improperly dressed. As she put her purse in between them and settled at the table, she caught a whiff of the smoky smell from the club left over in her fabrics.

"Hi, Valerie." Again, he smiled and addressed her with the comfort of an old friend. "Are you hungry?"

"A little."

As she ate her French Slam, she kept one hand in her lap, never an elbow on the table. She didn't take large bites or huge swallows of anything. Even though she was starved, she ate like she wasn't really hungry. He nibbled at his cheeseburger and fries as they talked. Valerie thought he was trying to match her pace.

He told her he was in technical writing and leaving in about three months to go back East to grad school on a fellowship to work on his MBA, a decision he had made after his divorce was finalized. It took him this long to get his crumbled finances back on line. The soft market had made it hard to sell his house over the hill in Phillips Ranch, so he took a big loss. His wife ruined his credit before they split. With a smile, he was starting from scratch.

"What happened to you and your wife?" she asked, then immediately felt like that was the wrong question. If she wasn't supposed to talk about her present husband, then she shouldn't bring up his ex-wife.

"She had a lot of men friends," he said, making light of his situation. "Which I didn't mind because she was military, and the military is male-dominated, and I'm not really the jealous type. Not much, anyway. She knew most of them before we married, so hey. But it seemed like it got to the point where I was always fighting for her time."

"Really?"

"She always had to go back on base at Norton for this and that. Always had to pick up one of the guys at March to run him here or there because of this or that. You know."

"And you didn't suspect anything?"

"She always complained like she really didn't want to do it. Fooled me. She *said* she didn't want to, but had to do it because of some bullshit, military-fraternal, brotherhood thing."

"Did you go with her and meet them?"

"Nope. She never really introduced me to them."

"You never met them?"

"No."

"They weren't at your wedding?"

"We did Vegas." He chuckled. "I guess that should've been an omen, getting hitched in a gambling place."

"What happened?" Valerie asked, then knowingly, "Say anything but the obvious."

"Yep, you got it. Then I finally noticed that she'd get a little bit *too* jealous when of one of her special male friends had a girlfriend around. She always had to go do something with or for him, unless of course he had another woman around. Then I guess she was off-limits and stuck with me."

"First one can't, second one can."

"Exactly. I thought her not bothering him when he had company was just a respect thing. Couple of times she spent the night on base because she said she had some late or early-morning military exercise crap to do, and that didn't bother me because it's a forty-minute drive and I wanted her to be safe. I guess I was stupid because she said he was like a brother to her. Took it at face value. I don't know too many people who ignore their husband and sleep with their brother."

"That's messed up."

"Ooops. Am I talking too much? Feels like I'm babbling. Let's change the subject."

"No." She winked. "I like the way you talk. You have a nice voice."

He smiled. "Thank you."

"Damn," Valerie said as she pushed her plate back. She did the ladylike thing and ate most but not all of her food. "Sorry to hear that. About you and your wife. You seem so nice."

"I found out later that a couple of the other guys she hung with and was always doing favors for, she used to date them, too. And they were married."

"For real? And these were her friends?"

"I guess all of her friends were a collection of ex-whatevers. Things she didn't want to let go of. I guess I was just another one of her chess pieces. Not even the king, just a pawn. That's how I felt, anyway."

"That sounds like how it was. Too bad."

He winked. "Hindsight is twenty-twenty."

"Tell me about it." She laughed. "Where's she now?"

He smiled. "She's married to her 'brother.'"

They both laughed. His openness, his welcoming her into his life, sharing his pain through the conversation made her comfortable. He was as human as she. She didn't feel like she had to be guarded with what she said or how she said it.

He scooted a little closer to her, his knee touching her knee. The conversation became mildly flirty. Friendly flirty. Each smiling on the other's words and complimenting. She told him she'd been watching him in her rearview mirror. She saw how he sweated and joked that she started to bring him a glass of water. He told her how fantastic she always looked and how he liked the way she danced. They both blushed and the talk went on to other subjects, mostly her family.

Walter's name never came up, so her smile never dropped.

On the wings of their words, four o'clock flew in quickly. She couldn't remember the last time she'd been out this late or even up this long. The middle-aged, stocky blue-haired waitress, Lucille, walked over to pick up their plates and smiled. "You two look so happy together. How long have you been married?"

Valerie dropped her left hand into her lap and didn't know what to say, but Daniel said a cute, "First date."

When Daniel stopped by the cashier to take care of the check, Valerie went to the pay phone to call Inda to let her know everything was okay and she was on the way back. Valerie habitually checked in with somebody to let them know where she was. Inda answered on the third ring, wide awake. Raymond had come over. They were "having a relationship discussion" and Inda thought he might try to spend the night because he kept hinting about how tired he was and was yawning and making sly remarks about how far away Long Beach was. She kinda wanted him to stay, but she was playing stone-hard to get. She said if she did let him take a nap, she wasn't going to give him any. Not much anyway.

"Lying heifer. I thought you were soooo mad at Raymond."

"Well." Inda blushed, and uttered a sweet shame-faced, "You know."

"No, I don't know."

"You sound much better."

"Anyway. Anybody call?"

"No, that piece of shit didn't call. I'll put some pj's, covers, and a pillow on the sofa."

"Don't bother." Valerie smiled and indecisively fingered her wedding ring as she looked at the patiently waiting Daniel.

Inda said a disgusted, "Going home?"

She bit her lip and sang, "Watch my back, Black."

"Whoomp, there it is! You go, Red!"

Valerie followed Daniel back to his apartment.

10 / **VALERIE**

Daniel had taken a short lease on a small one-bedroom in a large mauve stucco complex, only three long suburban stoplights from her home. Like most of the area, the buildings and boulevard were lined with Mexican palm, evergreen, magnolia, and well-manicured shrubbery. As she followed him, she practically passed by her own house. A house that every day felt less like a home. For some reason the fear of being recognized didn't make her change her mind. The thought of Walter finding out didn't bother her. Either something inside her was coming to life, or something inside of her was dying.

Daniel had very little furniture left. A solitary painted African-American portrait graced the living-room wall. Nothing else in the living room or kitchen. A few dishes were in the sink. A few packed boxes and a couple of U-Haul wardrobe boxes were in the dining area. When he turned the light on, fresh indentations in the powder blue wall-to-wall carpeting showed where a sofa, love seat, end tables, and entertainment center used to be.

He told her that he'd put ads in the local paper and sold almost everything in preparation for his departure to a different life. When they walked into the bedroom, she noticed that a small television was situated on top of a sturdy shipping box. He picked up a remote and aimed it at a mini-stereo. The CD player clicked on. A soulful, sexy ballad began to play.

"What group is that?"

"After 7," he said. "Want me to change it? I could put something else or the radio on."

"No, it's fine."

Valerie let her moving eyes make her seem busy, comfortable with exploration. She looked at the picture of Daniel's mother and father. Then at his plaques and awards from work. She looked at his conservative, regular-sized bed with the dark-colored quilt that had already been pulled back. It looked as if it was waiting for her. She quickly jerked her eyes away and made like she was more interested in the television. The size, the model.

"I'm sending my television back home to Toledo to my parents. I'm shipping my car to my baby sister. She's going to Howard and has been hounding me to give it to her ever since I told her I was selling it."

She shifted side to side, not knowing whether she should sit on the bed or wait for an invitation to whatever. She wanted him to hurry and do something. It was at those peak lustful hours, somewhere between late night and early in the morning, and she was in another man's apartment, ready to give of herself or take of him. She was confused and didn't know which.

She walked over and stood next to the bed, looked at the pillows, then back to Daniel. When she saw he was watching her, had been watching her the whole time, she looked down at her feet. "Eh. Err. Should I take my clothes off?"

"Depends."

"On what?"

Daniel smiled. "Do you love your husband?"

She threw her eyes deeper into the carpet. "Yeah."

"Does he love you?"

Valerie was about to lie, then she paused. She looked at Daniel and said a hurt, "I don't know."

"I could tell that when I saw you at the club."

"How?"

"I've never seen you with anybody. You're always riding by yourself. You smile, but it's not from the heart. You're not happy. Just like me."

Daniel hugged Valerie. He reassured her it would be all right.

"I feel so stupid. I got my nerves up to come over here. Now I don't know what I want to do."

He asked her, "You want to make love?"

"I do, but I can't. I mean I can, I want to, but, I mean, you know. I'm, you know."

He said a sweet, "Shhh. It's okay."

She wiped her face. "Maybe I should go."

Daniel said a very vulnerable, "Stay. I could use

your company. I don't feel like being alone tonight. That's if you can stay and if you want to."

"I want to. Believe me I want to."

"I don't know what your situation is at home, but I don't want to make it worse and I'd hate for you to get in trouble. But I'd like to cuddle with you."

She smiled then said warmly, "I'd like that, too."

He gave her some big fluffy towels, soap, and a new toothbrush. While he lay across the bed and watched television, she showered and changed into a pair of his over-sized, paisley pajamas. She sat up and tried to make like she wasn't tired while she waited for him to shower. There was something odd about the way she felt in his apartment. After a few moments, she realized what it was. Welcome.

She kept thinking that he was on the other side of that door, naked. She wondered what he was doing, how he looked in his birthday suit, wished she could talk to him while she watched him bathe. She was tempted to take her clothes off and be naked under the covers when he came out, *thought* about strategically putting her pajamas on the floor, a path leading to her nakedness. But she didn't.

The words rose from her heart and slipped from her lips, "I'm married."

A minute later, Daniel came out and brushed his teeth. They quietly flirted with their eyes as she watched his reflection in the mirror. He had the same patterned pj's, only his were a lighter shade. Her face smirked with disappointment that he was in full pj's.

She'd seen more of his toned body when he jogged, when she didn't know who he was.

When he had finished, he turned off the light, crawled into the bed, and snuggled up close to her. She liked that. She needed that more than the sex. She thought it was strange, to want to be touched. To need to be touched. To be so vulnerable to and denied such a simple wanting. If she'd slept with Daniel, if she'd let him live inside of her, she'd wonder if he was holding her out of obligation.

"Daniel?"

"Yeah? You comfortable?"

"Will you take your shirt off?"

He pulled his shirt off. She took off her top and snuggled her skin as close to his as she could. He did the same and they both laughed. His fresh smell, his warmth felt good against her too-awake body.

Valerie asked, "Doesn't it make you scared?"

"What's that?"

"Moving on. Starting over."

"Yeah. It does. But sometimes you have to step back to make enough room to run forward." He kissed her lips. " 'Night, Val."

She didn't really return the kiss, didn't open her mouth to invite his tongue inside, but she smiled at the nickname he'd already given her and hugged him. They began talking, but quickly drifted off to sleep.

11 / VALERIE

Valerie walked into Inda's place around one. Attack-cat didn't even look up from his comfortable spot inside the window sill when the front door squeaked open and bumped into the wall. The pleasant smell of Inda's plug-in lavender air fresheners met her as soon as the door opened. Two glasses of wine were on the coffee table, one with berry-colored lipstick on the rim.

Inda had already gone to church at AME in Los Angeles. She'd left Valerie a note that said Raymond was supposed to sing a solo, "Amazing Grace," at the second service and after that they were driving the two hours north to Magic Mountain, meaning Inda wasn't coming back until late night or early morning. And since Inda didn't work on Mondays, maybe not at all. Valerie smiled and pulled back the salmon curtains and teased comatose Carlton. He opened his eyes, looked at her like she was crazy, rolled his eyes, then turned his head away. He'd been like that since he got neutered.

Hazelnut coffee was still simmering in the coffeemaker. Its fresh aroma reminded Valerie of the way their moms's house smelled every morning before they were bused off to school back when they lived only twenty minutes west in Rowland Heights. On Saturday afternoons, when she was maybe eight or nine, she would sit at the dining room table in her pj's, her Crissy doll at her side and her homework in front of her.

Polyester pants were in and her mother would stay true to the fabric trend in pastel colors. Valerie thought her mother looked like a model out of a magazine because she had the longest legs, the most peaceful smile, and the longest dark brown hair she'd ever seen, hair that was always in two long braids on either side of her oval face while she did her housework. Their German shepherd, Poo-Poo, would be at the back door's screen, peeping in and wagging her tail.

Her mother would have the radio on the countertop playing something up-tempo, and if her mood were nostalgic, maybe an old movie with Ingrid Bergman would be showing on the small television while she smoked a Virginia Slims. Every time she lit a cigarette Valerie would scrunch her nose, then her mother would say, "This is my last one before I quit cold-turkey."

Brown would be in the den with his G.I. Joe, glued to the television and Scooby-Doo or the Groovy Ghoulies. He'd usually be inside the house because he was always on restriction for fighting at day care. Inda would walk in sporting ponytails and cutoff jean shorts, hear the crossover melody, poke her lip out, cover her ears, and head for the door.

Her mother would talk in a teasing voice: "Inda darling, come dance with me." Their mother never did the color game. "Come listen to the music with us."

"Can't. That music sound too white."

"White?"

"You know, like old-folks music they play on those corny radio stations you and Pops be listening to."

Her mother laughed. "Oh really? The Fifth Dimension is all black, all soul, and they're not old."

"I'm not jiving, Moms. They sound stale. 'Up, up, and away?' Call me if the Jackson Five come on." Right before she got outside, Inda asked, "Where's Pops at this time?"

"He ran to the store." Half of her mother's smile went away. The half that used to belong to their father. "He's working on his Mustang, then going out to the base."

"What was he mad about this morning?"

Valerie perked up and said, "Moms was mad because Pops just got back home and won't spend time with her, and Pops was mad because Moms is working again teaching P.E. at the high school and not here every day being a good wife. That's why he got mad and drove out to Sunnymead and didn't come home yesterday in time for dinner. Moms said that was just an excuse. Pops was saying, 'Mimi, I don't want you working because you got children and a woman suppose to follow her man,' and Moms was saying, 'Steve, I'm not following anybody and when are you going to pay attention to my needs as a human being.' Pops said, 'Mimi, there's food on the table and a roof over your head, so what else do you need.' Then—"

"Valerie, shush." Her mother's voice was somewhere between amused and irritated. "Stop being a parrot. Finish your homework so I can check it, then we can get out of the heat and go to the beach."

Inda said, "Hope we go to one with some black people this time."

"Inda, darling, go clean your side of your room."

"It's clean, Moms."

"Now."

"It's clean."

Valerie said, "Liar, liar, pants on fire."

"Buck-tooth paleface."

"Monkey-breath cootie monster."

"Skinny legs."

"Fat butt."

Their mother laughed. "Girls. Enough."

The sound of her father's car's engine rolled into the driveway. After he'd left the Air Force, he had worked as a systems analyst for the FAA, a job that kept him on the road more than Mimi cared for. He couldn't be home and she wouldn't stay home and wait. Whenever he came home, Inda would brighten up and bounce outside. Their chubby brother would be right behind her. Valerie would stay and sing with her mother.

Valerie walked into Inda's kitchen, ran her fingers across her hair, thought about the back length of her mother's mane and mumbled, "The way mine used to be before I cut it all off."
After Valerie ate a half bowl of Frosted Flakes and a blueberry muffin, she cleaned up the living room, put the cover over the computer and printer, then threw her own smoky suit into Inda's overflowing dirty clothes hamper and took another shower to get the suit's smoke out of her skin. Valerie rambled through Inda's walk-in closet and stole a pair of too-big ragged jeans. Holes in one knee and right below the butt. Like all of Inda's clothes, the dungarees were almost two inches too long on Valerie and an inch too big in the waist. So she cuffed them and found a wide, silver-studded belt. She went into the dresser and found a white, large-sized T-shirt with Donald Duck embroidered over the left pocket. When she slipped it on, it looked like Donald Duck was standing on her breast laughing his duck feathers off. She went into the bedroom, sat on Inda's rumpled down comforter and pulled on some thick socks before putting on Inda's hiking boots—the only thing that fit perfectly. Then Valerie saw something that made her laugh—several empty condom packages on the oak nightstand.

12 / **INDA**

Like the song that Toni Braxton sang, it was seven whole days later, only Raymond and myself had owned the perfect evening.

Now keep up with me. As you already heard back when me and Red kicked it last Friday at the club out in the boondocks where she met the dude that liked her, me and Raymond had been having more ups and downs than a roller coaster at Knott's Berry Farm. But ever since we spent last Sunday together, did church and the Six Flags amusement park with his cousins, everything had been better than good. This Friday was definitely my Friday.

Today he called me at work three times, each time damn near flirting me out of my drawers. And it didn't stop there. Tonight, he was in full swing. My man was in rare form and the romance was definitely on. Not just on, but *on*. The brotha was being spontaneous and taking charge. After work, he told me to pack a bag, then drove the forty-plus miles in unforgiving eastbound Friday traffic from Long Beach to Diamond Bar to pick me up, then turned around and drove another forty-five uncomplaining miles to take me out to dinner at the Cheesecake Factory in Redondo Beach. And a sistuh didn't have to go in her purse one time.

As he sat next to me and ran his fingers lightly over my palm, I kept blushing and staring and noticing the fine details of him; his skin that was just as dark as mine; his freshly trimmed sideburns and stylish goatee; his texturized fade, that subtle teasing hint of an alluring cologne that seemed to be coming from all around his dark green blazer and black slacks. The brotha was looking so good I could feel my sweater top slowly unraveling as my black mini-skirt glided toward my thighs to show off the African-American goodies in the feminine jewel box. After that, he took me to a movie up at the too-damn-expensive Universal, followed by a casual late-night hand-holding stroll through Universal City Walk, then stopping at gift shops and buying black movie star postcards and costly knickknacks.

With my souvenirs in hand, he drove me back to his one-bedroom apartment for a glass of wine. At least, he said for a quick glass of wine, but after the queenly way he was treating me I knew what was on his mind would have me rocking and rolling until the middle of tomorrow. The same damn thing that was on my mind after he kissed me and woke up damn near every comatose hormone in my body during the movies. Not a kiss, or a kiss-kiss, but a bona fide tonguing KISS-KISS. I swear to the African-American woman upstairs that created the world, after that kiss of all kisses, I was so sprung that the movie went blurry and I didn't hear a damn thing Denzel said. And, Lord knows, when Denzel talked, I listened, listened, listened. But tonight my fine bro-tha on the sky-high silver screen was nothing but a distraction and I just wanted him to hurry up and get the damn movie over so I could get close to my man and get kissed again and again and again: here, there, and everywhere.

Needless to say we barely made it from the car to his place because we were pawing, gripping, tugging like the world was coming to an end and we had five minutes left to fulfill one last sinful fantasy. And if he didn't drive that itty-bitty two-seater MR-2 with hardly enough room for a Japanese midget in it, we wouldn't've made it in the house. I'm talking about with or without my diaphragm and condom combi-nation, it would've been in and on. I would've been one reckless thirty-ish sistuh on the bucket-seat move, rocking and rolling, grooving and grinding, singing and moaning my blues away. Actually, the thought of some immature, juvenile naughty car ac-tion turned me on to the extreme. Hell, if the winds weren't blowing a too-brisk forty-degree September breeze (because even though it was hot as hell in the California desert all day, the temperature dropped about twenty degrees or more at night) I would've opted for a blanket and headed for Redondo or Man-hattan Beach and found a soft, secluded spot for some moonlit appreciation.

I've never made love on the beach, outside with

a nice gentle breeze where if I looked up I'd see dazzling stars and not dry-ass stucco. Didn't have the daring, but that's one of the things that's high on my long wish list of romantic shit to do before I die. I don't know about you, but I get sick of the bed. Even when you spice it up, it's still too damn predictable. A bed is a bed is a bed. I just didn't want to get busy in his car while I tried to find enough room to bend my back and crook my neck and keep a stick shift from slipping up the crack of my butt.

As we kissed on each other and playfully tugged on each other's already loosened clothing from dark room to dark room and stumbled our way to the bedroom, his phone rang. I heard the outgoing message on his machine come on. Before I could say a word, Raymond let me go, dove across the bed and answered, said a few words and happily announced, "Inda's over." He smiled an impatient smile that was exposed by his nightlight. "It's Derek."

I smiled and lay across his back, sliding my hand between his thighs to keep the fire brewing. "Tell Derek 'Hi.' "

"Inda said 'Hi,' " Raymond said. "We're busy. Guess. Yeah. Peace."

He hung up, and before I could steal another kiss, the damn phone rang again. This time he answered and dropped his voice. His shoulders tensed, and he gave no announcement of me whatsoever. He didn't even look at me. I was topless, pantyhose off, skirt unzipped, nipples hard, laying on top of him, but he moved my hand from his Mr. Happy and shifted me away so he could sit up. After I took the hint and scooted to the far side of the bed, I waited as he talked eight, nine, maybe ten whispery minutes. And I mean whispery. I strained to hear some of the ambiguous conversation that didn't even give a hint of him being in the middle of something. But still, I could hear her high-pitched voice laughing and talking from her side of the phone. When I cleared my throat, he got up off the bed and started moving around the room, acting like he was straightening up, probably to get some space. But it didn't matter, because within her first syllable her voice had changed my mood, softened my nipples, dried up Miss Sweet Thang, and unplugged my tub of loving. All of the good I had been feeling was rapidly funnelling out into a tank of pisstivity with each of his murmurs. Before I knew it, my heat had gone cold. He hung up and said nothing, then had the nerve to try and pick up where he left off, like nothing had happened. When he leaned over to kiss, I put my hand up and cut him short while I gave him the Inda-face. I said a calm, "I don't think so."

"What?"

"Don't even go there."

"What's up, Inda?"

"Who was that?"

"Gina."

"What she want?"

"Nothing."

"Uh huh. That was a long nothing."

"Aw, Inda—"

"You and Gina in love or something?"

He said an irritated, "Why you keep saying that?"

"You've had her picture on your dresser since you started seeing me."

"I've got other pictures on my dresser."

"Of your family."

"She has my picture on her dresser, too."

"I don't know anything about that."

"Of course you wouldn't, you've never met her."

"Now, what's really going on?"

"Is that a problem?"

"You've canceled with me because she needed a favor."

"She's my best friend. She's like a sister to me."

"You date and screw all your so-called sisters?"

"*Once.* I only slept with her once."

"I rest my case."

"And that was *over* a year ago. We're just friends now. I told you that, we're *friends.* Don't start, okay?"

"Why you get so mad when she has company?"

"Because I don't like to see her hoe'n around, that's all."

"Oh, if she finds somebody and gets off, she a hoe?"

He didn't say anything.

"She tried to sleep with you since we've been going out?"

"No."

"If she did, what would you do?"

"What do you mean?"

"Answer the question."

"What question?"

"What would you do if she made a move?"

"Depends."

"On what?"

"You always mess up a good evening. You jealous?"

"Would you stop her? If she made a move, would you let her?"

"Why you starting this again, huh?"

"Why didn't you tell her I was over? I'm quite sure your best friend could understand. That was so damn disrespectful, that shit you just pulled. You told your brother I was laid up in your bed, why couldn't you tell that heifer that I was over, huh?"

"She didn't ask. Anyway, we were just discussing some business."

"Business? At one o'clock on a Saturday morning?"

"It was an emergency. She's leaving town and needs me to take her to the airport first thing in the morning."

"Oh. Which meant you were going to kick me out

in the middle of the night or early in the morning. Why she ask you?"

"Because."

"You love me?"

"Don't start, Inda. *Don't.*"

"Answer the fucking question and I'll leave it alone."

"You jealous or something?"

"No, I'm not jealous. I'm not stupid either."

"Then, why you always get an attitude whenever I have to do something for her?"

"I don't get an attitude, it's you. You get evasive. When I try to find out what's up, you step around the heat instead of walking through the fire. Fucking elusive-ass Pisces. Shoulda known better."

"You've got an attitude now."

"No, I don't. You haven't seen a 'tude. Yet."

"Does my hanging out with her *sometimes* bother you?"

"It wouldn't bother me if you introduced us. Last time you stood me up, I found out you took her to Def Comedy Jam. I just want to know what's really going on. And the way you talk about her—"

"How do I talk about her?"

"All the time, you always talk about her. We can't have a decent conversation without you bringing up her name."

"Why you packing your clothes?"

"I'm taking my shit home with me. Where's my Betty Boop?"

"Because of a phone call?"

"It's obvious."

"Jealous?"

"Somebody you screwed *can't* be your sister. You don't fuck family. *Never.*"

"Want me to take the pictures down?"

"Your place, your pictures. Where's my picture?"

"I don't have one."

"I rest my case."

"Inda," he exhaled. "You're here, she's not."

"And I'm not jealous." I pulled my sweater back over my head and fingered my hair from my face. "I'm just being for real."

"Yeah, right."

"Whatever."

"Uh huh. Whatever."

"Don't touch me."

"Look," he said, "why don't we just go ahead and jump in the bed, end the evening right, and we can talk about this when we wake up in the morning?"

"I don't think so."

"Inda. C'mon—"

"You taking me home?"

"Tomorrow. Chill. Stop this and let's get in the bed."

"I don't think so."

"What're you doing?"

"Calling Red."

"Shhhhhiii," he exhaled and put his fingers up to the bridge of his nose. "Why?"

"Why you think?" I put my gold dolphin earrings back on and snaked out a sarcastic, "She's my sister. I'm quite sure you'll understand that. But then again, maybe not, because me and Red have the same parents and haven't ever slept together."

13 / **INDA**

"**H**as my life come to this?"

I was bone tired, but I couldn't sleep because while I was waiting that long hour and a half for Red to drive her cranky butt forty-five miles from Chino Hills down to Long Beach, I sat around drinking cup after cup of caffeine with a little coffee because I knew when she got down on Shoreline to the Hilton (where I had a cab drop me off because I wasn't going to spend one more minute in Raymond's apartment; I was going to stay at the hotel next to the Convention Center, but I didn't have any decent clothes, so I decided I'd best to go home and talk this shit out with Red) the heifer was going to make me drive back. When she pulled up by valet she hopped over to the passenger side before the car quit rolling. She looked like she planned to sleep from the hotel to my driveway. Not if I could help it. I turned the heat up too hot and blasted the radio. Other than giving me the finger, she grabbed the pillow from the backseat, tried to get comfortable, closed her eyes, and didn't even twitch.

I thumped her ear. "Wake up, Red."

"STOP-IT-BLACK-DAMMIT-I-CAME-AND—"

"Wake up."

"—got your ass now shut-up and drive."

I thumped her again. "I want to talk."

"You starting to piss me off."

She grabbed her pillow and tried to get closer to her side of the car.

I said, "That's your white-ass momma."

"Your black-ass daddy."

"I'm calling Pops and tell him what you said."

"Not before I call Moms and put her on you."

"Your Halle Berry–looking ass."

"Kunte Kinte."

"Your momma."

"Daddy."

"You're adopted."

"Test-tube baby."

Two seconds later she was fake-snoring. I turned down the heat and put the radio on low. My underwear had crept up my butt and I was fidgeting and changing the stations every few seconds. When I got on the freeway, Red raised her head with that familiar sad look on her face and sighed.

She mumbled, "Bastard."

"Walter?"

"Yep. He started sleeping in another bedroom."

"What?"

"Not that it makes any difference," she said, then waved me off. "Don't want to talk about it. Don't feel like crying."

"How's he doing?"

"Wouldn't know. I haven't heard his voice in a week."

"You're lying, right?"

She didn't answer. Two seconds later she was snoring for real. When I passed under the lights I could see stress lines trying to engrave themselves in her forehead. For a minute or two, I reached over and massaged her shoulder. When her body relaxed, I rubbed her short hair and took a few breaths to relax.

I drove up the 710 freeway north with Kenny G. blowing his horn, crossed the 405 with Miles J. crooning about his love and dedication, hopped on the 105 east with David Sanborn's sax playing "The Dream," changed to the 605 north with Chapter 8 led by sistuh Anita Baker, made it to the 60 east on the wings of Luther Vandross, and crossed the 57 with the Yellow Jackets. Off at Temple, then busted a left on Mission Road and back to the crib. This freeway driving was just like my life: a maze.

When we pulled up at my complex that overlooked three intersecting freeways, I asked Red if she wanted to come in. Since she didn't have shit at home waiting for her, I thought she might want to kick it over here for a while. Plus I still felt like yacking off some frustration.

She said, "No. I've got a meeting at work to go to at two."

"When you start working weekends?"

"It's just today. Today only and that's it."

"What kind?"

"Alliance dissolution."

"Anyway. You still haven't talked to that Daniel fellow?"

"Told you I threw his number away. I'm married."

"Forgot. You want me to come by later on and take you out to lunch at Claimjumpers?"

"Nope." She sounded distant and bitter. Then she almost snapped, "I'm going to be doing some grocery shopping and stuff."

"Thought you went grocery shopping yesterday."

"Will you get out of my business? Damn."

I paused. "Red, you all right?"

"Tired, Black. It's the middle of the morning. I'll get with you tomorrow or something."

"I'm worried about you."

"Don't."

"Love you, Red."

"Love you, Black."

Then she was gone.

14 / **INDA**

Now the damn streetlights were prying through my bedroom's venetian blinds.

I was sitting on top of my down comforter, still half dressed and in ripped hose because when I got in I was too mad to even take all my clothes off. And would you believe I was sitting up with my gold lamp on, reading the personals. And I don't mean flipping by to get to the next section, but looking over the stupid help-me-because-I'm-too-inept-to-find-somebody-on-my-own columns, I mean straight-up *reading*, word for freaking word, closing my eyes and trying to put a face with the longing phrases from the lonely. Before I knew it, I had considered calling a couple that didn't sound too cliché just to see how the voices sounded. But when I saw the ad had a 1-900 number that wanted $1.98 a minute, I didn't think so.

Look, I don't pay $1.98 a minute to talk to people I *do* know, so I'll be damned if I pay my hard-earned money to get lies from a stranger. If I wanted somebody to lie to me I'd call Raymond, collect.

But still, I kept on a-reading. "Has my life come to this?"

Then I looked at my answering machine and got more pissed. No messages from Raymond checking to see if I was all right and made it home okay. Can we talk about rude and insensitive for a minute? Not that I would've called him back, but that's not the point. Raymond's inconsiderate ass let me walk out of his place, in the middle of the night, in the cold-ass ocean air, deep in the heart of Long Beach's gang-banging Snoop Doggy Dog drive-by territory, by my damn self, in a short dress, no hose, high heels, hair every which-a-way, jacked-up makeup, and toting a bag full of dirty lingerie. The least he could've done was got in his funky MR-2 and followed me to make sure my sister picked me up. And me walking down Cedar to roughneck Burnett, then up hoodlum-filled Pacific, all by my damn self, and shit, I know how I looked because before I made it to the pay phones in front of the piss-smelling 7-Eleven on Willow and Pacific, I had been propositioned three times. It wouldn't have been so bad, but the first two had low-budget Jheri Curls and the last one didn't have any damn teeth. The circus must be in town and they left a couple of cages open.

Anyway, I closed the paper and threw it over in the corner where my fat attack-cat Carlton used to lounge. I forgot to tell you, but since last we talked, he jetted. Yep, the bastard is gone. A couple of days ago we had an aftershock to the Landers or Northridge or wherever earthquake—hell, we have so many damn tremors and aftershocks out here that I lost track of whose fault it was—anyway, his fat lazy selfish ass freaked out and jumped over the concrete fence and starting running toward Mission Boulevard like he was possessed by the Holy Ghost. Ran down Mission going faster than the 50 miles-per-hour traffic. He never came back. He never called or wrote or faxed me a picture of his little paw print to let me know he was all right.

Shit, when a woman can't get a cat to stay in her life, something is wrong. That's got to be one of the seven signs.

Still, back to the paper that was staring at me while I stared at it. I picked it up again and got back to reading.

Another thing that pissed me off, not that it's any of my business, was that damn near all the brothas in the damn classified were looking for white women. Brothas advertising for rednecks should be against the law. I mean, I know my moms is a bit on the pale side, but *damn.* Half the brothas in my age range were in the market for white women, the other half were on the next page under the section "MEN SEEK-ING MEN."

Is there no hope?

When I was in college, it seemed like there were nice-looking, positive-attitude, HIV-negative black men for days. Walking through a mall felt like you were floating through a black Heaven.

Again, before I knew it, my eyes had turned back to the paper. I went down the next column and started reading the lack of creativity that was supposed to find a Miss Right for a Mr. Hard-up. All the ones with any real possibility sounded either too corny or too horny.

"There is no hope."

I was going to watch Black Entertainment Television, BET, but all they ever had on after midnight was half-naked white women advertising them damn 1-900 numbers, sucking brothas over to the Caucasoid zone.

Later on, because Saturday was made for life in the city, I wanted to take Red into the heart of LA to this jazz place in Leimert Park where a lot of decent brothas and sistuhs hang out. All kinds and shades of black people—African-American, Jamaican, mulatto, straight-up African—kick it around there. I had been dying to get up there and hang out with some real culture at 5th Street Dicks, that nice shotgun style, split-level coffee shop that had some small bands jamming original and old-school jazz until the wee hours of the morning. That whole area has black museums, theaters, dance studios, comedy clubs, boutiques—it is definitely on. The thought of going there was making me excited, especially since I worked with white folks eight hours a day and lived where black folks seemed to be an endangered species. But Red's mood didn't seem too positive, and, to be honest, I didn't need the negative. Don't get me wrong, I love my sister to death, but sometimes,

Lawd-haf-murcy, her miserable life wears me down-down-down.

I hate going out by myself, and I don't have an alternative socializing partner, so my weekend was shot. I needed to stay home and power up my 486 and catch up on some court reports I had yet to fill out before Tuesday rolled around. Yep. I'd get a bottle of Spumante and recoup from some of those supervised visits I had to deal with all week. That's what I would do. Chill. Swim a bit. Relax in the Jacuzzi. Ride my mountain bike on the trail from here to Orange County and back.

Maybe.

But then again, maybe not. Oh well, what the hell. Nothing ventured, nothing gained.

Before I sat back on the bed with my remote, my phone rang. It was five a.m. About the time my moms rolled out of the bed on weekends.

When I picked it up, Raymond asked, "You home?"

"What you think?" I hung up and turned my ringer off.

15 / **INDA**

I guess I finally dozed off after I showered and it looked like I slept until almost noon. Almost six hours of resting for no reason. Not much sleep, but too much to waste away on a sunny day that was meant for heading to Los Angeles. Because, Lord knows, ain't a damn thing for black folks to do out here in this hot, dry-ass Inland Empire but hug a cactus, catch sunstroke, and shrivel up into a California raisin.

"So, tell me something about yourself, Linda."

"Not Linda," I corrected and rubbed the bridge of my nose. *"Inda.* Linda without the *L."*

"Inda." His voice smiled. "That's pretty. Linda without the *L.* Creative."

"Thanks. So, tell you about myself." I paused, "Like?"

"Describe yourself."

"Oh," I said.

This felt too damn awkward. Okay, so I broke down and called a 1-900 personals' number. So sue me and send me to hell, all right? But like I said the last time you were deep into my business, nothing ventured, nothing gained. I mean, after all, one of these brothas could be in the same predicament I'm in. I mean, I did look over the classified ad twice, and that's just one step away from writing one my damn self. This guy, Wiley, called me back less than thirty minutes after I left him a message. I had just put on my black jeans, jean shirt with Daisy Duck on the chest, grabbed a black leather jacket in case I didn't come back before it cooled at sundown, and was on the way out the door when I heard my answering machine click on. When I heard it wasn't Raymond's voice, I came back and picked up. At first I thought it was a radio station calling me, maybe that Theo from KKBT, because he had a too-smooth late-night DJ voice. That smooth tone that could get a sistuh into a lot of trouble real quick. "What do you mean?"

"I mean, are you tall, short?"

"How much do looks matter?"

His voice smiled again. "Exactly. Good. I'm glad you said that. I'd rather get to know a person, find out what the foundation of their soul is really about."

"The soul, huh? So looks don't matter?"

"Some." He laughed a little. "Not much, some. It don't matter what a person looks like because if you don't get along, you don't get along."

"Strong words from a brotha."

"Truthful words to a sister."

"You're full of it."

He laughed. A cute, boyish laugh.

"Your personal ad said, 'Six-one, 180, African-

American, ISO strong, honest sister,' which I liked. And you just wanted to meet for 'friendship, talks and long walks.' Right?"

"Yeah. That pretty much sums it up."

"First off, I'm divorced."

"Ties to your ex-husband?"

"Not at all. No rug rats. Divorced and recovered."

His voice smiled. "Sounds good."

I tried to lighten up and give one of those friendly, phony cute laughs—you know one of those sophisticated giggles that was a tad bit schoolgirlish and womanly at the same time; you know to show that even though I talk serious, I'm no stick-in-the-mud. "Let's see. I'm friendly and outgoing, I can talk as well as listen, and my legs work, so walking is definitely on."

"Let's meet. Uh, for a lunch or early dinner?"

"When?"

"I'll give you my home phone number and let you decide."

"Where do you live?"

"Long Beach."

My mouth curved down-down-down. I said a disappointed, "Long Beach?"

"Yeah. I know it's a distance, but don't worry, I'll drive to you. Or if it'll make you feel more comfortable, we can meet halfway at a neutral place so you'll feel safe."

I wasn't too thrilled about even having a two-minute conversation with another dog-ass brotha from Long Beach, let alone meeting him face to face, and that definitely broke the pace of the conversation. But still, the man sounded good. But so did Raymond when I first met him, and I met that fool at church on a Communion Sunday. So that goes to show, dogs are everywhere. But then something to look forward to is better than nothing. Damn, I don't believe I'm doing this. I'm thinking about all the brothas I met at clubs and all the numbers I threw away before I ever made it back to my car, remembering the faces of all the nice-looking brothas I kicked to the curb before they had a chance. And now I'm sitting at home looking for some company. Face it, girl, face it. It has come to this. I'm too young to be having this old-ass life.

I said, "You sound like a pretty nice brother, but the truth is I don't know you from Malcolm."

He said a reassuring, "I'll let you pick the time, day, and venue. And I'm just talking about maybe a few minutes of some friendly conversation, it don't have to be deep, or long, and maybe we can take a little public walk if we make it that far in the friendship department. How's that sound?"

I said a positive, "Sounds good. I'll call you in a couple of hours. Maybe we can set something up."

16 / **INDA**

Before I left the desert and headed toward civilization, I zoomed up the 71 and stopped by Red's house of pain, just to make sure she had to go to work and wasn't kicking me to the curb so she could sit up and be depressed. Because you know I caught her in a bold-faced lie. I'd bet a dollar to a doughnut she was in her pink pajamas watching one of those Cary Grant movies, *Notorious* or *Charade*, pausing it on the romantic parts.

A taste of music came through the front door. Sounded like some Everett Harp jazz. I knocked and rang the doorbell, but nobody answered. I peeped in the driveway and saw the asshole-called-Walter's car, but the Paseo was gone.

Before I could get back to my car, the next-door neighbor, a sistuh named Charlotte, pulled up in the driveway of her two-story peach brick-and-stucco crib. She had her short auburn hair sculptured back and was decked out in a long, light brown dress, which looked good on her somewhere between high-yellow and light-brown skin, so I assumed she was just getting back in from early church service. She was a Seventh-Day Adventist, y'know, one of those

102

people who hated Saturday-morning cartoons so much they went to church at sunrise just to piss their children off. She didn't have any rug rats, yet, but I'm quite sure that when she did, after they'd missed a year's worth of the X-Men and Power Rangers, I know they'd have their lips poked out clear to Zimbabwe.

"Hey, Inda girl."

"Hey, Charlotte."

"Looking good, Miss Thang."

"You looking better than me, Miss Thang."

"How's Raymond?"

"He ain't."

"Guess ain't nothing changed."

"Thank you for understanding the plight of the black woman."

"I've got you in my prayers." She laughed. "Where you heading off to now?"

"You know me. What you up to the rest of today? Want to ride out to Marina del Rey and drop in Aunt Kizzie's restaurant and get some soul food?"

"Can't today." She smiled. "Got me a dinner date later."

"I heard that. Cute?"

"And he calls when he says he's going to call. Would you believe it?" She smiled and made her eyebrows dance. "Wants me to meet his family. Holds my hand when we're walking. Grrrl."

"White?"

"A brotha."

"American?"

"From the Ivory Coast."

"Good for you! Say hi to the motherland for me." That made me happy because I didn't think she'd been on a date since she moved in next to Red. She's the only other African-American on the block. At least the only other one that wasn't married to a white man and still talked to black people. I pointed at her house. "Looks like you got a blooming package on your doorstep."

Charlotte hurried over with a smile when she saw the two dozen red roses leaning against her door. When she read the card, her smile poofed away, lips poked out, her shoulders dropped six inches, then she shook her head and went to the curbside trash barrels and tossed them in without a second thought.

"Let me guess." I laughed. "Your ex still trying to get back with you?"

"Every other day, home and work, sending flowers or cards."

"Can I ask you something?"

"What?"

"Did he ever send you flowers while you were together?"

She tisked. "Girlfriend, please."

"Didn't think so."

"Now even the restraining order won't make him back off."

I never told Charlotte, but right before Red introduced us, I met a guy at a club one night named

Clarence who, from the moment I stepped in, was doing all he could to get with me. Sending me drinks, notes, straight-up begging. Of course I kicked him to the curb so hard he can probably still feel the concrete on the back of his neck.

Come to find out, Clarence turned out to be Charlotte's flame. Or I should say ex-flame, because she had extinguished his cheating ass. The brotha messed around and got cold-busted on the downstroke with a married Mexican woman down in Orange County. Cheating. Caught up in the game.

The day after he came on to me, I recognized him standing in front of her house, holding flowers and wearing a puppy-dog face, screaming her name like she was the answer to all his troubles. Charlotte's Probe was in the driveway, so I knew she was home. When I stepped outside, I called his name, he saw me and almost crapped in his button-fly Levis. All of a sudden he had the urge to leave.

Before the sound of his embarrassment faded, the police pulled up with the lights twirling. When they left, with me being the concerned human being I am, was, and will always be, I walked over and asked my sistuh what was really going on. That was when she gave me the lowdown. To make it worse, like you heard her say, she already had a restraining order out on him and he still did a ride-by for a look-see every now and again. Nothing worse than a man who can't take a direct hint.

That's one thing I've never understood about men.

Why is it they don't really want you, can't really love you until you got suitcases in both hands and heading out the door? When it's over, when you've given all you had to give until there is hardly enough left to keep you sane, then they decide they wanna straighten up and fly right. Dog you out, then wanna come whimpering back with their tails stuck between their legs. And then, their getting right only lasts as long as the 24-hour flu.

So with hope in my heart I blew kisses to Charlotte, hopped on the 71 northbound, kicked it to the 60 freeway westbound, and tried to get a life by heading into Los Angeles. I don't know what was *really* going on, but the freeway was jam-packed, stop-and-go, mostly stop with very little go. The 60 was filled with herds of big 18-wheel trucks, so no matter how much I stretched my neck out the window or over the dash, I couldn't see two feet. It was that kind of piss-me-off traffic where everybody and their momma was cutting you off, jumping from lane to lane, then back to the damn lane they just jumped out of, getting nowhere fast. I know because I lane-traded, cut-off, and flipped-off a few myself. And the smog blowing in from LA added to the oh-so-fresh cow smell from Chino, plus the carbon monoxide all the slow-ass trucks were kicking back in my face didn't seem to help any. Less than fifteen nerve-racking miles and over an hour later, it finally hits me to put the radio on KFWB, the all news/traffic station. Come to find out that some fool's semi unhitched, flipped over, and left oranges everywhere. When I finally got to an exit, the police had put down those flares and cones and made us all detour south. Toward Long Beach. I could take a hint.

17 / **INDA**

Since I was in the area, I passed by Raymond's apartment. Just did a cruise-by for a look-see. Force of habit. Anyway, his car wasn't in his stall. He was supposed to be at church practicing for an upcoming concert. That is, if he wasn't out doing something for his "best friend." Didn't really matter, I was just going to pop in and pick up my Betty Boop T-shirt, y'know, the one I left over there just in case I needed a reason to go back, the lipstick-stained one I left hanging up in his closet to mark my territory. I know it sounds stupid. It's an Inda-thang. But the more I thought about it, I didn't really see the point. But still I decided to leave a note that I wanted it returned to me. Ain't it funny how a little argument can make a sistuh want the most trivial things right now?

Since the two-laned Cedar Avenue was packed on both sides, I had to park around the corner on Burnett. The empty space that I had just passed up because I thought I could get a closer one was gone. A sistuh in a blue Miata had stolen it before I could get back. While she struggled to parallel park, she looked almost as frustrated as I felt. I had parked half a block down and had strolled back up to her before she got out of her car. I passed by and looked at her neat, short reddish texturized Afro as she let her top up. I said, "I like that hair, girlfriend."

She gave a generous smile and said, "Thank you, my sistah."

I was rumbling through my little handbag when I realized that I didn't have a pen or paper. I stomped my foot. "Shoot."

"Cheer up, girl." She said it in a very positive tone that sent me a wave of confidence. I turned and looked at my Afro-Sistuh, dressed in black jean shorts, a white sweater, and trendy combat boots. She grinned as she bounced out of her sports car, beaming, looking like she owned it all. "Today's too sunny and pretty to be frowning."

I smiled. "I know that's right. See you riding 'round with your top down."

"Letting my hair blow in the wind."

We both laughed.

I said, "You go on with your bad self."

Girlfriend was getting a gorgeous tulip arrangement and a couple of travel bags out of the car. She seemed pretty cool, so I asked, "I don't mean to put you out, but do you have a pen and paper I can borrow real quick? I need to leave a note and don't have a thing in my purse to write with or on."

She fidgeted around her purse, then looked around her car before she said, "Not on me. Let me run up the street to the house and get you one. I'm heading right up that way."

"No, that's okay. It's not that important."

"No biggie." She smiled and reminded me of my late-blooming baby sister. "C'mon."

"I'll help you carry some of your stuff so you don't have to make two trips."

She sighed and gave a relieved "Thanks. Lord knows I'm trying to carry too much stuff. Sure you don't mind?"

"I don't mind. Got nothing but time. I'm Inda."

"Linda, I'm Chiquita."

"*Inda.* Linda without the *L.*"

"Inda. That's pretty. How'd you get it?"

"Misprint on the birth certificate." I smiled because nobody had ever asked me that before. "Moms liked it and kept it."

"Smooth name. Unique and pretty."

"Thanks, Chiquita. That flower arrangement is boss."

"I sorta dissed my man," she said in that girl-to-girl tone of understanding, "so you know. Trying to correct myself before I wreck myself."

"Tell me about it. Been there, done that."

She laughed and picked up her big purse and garment bag. I grabbed and sniffed the flowers, which smelled like true love and undying friendship. So, me and my homegirl with the Mexican-brown skin took off, chit-chatting, laughing about men, slow walking like we were old friends, carrying stuff back down the street. The flower arrangement was kinda big and awkward, and after a few yards I was wondering how far she was going to walk, because we were just about to pass by Raymond's, which meant we'd have to cross the street. Then, she turned right up in the walkway that led to two apartments: Raymond's, and his next-door neighbor's, who happened to be a very old, very white man. My end of the conversation sorta died down when she swerved to the right and headed toward his crib. Then, of course, she didn't knock on Raymond's door. Nope, she just put her bags down and started feeling around her purse, like we sistuhs do when we're looking for the keys.

Now, correct me if I'm wrong, but when I left last night, Raymond didn't have a roommate, and as far I knew, I was *the* woman. But then again, I didn't have a key.

You know I wanted to go off, but I tried and kept my tone lively while I looked around the damn lawn like I was a tourist and this was the first time I'd been here. "Nice building."

Then she reached into her purse and took out her keys. "His car's gone, so he's probably at the church rehearsing."

"Church-going man, huh?" I said as I looked the sistuh over, now in a different way. We had nothing in common, so far as appearance goes, but this was Raymond's whatchamahcallit? She even had keys to two of the three new locks on Raymond's door. And the keys were on a heart-shaped key ring that had their cut-out picture on it, snuggling and grinning like the dickens in one of those dollar booths.

She smiled. "Yeah. I was supposed to come down last night. I'm a flight attendant and I was going to catch a shuttle and fly up, but we had a misunderstanding yesterday morning and I tripped out and canceled."

"Really? So y'all already had plans in the oven for last night and *you* canceled?"

"I had a stupid attack. He had already made reservations and got advanced tickets to the movie. I felt bad about it when he called me about one this morning to apologize, said he missed me and loved me, and I hung up on him."

"What movie?"

"Huh?"

"What movie were you going to see?"

"The new one with Denzel Washington. The one where he's an action policeman. You seen it?"

"Not really."

If she had turned around right then, she would've seen my mud face grimacing as I bit my tongue and shook my head. She slid her shiny love-keys into the liar-locks. The first one clicked open; the second one clicked open; the third one wasn't locked.

"I'll find you a pen and some paper. Make yourself at home."

"Okee-doke."

When the door opened, it was dead quiet inside.

I'd been coming down here for the last six months, now I was playing the fool by playing it off and acting like a damn stranger. And you know it ain't easy for me and my mouth to let it be. I was kinda hoping Raymond would walk in. She headed straight to the bedroom, which verified what I already assumed. The place smelled like breakfast and something else. Just then, Chiquita let out an earsplitting scream that coulda made the dead roll over. Her scream escalated. Then another scream of equal magnitude added to the nerve-racking sound. Shit scared me so bad, my skin goose-bumped up and I think my hair de-permed and stood up Buckwheat style. I almost dropped the tulips and ran back out.

"Raymond, what the hell is this! Why!" That was Chiquita.

"Oh, shit," I heard Raymond shriek, sounding like he was just waking up. "Chiquita! What you doing here?"

Chiquita screamed, "What's *she* doing here?"

Another sistuh's voice screamed, "Who are you and what are *you* doing in here?"

Chiquita had her hand over her mouth, wide-eyed, as she stumbled out of the bedroom, ran right past me and straight toward the door. I tried to slow her down, but I was still gripping the tulip arrangement, so she damn near knocked me over. She was crying like a banshee and sprinting like a roadrunner. A couple of seconds later Raymond flew into the room, stumbling his greasy face around the corner, his drawers halfway on and inside out. He almost crapped on himself when he saw me standing there, stonefaced with flowers in hand.

His eyes damn near popped out of his head. "Inda?"

I smiled like I was June Cleaver and said my sweetest, "Good morning, honey."

He tried to cover himself up, like I'd never seen him butt-naked. He let out one of those overly dramatic, soap-opera-ish gasps and damn near fell down from the shock. When he froze in his hoe-tivity, I sidestepped and said, "Don't stop chasing Chiquita on my behalf."

"What—How'd you get in?"

"Through the door."

Just then the other sistuh hurried around the corner. And guess what? She had the nerve to be wearing my damn Betty Boop T-shirt, inside out and backwards. She looked just as mad-hurt as Chiquita looked hurt-mad. And I realized what that other odor was that was mixed with the breakfast smell—them.

She looked just as rattled as him as she looked me up and down and asked, "Who're you?"

I shifted and exhaled my calmest, "Who're you?"

"Well, I'm Gina. Raymond's fiancée."

"Oh. I recognize you from the pictures in the bedroom." I nodded my head. Raymond had swallowed his tongue and gone mute. I said, "My name is Inda. You have heard of me, right?"

"Oh, I'm so sorry," she said and covered her mouth, like she was apologizing for her hard 'tude. "You're Raymond's sister."

"*What?*"

She turned to Raymond. "This is your sister, right?"

Raymond dropped his head into his hands like an ostrich trying to stick it deep into the burning sands. And just because you can't see us don't mean we can't see you, I thought. Your ass is showing.

She looked at him then looked at me and rattled off, "You're his half-sister, right? The one that was over last night so he could run her to the airport this morning, right?"

"I was over last night. I thought you were his platonic friend that he was supposed to be *taking* to the airport this morning?"

After she looked at his dark skin, then looked at my dark skin, she gave me a look of stupidity then said, "He's not your brother?"

"Brother?" I gave her the look of stupidity back, then said, "And that's my Betty Boop you got on, Gina. My favorite T-shirt I left over here *months* ago."

She asked me, "Who was the other girl?"

"She had keys and flowers and a travel bag." I sorta hunched my shoulders. "Ask Raymond. Eh, Raymond, what you got to say about Chiquita, baby? Or you done forgot how to talk."

Raymond's mouth was wide open as he looked back and forth. The way his face twisted and contorted like he was constipated, which would explain why he was so full of shit, he looked like he wished he had clicked on that third lock. He looked like he wanted us both to leave.

Gina exhaled, and as quick as she could blink her watery eyes, she gave up her denial; her brown skin turned fool-red and the tears ran out of her face almost as fast as Chiquita had left. I wanted to feel for her, but I was too hurt my damn self. I wanted to have an "Inda-moment," one of those moments where my emotions went extreme, but I wasn't going to drop my wall as of yet. If I was going to cry I definitely wasn't going to do it in front of them. She long-screamed, snatched her ring off, threw it, doubled up her fists, began hitting Raymond, windmilling her arms. He tried to catch her hands, she scratched him, he backed into a corner, then she started throwing all of his CD's and plants at him. The hood-rat was clocking him with the plants I gave him. I wanted to drop my white-collar attitude and flip to the ghettofied, join-in-and-take-this-to-a-lynch level, but I just shook my head. Inda is too much of a lady for games, but not too sophisticated to peep at the fireworks.

While I enjoyed the show, I calmly put the tulips down, ran my fingers through my hair, rubbed my neck, cleared my throat, put my shades on, picked up the tulips, and walked out. I was tempted to get my .380 from under my front seat, but Raymond ain't worth the bullet and ain't worth the time. Besides, the ruckus from the wailing and ass-kicking Gina was dishing out was so loud that the neighbors had either come to their doors or stepped outside. Even people walking down the street had stopped. Too many witnesses.

18 / **VALERIE**

Downtown Los Angeles.

Since she'd stopped going to UCLA, Valerie could count the number of times that she'd ventured as far as downtown alone. After living and working in the suburbs, the urban areas seemed so filthy and untamed. Dangerous. Homeless people strolled the streets and camped out on most every bus stop, even right in front of Parker Center, the police station, talking to everybody and themselves, asking for money like it was owed to them. The spaghetti system of freeways was always congested, something she didn't expect early on a Saturday afternoon. The criminal courthouses and sky-high concrete-and-steel banks hovered over the heart of the city, some with ten-story artistic scenes painted on the walls. Some with unintelligible graffiti to let the people know which gang was in charge.

But the garment district at Ninth and Los Angeles that was lined with building after building of storefront sale after sale—a woman's ten blocks of fashion paradise—used to be her favorite hangout. A nice day of shopping and bargaining, then a drive on the other side of the 101 to Chinatown to grub on some bona fide shrimp fried rice. That was when she and Walter spent weekends doing sociable things together.

With dark shades covering her eyes, Valerie drove her car up the hill on Temple and parked across from the Ahmanson Theater. A well-dressed crowd was driving into the seven-dollar lot and rushing to make it in time for the start of the play. Like she'd done so many times before when she was out by herself, Valerie glanced around at the people. The event looked like it attracted mostly couples that were holding hands as they crossed the streets and hurried up the stairs into the concrete building, a contemporary monolithic structure that looked like an architect's dream come true.

More couples swarmed in from all directions. Men and their dates. Women and their husbands. Couples and their children. A group of pregnant women. All walking and laughing and smiling and talking together.

When she made it upstairs and got her bearings, she saw some people were heading toward the other side of the structure, a section that had another performing arts hall that was showing Gershwin's opera *Porgy and Bess*. That made her think about one of Maya Angelou's autobiographical books she had read, the one that talked about when Maya herself performed in the production many years ago. It also made her think of her mother playing Nina Simone records and singing *Porgy*.

Valerie stood in the shade of the building and double-checked her ticket to make sure she was heading for the right show. Valerie followed the banners and sign and veered into the glass-fronted lobby of the place that had an early afternoon performance of *Miss Saigon*.

But still, even though the tickets cost at least sixty-five dollars and were almost impossible to get, she stared out at the city and wondered if she should just go back home.

After stopping by the ladies' room, checking her teeth, freshening her breath, adjusting her pale yellow suit and putting on another coat of lipstick, Valerie took a deep breath and stared at her tiered bangs. Exhaled. Gritted her teeth. Tisked. Glowered at what was left of her mane. No matter how many compliments she got, she'd never get used to it being that short.

A middle-aged woman wearing a red evening dress, her blond and white hair in a back-length braid, tapped Valerie's shoulder and smiled a blue-eyed smile. Valerie didn't know the woman, but she smiled in return, force of habit, and said a polite, "Yes?"

"I thought so." Her voice was strong, raspy. "I know you."

"I don't think so."

"Aren't you married to a ball player of some sort?"

Valerie's breathing shortened. "Why, yes I am. My husband played ball."

"I loved your movies. Especially the Alex Haley miniseries." She thrust a black journal in Valerie's face. "May I have your autograph, Miss Berry?"

Valerie shifted away and frowned. "I'm not Halle Berry."

"Oh yes you are." The woman laughed and smiled wider. Held the book closer. "You can't fool me with those shades. I saw you in the *Enquirer*, in that short dress, dancing all over those male strippers. It's too bad you and your husband are having marital problems."

Valerie quieted the slight temper that tried to flare and turned around. She groaned and headed for her seat.

"You might fool some people, Miss Berry," the woman's voice chased her, "but you can't fool me."

Just as she got inside the auditorium, a city-sized room packed with people and buzzing with chatter, the lights flickered high to low, letting everyone know the show was about to start.

With her purse in front of her most feminine parts, Valerie bumped down the aisle and found her seat. Daniel pulled the lap of her regal chair down. He smiled ear to ear. So did she.

Right before she sat she saw two African-American sisters walk in, hand in hand, one leading the other. One had braids, the other a butt-length weave. When they sat down two rows in front of them, the twenty-something women rubbed each other passionately, then got settled right up under each other.

Valerie sat in a way that made it look like she and Daniel weren't together, but a moment later she leaned toward him. Not much, just a little. Enough for him to know she was grateful for the invitation. The room was packed with what looked like thousands of people and she'd seen less than ten black people there for the sold-out musical. Row to row, there were mostly Asians and Caucasians. With her and Daniel sitting right next to each other, based on complexion and grins, it would be obvious they were together.

The African-American ladies below them French-kissed and laughed. They were in their own world. Nobody seemed to care.

When the women got a bit more involved in the tongue exchange, Valerie said, "Yikes. It's getting a bit ridiculous."

"Guess you haven't been to LA in a while."

"Now I remember why."

"Looks like they're making a political statement."

"Love."

"I guess." Daniel chuckled. "Nice-looking women. Wonder what made them like that?"

"Probably a man."

Daniel told her how nice she looked, complimented her hair, and her natural-colored lipstick. She always looked forward to that, the attention, the way he noticed the little-bitty things about her. When she wore the new lipstick, when she changed to a natural nail polish. The nice words that flowed so easily from his lips warmed her head to toe. Each syllable felt like it came from the heart. And that type of kindness could be addictive, as refreshing as a cold Snapple on a hot summer day. It could also be a scary sensation for a married woman. A woman who felt like a little bit of her heart was dying every day.

Without a thought she slid her hand in between his fingers and told him how nice he looked in his gray slacks, white mandarin-collar shirt, and black vest. Her eyes walked around the room and didn't see anybody she knew, and that eased her mind enough so she could relax her posture. A moment later she inhaled his Wings cologne and smiled.

She whispered, "Thanks for the ticket."

"What ticket?"

She elbowed him. "The one you left at the lobby of my job."

He chuckled. "I didn't leave you a ticket."

"Oh, I see. Somebody with the initials D.M. drove twenty minutes to Rowland Heights and just happened to leave me a ticket, and our seats just happened to be right next to each other."

He sang, "That's right."

"What a coinky-dink."

"Yep. Coinky-dink."

"Well, Daniel Madison, I wonder what D.M. would've done if Mrs. Sinclair"—the pace of her words broke when she said *Mrs.*, some of her liveliness withered, but she cleared her throat, held on to her blush, and continued—"if Valerie hadn't shown up."

He stroked her hand with his fingers. "It's like you said, we're not dating, and I don't get involved with married women, which means we won't be going anywhere together. But if we both happen to be at the same place at the same time, there's no reason for us not to be cordial."

"Shhh."

"Just because we happen to run into each other at the grocery store outside of our neighborhood, or I just happen to see you at the movies a couple of times this week, again alone, again outside of our—"

"Shhh." She snickered and felt her age. The weight from the guilt, the self-blame that made her feel too damn old to be that young, had lifted away. The way it always did when she was with him.

He whispered, "Just because you cuddled with me once—"

She lightly pinched his hand. "Shhh."

Other than being set in the Vietnam era, Valerie didn't know what the musical was about. While most people were amazed by the choreography, vocal ranges, and different sets—that smoothly went from scene change to scene change right in front of their eyes—Valerie was completely caught up in the story. Not the political story about the biracial babies the American soldiers left behind. But a love story that pulled her out of her life and deep into theirs. A tale of two people swearing an undying love at one point in their lives. A love at first sight. An affair where he was her first.

Through songs and scenes of longing, they both breathed intensity and passion for each other. They married, made vows to God. Promises to each other of a forever together. So much desire in each word, she thought, so much craving in every touch. All of it combined to create enough emotion to steal some of Valerie's breath and chill her body to the point of a sweet numbness.

Then without a warning, the stage lights flickered, the scenery altered. The man's love for her had changed while the woman clung to the promises of the past. In the end the woman put a gun to her head and ended her misery. An abrupt end to what Valerie had trusted would be a Disneyland fairy tale.

When the lights came up and the audience rose to their feet with thunderous applause, Valerie was too shattered to stand and send her own appreciation to the performers at curtain call. She felt like everybody on that damn stage knew her, had mocked her, that everybody in the room had been peeping inside of her.

First Daniel's hand touched her damp cheek, then she felt the softness of his handkerchief on her face. He leaned close and asked, "You all right?"

She shook her head, stood, and bumped through the crowd that was still applauding, cheering as the calvary of actors came out to take their final bows. For them, the show was over.

Outside, the sunlight looked different. Brighter. Even though she'd stopped by the railing that looked out over the streets, the insides of her body were frigid. All the couples passed by, this time rushing to get to their cars to beat the traffic. All Valerie could see was the last tragic scene, the young heartbroken Vietnamese woman running into her room with a gun. Then a loud bang that made Valerie throw her hands over her mouth and want to scream *Noooooo*. Then the lifeless body that rolled down toward the front of the stage like it was offering her some sort of reality.

Daniel asked, "You okay?"

"No, I'm not okay. I haven't been okay for a long time." Again, Valerie shook her head. Then her words were abrupt. "I'm not going to see you anymore."

She felt the hurt in his voice when he said, "Okay."

"Sneaking around like high school children." Valerie fingered her ring. "I mean, who the fuck are we kidding, right?"

Daniel's eyes blinked. His words were soft. "Yeah. You're right."

Valerie reached out and they shook hands. Softly, briefly. Then she took her hand back. She opened her purse and asked, "How much was the ticket?"

"No. Don't. It was on me."

But she still wanted to give him the money so she wouldn't feel like she'd betrayed or misled anybody.

She handed him some twenties, then closed her purse. "Thanks for the play."

"Why're you upset? Did I say something wrong?"

Valerie didn't answer. When he reached for her hand, she backed away. He raised his hand in apology.

"I really don't know what to do," Daniel said. "Want me to walk you to your car? Maybe we could get something to eat and you could tell me what's bothering you."

Valerie turned away. After a step, she didn't hear him moving away, didn't hear the sounds of his shoes fading on the concrete. She stopped and turned and stared at him, saw in him what she wished she could see in Walter. Admitting that to herself, even in silence, aggravated her soul to a new height. And sunk her heart to a new depth.

"Val, are you all right?"

A moment later her lips parted. "Can I stop by your place before I go home to my husband?"

He nodded.

19 / **VALERIE**

"Kiss me."

That was what Valerie mumble-whispered when she stepped inside Daniel's apartment and faced the solitary portrait on the living-room wall. An oil painting of a black-suited man on his knees, pulling a shapely black woman who was outfitted in an open-back red sequin dress and matching high heels, bringing her love closer to his face, his hand gripping right under where her rotund backside stopped. Him wanting her.

The venetian blinds were drawn tight enough to block out most of the sunlight, only slivers came inside. The black ceiling fan was rotating, cooling the room. Without a sound, Valerie rested her back against the door like a woman tired. Closed her eyes like a woman denied. Dropped her hands to her side like a woman humbled. When her arms lowered, her purse and overnight bag fell free and landed on the carpet with a soft thump that sounded like one faint heartbeat. Maybe a last heartbeat before a dying wish. Maybe the final breath of Miss Saigon.

The words floated from her lips, "Kiss me."

Then she felt the heat. His body eased next to hers.

When he touched her, both legs weakened, her back went deeper into the door. She felt his lips on her shoulders. Then his tongue slowly stirring the nerves around her neck, then grazing her sensitive earlobes. Toes curled inside her pumps. Everything quivered. Her mind tried to push him away, but her heart pulled him closer. His breath felt good on her skin, the soft inner wind that told her how bad he wanted her. Daniel's mouth moved closer to hers, so close that she could almost savor the spearmint flavor on his lips. She said, "No tongue."

"I know."

"Put your mouth on mine. I can't let you inside of me. Not even your tongue."

She felt him nibbling her lips, kissing her closed eyes, licking the traces of salty tears. Then her hands reached and guided his palms to her breasts. Soft squeezes that made her chest rise and fall. Valerie led one of his hands between her legs, held it firm at her womanhood and chewed her lip. Both pressed closer together, reciprocating grinds while his hand slid downward and pulled her skirt up. Her eyes eased opened and she released a sigh when he touched her there. Tingles became shudders. It had been too long since she'd felt anything like that. Her hand went down and helped him massage her love. Slow. Small circles. Heat. She wanted to feel him, touch him in the same way, but she closed her hands tight, clenched her fists like she had to crush the wanting and frustration out of her life. With her legs squeezed around his motions, she pulled his mouth back to her neck. That helped ease the pain she had from not allowing herself to taste him. Not even one kiss had she ever given him. A second later she moved his affections away because she didn't want her neck to get bruised. But she held on to his hand.

She moaned, "There. Harder."

Her responses grew. Twitches rose to that point. Then she extended her arms and gently pushed him away. Even at arm's length, she felt the tension, saw the anxious movements in both of their bodies. The cool room was now warm. Humidity lay on both of their faces. Heavily breathing. Her lipstick had been quietly smeared away. Their clothes disarrayed. Her secrets, wet and aching.

Valerie shivered as she picked up her overnight bag and went into the bathroom. A few minutes later she came out dressed in jeans and a T-shirt. Teeth brushed again. Face washed. Makeup redone. While her hand gripped the handle on her overnight bag, her eyes didn't raise from the powder blue carpet.

At the front door, she turned back long enough to say, "It was nice meeting you, Daniel. Thanks for the movies and, you know. The play was excellent. Sorry if I wasn't good company."

She thought he would say something, but he stood there and looked at her. It felt uncomfortable that he let her babble while he watched with emotional eyes. Eyes just like hers. Valerie felt that he was studying like he was trying to capture every little detail about her. She'd already done the same when she took her last stare at him.

"I want you to be all right."

"I will," Valerie said. "Please, when you go running, try not to pass by my house."

He nodded.

"Take care of yourself."

He whispered, "Good-bye, Val."

"Good-bye."

20 / INDA

Despite my heated temper, Shoreline Village was pretty cool. I could see the sun was shining bright a few miles out, but the shoreline was having an overcast Saturday afternoon, so the air was a bit breezy and the temperature was a bit on the chilly side. Felt like a winter breeze in early September. Relative to everything else that had monsooned over the last thirty minutes, it was a calm after the storm. It had a nice view that I was too enraged to see and a good breeze that I was too hurt to feel, so I figured this was as good a place as any to try to think and walk this off before I attempted to drive back home. The last thing the freeway needed was me in traffic. Even though I'd managed to keep my dignity and composure in Raymond's apartment, I was too upset to sit still and chill, so I had to keep moving and try to shake this negative groove.

Since I parked on the boardwalk by the seafood tavern, I had walked circles around the restaurants, candy emporiums, gift shops, bookstores, and coffee shops. But no matter how far I went I dragged my bad feelings and temperament with me. And if you dragged something long enough, the shit started to get too damn heavy. And emotionally I felt wore down to the ground. Hate to say it, but not even Inda liked being played like she was Boo-Boo the fool. But experience with my ex-husband had already taught me this shit don't go away that easily.

It was too breezy and too cool out by the water, but I didn't care. I threw on my dark shades, bundled up in my jacket-of-hurt, hid my face, then meandered away from the crowds and cried a little bit. All I could think was, if I had stayed the night at Raymond's, that would've been me butt-naked with my coochie in the air, waking up and gawking up at Chiquita's face. But then again, maybe that was why he wanted to do me and get me out of there as soon as possible in the morning so he could go to the airport. Probably the real reason he let me walk out last night. Guess that middle-of-the-night phone call threw a monkey wrench in his scheduling for the downstroke.

I was wandering down the concrete strip where the thousands of boats were docked, with the *Queen Mary* out in the ocean on my right and the buildings of downtown standing sky-high on my left. When I blew my nose and glanced around for a trash can to toss my snot rag into, I saw a blue Miata parked crooked by the public bathroom. Parked across two spaces with the top down. Nobody was in the car, but I could see a travel bag recklessly thrown across the front seat. A few feet down the concrete boardwalk, sistuh-Afro was leaning over the rail, crying and shaking, looking a little like she was about ready to jump face-first down on the jagged rocks, but mostly like she needed a friend to lean on. And since I had two empty shoulders, I wiped my watery eyes and walked over to her. Misery loves company. I just didn't know if I was the misery or the company.

I put my hand on her shoulder. "Where's your coat?"

She didn't move when she mumbled, "huh?"

"Chiquita, where's your coat? You're freezing cold."

She turned around and looked at me, more like through me. At first I could tell she was too dazed to recognize me. Her nose was running a little bit, dripping over her red lipstick and she sounded stopped-up and hoarse when she cough-cleared her throat and said, "Brenda?"

"Inda. Linda without the *L*."

"Hey. Uh, my coat's in the cry." She wiped her face and smudged her already smudged makeup. "I mean the car. In my bag."

"Where you live?"

"Stupid me drove up from San Diego."

"You got somewhere to go or somebody to call?"

She shook her head then looked at her hands. She sounded like she was in a trance. "I've got a girl-friend I work with named Shelby who lives up in LA. I called her, but her man said she's on a two-day trip to the East Coast. That's the only other person I know up this way."

"It's getting cold." I took her hand. "No need being sad and sick over somebody who ain't sad and sick over you."

"Thanks, Inda. I'm sorry about leaving you back there."

"That's okay." I sighed.

"What's wrong?" she asked. "Why're you crying?"

It pained me to tell her, but I thought she deserved to know who she was talking to. "I was leaving Raymond a note."

"Raymond?"

I nodded.

Her grieving look asked me a question.

My red-rimmed eyes gave her the answer.

It was awkward for a long moment, almost like we were deciding if we were going to start acting stupid with each other. Then we sighed then tried to hug away each other's hurt. When I looked down at the concrete I saw she had ripped up the picture that was in her key ring. We looked at the ripped-up picture, then looked at each other. Then we held each other a little tighter.

"Excuse me," a polite voice came from behind us. A brotha in ragged jeans and a hooded black leather jacket was walking by carrying some canvas and other artistic supplies. "You ladies all right? Everything cool?"

We stood there, patting each other's back and nodded. I recognized him from seeing him sitting out on the docks painting big-headed, small-bodied caricatures of people for a donation. I think he'd spoken to me a time or two in passing. I sorta nodded and kept on moving.

"We're okay," Chiquita said and pulled herself together.

"Thanks," I said. "It's all to the good."

"Just checking. Wanted to make sure it was all right."

He saluted, smiled, and walked off. I guess he was heading to his corner spot on the boardwalk that faced the merry-go-round and yogurt shops so he could make his living.

We walked to the Miata, quiet and shaking our heads.

21 / **VALERIE**

On the two-minute drive back to her house, Valerie wished that she'd spent the warm morning doing laundry, then maybe the heat of the afternoon in the coolness of Lucky's getting groceries. Then going into the video store and renting two or three old black-and-white movies. Movies she'd watch while the laundry was being done. Doing the usual things she'd done over too many weekends to keep herself busy. Safe things so she wouldn't have the guilt from sneaking out today. Guilt that blended with too much anger. So much animosity was swirling inside of her. It had swollen her chest. Burned in the pit of her stomach. Spasmed in her head. A perpetual aching that had moved into her life and seemed like it would never go away.

The Asian and Caucasian neighbors' kids were riding bikes and skateboarding up and down Garden Court. Just as Valerie cut her car off, her next-door neighbor, Charlotte, bounced outside. She was holding hands with a medium-height cinnamon-colored brother with a faded haircut. Both of them were dressed in pastel linen shorts and conservative Old Navy T-shirts. Neither noticed Valerie, but she watched them. He opened the car door for Charlotte. She leaned over and unlocked his side of the black Mustang. When he got in, they kissed like teenagers. Charlotte wiped her lipstick away from his mouth. Giggled. The car revved. He let the top down. They drove away. Valerie imagined Charlotte's hand was on top of her date's hand, touching and massaging each other as they flirted and sped off to wherever they were taking their happiness.

After sitting out in her driveway for almost thirty minutes, she finally pressed her garage-door opener and waited for it to whir and rattle open. Walter's BMW was taking a siesta on his side of the garage. On the left of the imaginary line. She parked on her side. Then she turned off the engine and sat there. Head hurting. Damp hands gripping the steering wheel.

Valerie went into the house. Walter was just stepping out of the shower when she walked into his bedroom. The guest bedroom. He came out of the bathroom naked, but when he saw she was home, he wrapped a towel around himself. He maneuvered around her, went over to the dresser, and looked in the circular mirror as he put on his deodorant.

Valerie said a sweet, "How're you feeling today?"

He spoke a dry-ass, "Evening," then turned his back to her and started putting cocoa-butter-scented lotion on his thick, hairy legs. After what Inda said on the beach, coupled with what Daniel had asked her the night she stayed with him, Valerie had gotten up the nerve to ask Walter a question. Her mouth opened and closed several times, but nothing came out. Again she was intimidated. Not by his size, but by the answer he might give. Walter pulled his gray slacks on over his black boxer shorts, then sat in the corner wingback chair and started pulling on his black socks. When she deliberately dropped her heavy purse where she stood, he didn't look up. Valerie exhaled, rubbed her neck, massaged under her eyes, then walked over and kneeled in front of him. Not too close, but close enough.

Valerie said, "I need to know something."

He barely glanced at her and didn't miss a motion with his dressing. "What?"

"Walter, are you sleeping with somebody else?"

"Why?"

"Are you? If you are we can fix it."

"If I was, I wouldn't be wasting my time here every night."

"Walter." She inhaled, rubbed her hands together, then whispered, "Do you love me?"

His eyes met hers. That was the first time they'd made that much contact in months. It lasted less than a second.

She said, "Do you love me even a little?"

Walter frowned like he had a sudden bad taste in his mouth, shook his head and said a definite, "I don't even *like* you."

Her eyes widened. "What?"

"I said, I don't even like you."

"What did I do, huh? You used to love—"

"Valerie, there's *nothing* in you for me. It's been over for a long time. I know it and you know it."

She choked on her words. "You want a divorce?"

"Let me put it like this. I don't want you."

Valerie collapsed back on her butt and cried, "Why?"

She wanted to flee the room but she was frozen by his harshness. His tone pinned her down and made her listen. For weeks, he hadn't said a word to her. Now he growled out everything he'd bottled up. The more she cried, the less she wanted to hear, the more he forced out what he felt. He kept reassuring her that he didn't like her; that he never would like her; that he didn't understand why he ever liked her. He screamed that he'd only been going through the motions and hoped her "dumb ass" would catch a hint and leave; that she was boring, with no life; that she was so lost in him she didn't even have a "fucking personality"; that she'd changed and become the last thing he wanted to marry, a boring wife. He wanted an exciting, ambitious woman he could build something with but ended up with an "uneducated bitch who's content with wasting her time making minimum wage" and leeched off his paycheck. He added that if she had had ambition and had put forth the effort and found a decent job and contributed, they could've had more, but everything they had came from him. She was sucking the money out of his pockets and the life out of him. It didn't make sense to her, but he blamed her for his not making the NFL, for his not being "out there making real money."

"How are you going to blame that on me, huh? All I did was support whatever you did."

"If your ass hadn't been following me everywhere I went, if you had stayed where you belonged and stopped running up behind me, I wouldn't have been so distracted and drained when I went for tryouts. My life was all right until I hooked up with you."

She didn't know when he stopped badgering; she didn't know when he left. All she knew was that in between her whimpering, she realized she was alone. She shook as if someone had sat her on a block of ice.

All she thought of was the last six years. She'd given her all, her best, to him for six years. In college, when he was down on luck, she took her last money and fed him. He never offered to pay for any of the three abortions he coerced her into getting because "the time wasn't right." But she was strong and understood why he didn't want to take her to the clinic. His status was important and he couldn't "risk being seen at one of those places."

When he couldn't get the money to fly back for pro tryouts, she applied for a student loan and gave him the money. He asked her to go along. She never asked for a dime back. He never offered. He was such a nervous wreck before tryouts, so stressed, that he needed somebody to hold his sweaty hand. She was the one who was tired, but she'd sit up all night and listen to him vent about how excited he was from not getting cut the first day. Then she rubbed his shoulders and consoled him when he complained about how "they" had wrongly cheated him by cutting him. New York. New Jersey. Anaheim. Los Angeles. She was there for him. Making sure everything was in order, making it easier for him. And that made it harder on her. All the bills she amassed, all the debt she went into because of him. Up to her neck in debt, she couldn't afford to go back to school and wasn't going to ask her parents for help, especially since they'd given them the down payment for their house as a wedding present. With three-fourths of an accounting degree, she was lucky to find a job paying as much as the one she had that didn't involve cleaning something. At least it kept her mind oiled by doing books and accounting-related work. Even though it was a dead-end job, it paid more than minimum wage.

But all his failures were her fault. If that was true, then whose fault were her failures?

She cried, "How could you blame me for being in your corner, for sacrificing my damn life? I ain't got shit to show for *me*. I gave up my dreams for you."

She cried more when she realized she had nothing left to care about. After her tears dried, her heart hardened. The things he said, the way he'd been treating her, were unforgivable.

22 / VALERIE

After Valerie calmed as best she could, she made her plans. First, she tried to still her shaking hands and dial Inda's number. Where she usually could dial big sister's number blindfolded by heart, it took her three frustrating tries to get the number right. When Inda's answering machine came on, Valerie's voice cracked. Her head hurt as her swollen eyes welled and she started crying again. It took her almost three minutes to choke out: "Black. By the time you get this message, I don't know where I'll be, or what kind of trouble or shape I'll be in, but either way, I love you. And I want to thank you for always being there. I'm not calling Moms or Pops. And don't call Brown. I don't want Brown tripping. Not yet, anyway. Black, Walter went off on me and I got to take care of it. By myself. If I can manage to get away, I'll call you."

Next, after she gained more control of her voice, she called Daniel and left a softer, more composed message. "Daniel, Red. I mean, Valerie. Today meant so much to me. I hope that I didn't disappoint you. If I had today again, I'd, eh, I'd, hell, I'd go all the way. Oh, God. That sounded so corny. I'd have sex with you. You're nice and if I don't talk to you any-more, I hope everything turns out good for you back East. I'm sure going to miss seeing you running."

After she packed a few of her things into two big suitcases, she dragged them out to the car and stuffed them in the trunk.

23 / **INDA**

My life had come to this.

In the time it took for me to slowly walk Chiquita to my car, hand her the tulips she left behind, watch her throw them away, go back to her Miata, drive me to my car, then for me to get into my Camry, I relived the pain of the first time I went through something like this. The wounds weren't open, and the scar didn't show, but the memory was Ziploc-fresh. Back then I was sorta like the way Chiquita seemed to be now—hot to trot and good to go—but worse.

As quiet as it be kept, my first and only husband was white. Like the fool I was, I had married Andre damn near on the day he asked me. I'd only known him two months, if that long. But the man was *fiiine*. And had a j-o-b. From the moment we lip-locked, it was on till the break of dawn. We took blood tests and hooked up with the justice of the peace, and the next thing I knew, wham-bam, his Lava lamp and Hush Puppies were at my apartment in San Dimas, and I was Mrs. Inda Lorraine Johnson-Swift. With a Kool-Aid smile. My moms was mad as hell because we didn't have a four-star wedding. I think Pops was happy because he didn't have to spend any money. His cheap ass.

Before the three months had come and gone, things changed. Sorta like that ninety-day warranty you got on a television or VCR. Then on the ninety-first day, shit started acting strange.

But that's what happens when you don't really get to know a man.

Real quick it got to be little things like the cap being left off the toothpaste and clothes left on the floor. Then it got to be about him saying he'd be home at two o'clock in the afternoon and showing up at five a.m. Not often, just a couple of times. Then the phone started ringing one or two times and nobody was on the other line when I answered. But as soon as I hung up he'd have to run to the store for something important and come back two hours later empty-handed. That was enough. Especially after I called the grocery store he managed, called in the middle of third shift, and they said he wasn't scheduled for duty that night. His off day.

Red thought I was overreacting. She was so in love with Walter then. And mentally, we were at opposite ends of the relationship spectrum. I might've been at the point that most sistuhs got to sooner than I expected. That place where we'd had so many fucked-up relationships where our "monogamous" brothas were passing out their dicks like it was cotton candy that I just didn't trust anybody even when they deserved the benefit of the doubt. The slightest shift in the wind made me want to run in the other direction. It made a sistuh do crazy things. Like keeping a silent tally on the condoms. Then after the loving, checking the stupid latex to make sure he had climaxed enough juices inside the reservoir tip to satisfy our half-crazed minds. Made you want to run down to the market, grab a silver scale from the produce section and weigh the Trojan to make sure he'd pumped enough baby-juice to let you know he hadn't been donating anywhere else in between times.

And of course, Inda had to do her own investigating. And I know I was tripping when I started taking off work early, renting a different car, getting to his job before he left work, parking and waiting, then following him to wherever he went.

Took me a minute or two to realize what was going on. Mainly because I was working twelve hours a day, driving for two, and trying to get some sleep in between. And even then, like the most of us, I didn't want to believe the obvious. So in my denial, I went to the extreme to disprove my intuition.

With the windows up and the rental car seat reclined so that anybody who drove by couldn't see me, I sat underneath the condominium's bedroom window and chewed my nails down to the cuticles. The crib I had seen him go in three or four times. We didn't own property, didn't have any friends in the city of Upland, so Inda's well-developed radar-lie detector said it was something that needed to be looked into. I had even jotted down the address and went to City Hall to find out who owned the property. I knew I was in the right place because my husband's Camaro with the personalized plates was in a numbered stall that belonged to the unit.

At first all I wanted was to see who he came out with. See what and who I was dealing with before I stepped up to the plate. Because it could've been rented out by the owner. But time had ticked on by and I wanted to know what was really going on. With each tick of the clock, my heart was on fire, blazing like the desert sun that made me keep fanning my blouse. My forehead would sweat, but I was so hot the humidity would sizzle and steam before it left my pores. And there was nothing but ruthlessness in my chocolate-covered veins.

When the lights inside the place went off, something deep inside of me clicked on. Part of me wanted to walk up and bang on the door for a face-to-face. Part of me wanted to chill and see for sure before I made a fool of myself.

Anyway, after sitting for seven hours, I was too anxious to get it over with. It was two a.m. I had to be at work in five hours. He hadn't come out yet. I'd even left a few times to go to a pay phone and check our answering machine. He hadn't called home either. Men do start to get bold with their nonsense after a while. And I was just as bold. I took my .380 out and looked at it. Made sure it had a hollow point or two in the clip.

My hair had lost any kind of style because I had sweated all day. It was cool at night but the day was damn near triple digits. The glow from the new moon, the clear skies that let the Big Dipper shine down, made it a wonderful night for lying lovers to croak in each other's arms. Shit, I could jack them up, go home for a nap, shower, and be at work before they made the news.

The condominium's security guard drove by in his white Ford, flashing lights at the parked cars to make sure nobody was breaking in. When he drove off, I took a deep breath and opened my door. The inside light didn't come on because I'd taken the bulb out. A little trick I'd learned from television.

Sixteen stairs led up to the second floor of the tan stucco building. I'd counted them the time I came and got the address. At first I hiked to the front door and stood there for a while in the gentle breeze. Then I knocked soft, like I was Avon calling, and stepped to the side of the peephole. The only way they would hear the taps was if they were in the front room. No answer.

Then I went back downstairs and looked up at the patio door. It was open. I was twenty-nine, flexible and agile. And we all know when a sistuh gets mad, a sistuh gets athletically creative. Whether she's wearing a dime-store micro skirt or a thousand-dollar evening dress, she goes with the flow because she's gotta know what she needs to know.

After I came out of them heels, it took me less

than two seconds to act like I was trying out for the Olympics and pounce up on the rail of the first-floor balcony. Another second to make it up on the second-floor balcony and pull myself up to that patio. And that surprised me because I didn't know I could do that my damn self. My brand-new silk blouse had ripped. Hose had runs. Two nails broke. Green skirt ripped. But I was up there. Barefoot with my drawers riding up the crack of my ass.

Then I felt like Boo-Boo the fool because I wondered what the hell I was doing. I told myself I had too much sense and too much education to be doing some dumb ghetto shit. And with my acrophobic butt, there was no way in hell that I was gonna jump back down without an earthquake giving me a boost. Shame or no shame, as far as I was concerned, the only way out was through the front door. And if they were lounging in the living room, I'd speak and walk on through like I was the mailman.

The patio sliding door was open. Not even closed all the way. Cracked enough to let in some of the night breeze. It slid open real easy. I went through scared as hell.

Light love songs came from the CD player in the marble entertainment center. Speakers were anchored on all the walls. Somebody had taste and money to waste. A pizza box was on the floor. An empty bottle of Chablis was on the smoky glass coffee table next to two wineglasses. A pair of trousers were next to a polo shirt. A white polo shirt that I'd bought for my husband at the Gap. That was when I took my gun out of my purse. And let me tell you, my blood pressure was on the rise. I had already seen enough, but you know me. Inda had to see it all.

A few seconds later I was creeping down the hall to the bedroom. The venetian blinds were open enough for the moonlight to lay on their skin. Hers glowed like a porch light. I don't know how long I stood there with my fists clenched and looked at that four-post bed. Neither moved. I was in a corner by a ceiling-high plant and watched them cuddle and sleep next to each other under the spinning ceiling fan. My man and his clean-up woman, getting all the love I left behind.

A car's horn blew outside. My husband mumbled, moved, looked across the room at the digital clock on the nightstand, then checked the watch on his arm. As the car passed, he rubbed his eyes and leaned toward the window. Andre had beige skin, goatee, curly hair faded on the sides. A slim six-footer. So with my trembling hands fighting to be patient, I inhaled, exhaled, and waited. Then he eased down again and cuddled in the spoon position.

There was so much horror in my soul because I didn't know what to do. I had the gun pointed. Finger on trigger. Trust me, the shit ain't as easy as you think it is, especially when you hadn't ever shot anybody before. But I knew I was on my way. All I could think about was thick Plexiglas between me and my family while they visited me at Sybil Brand every other Sunday for the next ninety-nine years.

By then gobs of sweat had rolled over my lips to my chin. Makeup was just as runny. My blouse had stuck to my back like a second skin. And to make it worse my twelve-hour deodorant had clocked out. Nothing worse than a mad, musty sistuh.

Then Andre stirred. And inhaled. Eyes opened. For a second I thought the man smelled and remembered my sweat and perfume.

They started kissing. First the sounds of little soft kisses and mumbles, then slurps from deeper and longer tonguing. Andre rubbed her private parts and ran his hands over her shoulder-length blond hair. Then her hand slid between his legs, made up and down motions that made the sheets rise and fall.

"Mmmm." Andre chuckled. "Want me, baby?"

"Got time?"

"No rush."

Andre took the latex out. Rolled it on. And they became one ghostly shadow. Soft pulls and delicate screams that made my heart speed up while I gritted my goddamn teeth. It felt like I was somewhere else, somebody else, imagining the worst thing that could happen in my life. Had my life come to this? And all I had the strength to do was stand there and let it happen.

Tears ran down my face. I didn't know what to do.

Headboard rocked. The mattress squeaked a jazzy rhythm.

My legs were aching. Shaking. I held my breath and wanted to break for the door. But Inda was stuck where she stood. Like the damn fool she was. Good at her day job, but after five, shit was always falling apart left and right. And I couldn't move. But that's how it was. You want to see shit with your own eyes, then when you did, you wish you hadn't seen the shit with your own eyes. I would've settled for reading about it in the *Enquirer*.

Their exchange grew into something rugged. They slid down the sheets and fell from the bed to the floor, kicking the covers away while they melted into the carpet, never stopping, almost like they were chasing each other into ecstasy. With his pushes, they scooted back. Their heat and nasty-ass aroma drifted over to me like it wanted to add insult to injury. Then they were at my feet, my man on top with his eyes closed.

"Oh, Donna," he moaned, "I love you so much, babe."

Hearing that four-letter word put me to shame. And her hair was almost on my toes. Her face was in a sliver of light. Then the blue eyes popped open like a jack in the box. What was freaky was in the middle of what I was watching, I thought, I'd never seen eyes that blue. That peaceful. I'd never seen anybody look that happy to be with a man. Somebody who was happy and knew how to enjoy what she had while she had it. Even when she didn't have shit worth having.

The blue eyes stopped in their tracks and widened. She quit breathing and stared upward like something was definitely lurking in the dark. Something in a dirty white blouse, wild hair, and jacked-up warpaint. One of my tears rolled off my face and fell in the middle of one of the blue eyes. I swear to God I heard it plop like a drop of water falling out of a faucet into a puddle. Then blondie found enough air to choke out a low scream—a shuddering sound that came when somebody was too afraid to admit their real terror. My breast swelled. Chest tightened. But my newlywed husband gripped harder and bucked faster like he thought the trembling and wail from the person under him was a cue to kick into fifth gear and drive through the doors of seventh heaven. I never knew Andre had those kinda bedroom skills. Maybe it took a woman of a different shade to excite him to that point.

"Ahhh! Andre! S-s-somebody—"

My insides had spasm after spasm. I reached behind me to the nightstand and clicked the 40-watt light on. Andre roared and scared the shit out of me, made me yelp, then he jumped out of Miss Thang like he realized he was inside a burning poison. My husband's mouth was a big *O*. Both of their faces cringed.

Through my stopped-up nose I said, "Hello, honey. What time were you coming home tonight?"

"Ohhh—" That was Andre scampering when he saw my feet near his face. I stayed statue-still and glowered. Then I grimaced at the forty-something woman with D-cups and bikini tan line.

"Oh, excuse my manners. My name is Inda Johnson-Swift. And you are?"

Her words dipped into disbelief. "Don't rob me. I mean, rob me. Don't hurt me. My purse is right there. Take the IBM laptop and the Rolex."

"What?" I shook my head and tisked. A white woman sees an angry black woman in her crib at two a.m. with a loaded gun and the first thing she thinks is she's about to get robbed of her riches. Now ain't that a bitch? "Andre Swift is my husband."

"Bastard!" She wiped her sweaty face and snapped at Andre. Even slapped his arm. "You're married!"

Give me a break. That had to be the sorriest attempt at acting ignorant that I'd ever seen. Especially since he had a big-ass band on his finger.

They saw the gun. Heads shook. Mine slowly nodded.

Now all I know was I was numb. And when you went numb any damn thing could happen because you latched on to the first emotion that came strolling along. And trust me, that was what I was waiting for. A sweet sensation to tell me what to do.

Andre whimpered stupid-ass apologies through his thin lips and tried to scoot away, moved backwards fast enough to make his brunette hair bounce and get first-degree rug burns from his neck down his backside. The bony woman with the wide hips, washboard butt, and leathery skin froze for a moment, then bumbled around the floor, cursed and whined and grunted and groaned in circles like a stray dog that had been splashed with hot water. Andre did the same Three Stooges move with the condom dangling off the tip of his thang, his eyes darting every which-a-way like he was trying to measure the distance between him and the front door. When he tried to get up, I pointed the gun at him because I thought he was coming after me, but he gasped and looked like he was about to faint, slipped on an empty wine bottle, then fell on the tip of his dick and screamed the scream of all screams. That woke him right back up better than smelling salts.

"Andre," I said. "Shut up."

And it got quiet. Inda was in charge.

Sweat of regret dripped from Andre's forehead. "What are you doing here?"

"What are *you* doing here?" Dumb question for a dumb question. I asked, "How could you do some shit like this to me?"

The woman with the vibrating bottom lip was beet-red now. So was Andre. I had turned twelve shades of black.

Tears of fear rolled down my loving husband's face. Well, at least I knew his secret. Inda had been put in a serious trick bag. Drops of anger splashed from my face. I was trembling so bad everything was wobbling—except the gun in my hand. He wore a blinkless stare that said he doubted he'd see his twenty-eighth birthday.

"Aww, W-wait." His voice cracked. "P-please? I can explain."

The begging pissed me off. Why did a man always have to beg? Was there no dignity in shame? I mumbled, "Pah-leeze."

Then came the other babyish weep. "No, don't, Glenda."

I looked at her and said, "Inda. Linda without the *L*."

We all trembled as my finger tightened on the trigger. And it got quiet like I supposed it did when death came a-stealing.

Then I put the gun down to my side and went into the woman's kitchen. What tripped me out was that the first emotion that hit me was hunger. That crazy urge to peel a cap and set the record straight walked away because I knew the truth and there wasn't a damn thing to do about it. My curiosity had been more than satisfied.

There was so much frantic noise in the bedroom. Deep breaths. Struggling to get clothes back on, wondering how I got in, how I knew, where I came from. Just plain old wondering.

I said, "Andre Swift."

"Yeah." And talk about a man who sounded pathetic.

I was too strong for him. And I realized that then. Maybe when a man felt threatened by a sistuh he ran to a weaker woman to build himself up. I was about to give the Q&A routine, but then it didn't matter. Over is over is over. The reason why was obvious. His excuse would be an old story. Confused. Always confused. Either that or scared. Too scared to talk about it, but not too scared to take his jimmy for a midnight stroll.

"Your drawers are in the living room on the ottoman. Right next to the shirt I bought you," I said. Then I yelled, "Woman with my husband. What's your name?"

She stuck her head around the corner. Lips twisted. A yellow robe was on her, tied up tight. "Donna Emerson."

"You love him?"

She said, "Well . . ."

"Sweetheart, Inda is tired and cramping like a big dog. No games, okay? A simple yes or no."

"No."

"And you've been seeing him since when?"

"Few weeks. We barely know each other."

"Good for you." My stomach growled. "Donna, what do you have to eat?"

Her voice trembled and she held her hands up like she was a POBW, Prisoner of a Black Woman. "What was that, ma'am?"

Then I realized the gun was still in my hand and I was waving it every which-a-way with each of my snappy words. I stuck it inside my waistline like they did in the movies. "Put your hands down. I'm cool. I'm too wore out to shoot anybody."

She did. "What did you want?"

"Food." I had been sitting out in that damn car so long I had hemorrhoids and was hungry. "I'm starving like Marvin."

"Marvin?"

"Never mind." I exhaled and rubbed my eyes. "What you got to grub on?"

Her eyes blinked like butterflies. "Nothing much."

"I kinda figured that by the pizza box. You probably shouldn't leave it out on the floor because it's hot. Over a hundred degrees before noon. Ants will be all over the place. Have Andre bring you some repellent from his job."

A pint of butter pecan ice cream was in the freezer. Ben and Jerry's. The good stuff. I put the cup up to my face, rolled it up and down my neck, over my arms, under my funky armpits.

Donna tripped out but stayed away from me. "I'm sorry for—"

I said, "Donna."

"Yes."

"Shut up."

"Okay."

I said, "Andre."

He slithered into the living room, the sheets around his body. He yacked about being sorry, but the Inda-face made him shut up.

"Keys."

"Inda, listen."

"Now."

It took him a second to get his pants unknotted and hand me the house keys.

I said, "Donna."

"Yes."

"You got Andre." I raised the ice cream. "We're even."

Then I got a silver spoon from her dishwasher and left. Eating the ice cream and yawning. Damn near three in the morning. At the bottom of the stairs I picked up my pumps and finger-combed my hair. My hair was probably filthy enough to leave dirt under my nails. I'd been in the sun so long that my hair had dried so I think I had cornflake-size dandruff. Security passed by and waved. They drove slow and made sure I was safe inside my car. Then I gave a Miss America smile and waved back and left. Left so fast my tires screeched and rear end fishtailed. A sistuh fuming. But in control. Always in control.

And I rationalized to myself why I didn't blow up like I could've, should've, and thought I would've. I knew in less than ten seconds. First off I loved his Chippendale body and financial potential. The sex was okay. Better at first, but I guess his interests were elsewhere. Or everywhere.

The main reason was because I wasn't in love with him. Add it all up and I married for all the wrong reasons. Plus he said he loved her. Which was cool. You marry a white man and he tips out to be with a white woman, ain't much you can say.

It wasn't curiosity. Couldn't call it racism or jungle fever.

It was just him going back home.

To the Otherland.

And that was where Inda went that night.

Home.

To the motherland.

With an extra set of keys.

24 / **VALERIE**

Valerie's mind was still hypnotized by Walter's abuse. She didn't remember moving from place to place, doing all the things on her mental list. All she knew was she kept going. She'd committed to what had to be done. He would regret his unforgivable actions.

I don't even like you

Valerie drove north to the busy Pep Boys in Montclair, thirty minutes away from where she lived. She didn't want a remote chance of being recognized later. She paid cash for a large gasoline container. Then she drove to a hardware store.

uneducated bitch

"Excuse me."
"Yes?"
"Is this chemical flammable?"
She filled the metal container, then gassed her almost-empty tank. She didn't know how long or how far she might have to drive to get away. She

didn't even know if she would get away. That didn't trouble her. She might not make it out of the house, but that didn't make any difference. When you had nothing to lose, nothing mattered.

25 / INDA

"**S**he did what?" Chiquita doubled over laughing, spitting part of her crab salad dead into my eye. I ducked too late. "Damn, girl!"

"Ooops!" She covered her mouth. "Sorry, Inda."

I laughed. "That's okay."

"She drove down the freeway in broad daylight, doing eighty, throwing Coke bottles at his car?"

"Then she painted a message on the front door to his crib."

"No! What she write?"

"She carved it in the wood in big red letters, 'The dog-ass nigger who lives here ain't about shit and will fuck your best friend if you turn your back.'"

"You lie!"

"Even took the time to dot the *i*'s and cross the *t*'s."

Chiquita and I were sitting upstairs in a corner booth at the Shoreline Village seafood restaurant, Parker's Lighthouse, a two-floor oceanfront place that looked like a light tower. We were chowing down and swapping relationship horror stories. She'd tell one, I'd tell one, then we started telling our girlfriends' stories, and so on and so on. And it got pretty amazing how many times so many people had gone through a version of the same bull. I thought it would be hard to talk about, but nope. We just waved our hands and traded stories, sorta like brothas did when they got back from Vietnam. And our battles with relationships were definitely a war. Our tour of duty. Their lies were the shrapnel they left behind. All of which were painful at the time, but got to be pretty funny, after the fact. Way, way after the fact. The worst thing Chiquita admitted to doing was seasoning a few brothas' chocolate cakes with Ex-Lax and keying a coupla cars. Nothing unusual.

She twisted her smile. "And I make a damn good cake, too."

"I heard that. You ought to drop down that recipe."

"As soon as you hook me up with some Ben and Jerry's."

Me myself, other than what you've already heard, well I'd cut up a few suits and thrown a brick or two through an ex's bedroom window and put pounds of sugar in a few gas tanks back in my untamed days. But brick slanging was my claim to fame. Ain't nothing worse than a sistuh scorned.

Chiquita's twenty-five and met Raymond a year ago on one of her flights, then ran into him again right after that when she was up in LA clubbing on the west side. That was near Brentwood at a hot spot called Savannah West. She told him what type of relationship she demanded and he dropped her his door keys right off the bat. Then, of course, he added a third deadbolt.

I guess we were trying to figure out when he had time to be Ping-Ponging three women and working a nine-to-five five days a week. He probably crawled into work sipping on a gallon of orange juice, looking for an empty cubicle so he could get his beauty sleep. Because of the distance, I rarely saw the dog on weekdays and I know I always called before I went over. Chiquita never went to church with him and only came up when he called, which was usually during the week, but not every week. She'd never seen Gina's pictures, so I guess he took them down when she came to town, meaning I was definitely the low woman on the scrotum-pole.

Chiquita said, "Engaged, huh?"

"That's what she said. He didn't deny it."

"Think she'll stay?"

"I hope not. The sistuh deserves better."

"We should go rescue her."

"She's grown. She knows what's going on."

"I hope she ain't no fool."

"You never know. As much as I hate to say it, she was the fiancée. But then again, you had the keys."

"Only two."

"I didn't have that much. I just got a phone call every now and then. Every third day if I was lucky."

"That sounds about right." Chiquita stopped eating and looked out the window toward where we left our problems.

"If he called you," I asked, "would you go back?"

Chiquita snapped out of her trance and shook her head. "Heck no. You?"

"Nope, never, nada. Not even if he dropped on his hands and knees and blew fire out of his trifling ass."

"Good." Chiquita paused and shook her head. "I don't understand. You?"

"What?"

"Why would a brother go through that much trouble to hurt that many people? All he had to say was what I offered him wasn't what he wanted and let me go on with my business. If he had somebody else from the get go why couldn't he just say so? I would've just packed up and moved on. I wouldn't have made no noise 'cause I ain't the type. I'd've walked on, that's it. Why brothers trip out like that?"

"Not all brothas. A few dogs give the good ones a bad rap. I've been the villain and given a few brothas the short end of the stick a time or two. Some are good down to the bone."

"Most are dogs. Trust me."

"A lot of 'em. And that fool's a rover rolling over if ever I saw one. Looks like he had at least two good women."

"And who knows who didn't show up for the party."

"It was starting to look like a *Soul Train* line."

Just then the brotha who painted caricatures on the docks walked up and stopped by our table. "Glad to see you two ladies are doing better. Keep those delightful smiles."

Neither of us said anything because he caught us off guard with a mouth full of salad. So he walked on by.

"Inda?"

"What?"

"He likes you."

"No he don't."

"That's *twice* he's looked at you like that."

"Like what?"

Chiquita tilted her head and made her eyes go sexy. "This."

We both laughed. A piece of salad flew out of my mouth and landed on the tip of her nose. She ducked too late.

She wiped her nose. "He *really* looked at you again when you walked by."

"So?"

"And when I looked back he'd stopped painting that Mexican couple and was breaking his neck to see which way you were going."

"You lie."

"Nah, uh. Nice looking, too."

"Must've been looking at you."

"Nah, uh. You."

"Nah, uh. You."

Just as we laughed and high-fived each other, the brotha came back up the stairs and walked straight over to our table. He politely looked at Chiquita for a quick sec, but he stopped in front of me. He looked nervous, almost like he had got all of his nerves up to walk back over.

"I don't mean to bother you ladies, but I work down on the dock and I would love to sketch both of you. I'm a part-time artist." He cleared his throat. "My name's Michael."

"Well, Michael," I asked, "how much?"

"Complimentary." He smiled at me and gave me that look of interest Chiquita was talking about. The way he was subtly shifting from side to side, I could tell he was a tad bit on the shy side, and actually today shy seemed kind of cute. So I kind of broke down and gave him the sweet-eye look, just because. I didn't want to run him off, not so fast anyway. And I know we just broke it off with dog-ass up the street, but hey. After all I am a woman, dammit.

"Complimentary as in free?" I said. "That fits my budget."

He fidgeted around his jean shirt pocket and took out a gold business card and politely placed it on my side of the table. "If you have time. I'm here every evening."

Chiquita grinned and made her eyebrows bounce.

Michael politely excused himself for intruding, then grinned at me and walked off. When he turned around, me and Chiquita both cut our eyes at his butt and gave each other girly faces.

Chiquita called out, giggling, "Excuse me, my girlfriend wants to know if you're single? She thinks you're cute.''

''Chiquita!'' I said. She made me blush so hard I know I turned purple. I playfully slapped her hand and said, ''No, you didn't!''

Michael pretended like he was whispering to Chiquita, ''I think your friend's got it going on. She's all that and ain't nothing left over.''

I said, ''Thank you. Does your wife know you walk up and down the pier following and flirting with women?''

Michael said, ''S.I.N.C.''

I smiled. ''What's S.I.N.C.?''

''Single Income, No Children.''

I tried to be cool, you know hang on to that strong black woman persona I'd developed over the years, but me and Chiquita bucked our eyes and said, ''Mmmm.''

Chiquita asked, ''You live with your mother?''

''Afraid not,'' he said and looked confused. ''By myself.''

''Rent or own? Can we see your last two tax returns?''

I slapped her hand. ''Chiquita! You are so silly!''

''Shush.'' Chiquita fanned me off. ''How old are you?''

''Thirty-three next Friday.''

I mumbled, ''Hmm. Thirty-three's good'n stable.''

He asked, ''Stopping by?''

I said, ''Your house?''

"No, I meant the pier." His face turned red. "To get your beautiful face captured on canvas."

"Ooo*Ooo!*" Chiquita looked at me. "He's talking to you."

I held my blush in check and said a soft, "Maybe."

"Well if you don't I hope you ladies have a lovely evening."

Chiquita's high-pitched giggles made me giggle. He sorta laughed and almost tripped when he walked down the spiral stairs. I waltzed over to the top of the staircase and watched him until he got to the front door of the restaurant. He looked back and saw me watching. He smiled and waved. I waved, but I didn't smile. Not much anyway. I guess because before I could show my pearly whites, I had a quick flashback—kinda like I heard brothas who had been on the front line in hand-to-hand combat had experienced—from all the other relationships that started off so sweet and ended up so sour. At some point I'd think I'd know the difference between fresh Kool-Aid and day-old hot piss without having to drink the whole damn glass. But still, he seemed like a nice guy. But I guess *seemed* is the word of the day. As I sighed and twisted my lip, I lost that oh-so-good feeling he had brought up the stairs to sprinkle over me. My head slightly dropped as I strolled back over to the table-of-hoodwinked-and-bamboozled-hearts.

"Chiquita?"

"Yeah?"

"Why we always overlook brothas like that and end up with a Deputy Dawg?"

Her unsmiling face looked like it had the same feeling that was in my heart. She looked out the window and hunched her shoulders. "When I find out I'll send you a memo."

"Fax it to me."

"You got it."

I tapped the card and let out a nervous gun-shy Inda-sigh.

Chiquita asked, "Well?"

I shook my head. When we left the table, I looked back at the artsy card. Sometimes a fantasy was better than reality.

26 / **VALERIE**

Eleven P.M.

Valerie called home. Walter answered. She hung up. She drove through the back streets and parked around the corner and waited. None of his brothers or his friends came by, so he was home alone. Around midnight, all the lights were turned off. She had no excuse not to do it.

27 / **INDA**

We danced a bit, then sat over in a corner and kicked it over a couple glasses of wine. Most brothas were suited up, most sistuhs were short-skirted down, a few dressed so risqué you'd think they were auditioning to be centerfolds in *Black Tail Magazine*. As usual, a couple of tacky sistuhs looked like they wanted to be the next Divine Brown.

All the top R&B remixes were thumping hard enough to make the Mardi Gras windows—the ones next to the six-foot speakers—vibrate like they were in the middle of an earthquake. The place was packed and getting more packed by the minute. It got that way right after we walked in just in time to beat the "Ladies-Free-B-4-10" curfew. Some brotha, who was playing Mr. Anonymous, had sent us two drinks back to back, so we relaxed and soaked up the flattery and tried to figure out who was on the prowl. It was a night of plenty of melanin-filled men but not one knew how to start a decent conversation.

Since she'd packed for the weekend, Chiquita wasn't ready to go back to San Diego, and, Lord knows, there wasn't a damn thing in the dried up Inland Empire calling my body, so we hit the mall for some therapeutic shopping, then both got rooms at the Hyatt. They had been blasting commercials on the radio station advertising this twenty-one-and-over club that was right across the street from the hotel, right on the boardwalk, so I figured what the hell and drove us back over to this hip-hop joint.

And my girl Chiquita knows how to party, just like myself, and unlike my poor sister, Red. We both needed to get rid of some negative energy in a positive way. Before we could get a good table, brothas had snatched us up and we were out there in the shoulder-to-shoulder crowd dancing our butts off. Not literally, I mean I had the butt, but I wasn't strutting the butt. I was being sorta mellow because I had bought a nice classy, double-breasted gray pantsuit and wanted to play the sophisticated role. Chiquita was acting the same way in her green skirt and gold jacket.

We were calm, easy dancing for about five minutes, but we started tripping when they mixed in some strong Reggae. We hit the floors and got a tad bit risqué; broke out doing the butterfly so good we both looked like Butterfly McQueens. We were two sistuhs who refused to be outdanced by any brotha. After those carnal dance moves, practically every mack-daddy tried to pick us up before we could get our sweaty faces back to our table. And we had to kindly brush off the two we were dancing with, because they got too attached too quick and they were too young and too anxious and too broke to even offer us two Diet Cokes.

Trust me, if all a brotha can find to say is how good your ass looks and he'd "sho'll like to git wid dat," he got some ways to go. And that's just in the grammar department. Brotha needed to buy a vowel and rent a verb, then get a roll of duct tape slapped on that broken English.

I mean, I am human, got feelings and desires, and might ultimately want the same thang, but can I get a moment of mental stimulation first? He kept following me like he was a lost puppy, that was until I politely told him to run home and let his momma change his Pampers because his shit was starting to smell. We were still laughing about the sad look on his face when Chiquita cut her eyes across the room.

Chiquita smirked. "That brother's staring at you."

"Please tell me it's not the same one."

"Nope, it's not the one that was so doggone rude and talking to your breasts."

"Butt-ugly-ass pervert. Ugly men are never shy."

"Tell me about it." She whispered, "I think it's the brother who paid for the drinks because when our waitress went over, he looked this way and pointed. It's your night three-sixty."

"Three-sixty?"

"All the way around." She smiled and drew a small circle in the air. "At three hundred and sixty degrees."

"Oh." I straightened out my jacket. "Where?"

"Behind you to your left. The kinda tall buffed brother with the tan pants and busy vest with no shirt."

"No shirt?"

Of course I turned around, and of course he waved. The brotha's not as tall as Chiquita's voice made him sound. I'm five-nine-and-a-half; he's about five-eleven, but then again Chiquita's probably five-six and some change, so I don't know what's tall to her. Anyway, when he grinned at me, I gave him the middle finger. The kind look in his hard-core face turned cold; he frowned, called me something obscene and had the nerve to give me the finger back. He scrunched up his face some more. I rolled my eyes at him, and again, I gave the finger.

Chiquita pulled my finger down and patted my hand. "Don't start nothing with that brother."

I said, "You got my back?"

"Leave him alone. He might be in a gang down here. He got muscles like he's been in jail or something. Maybe we should leave and go somewhere else."

When I looked back he was still staring at me. I shook my head and said, "And I know his momma taught him how to dress better than that."

"Maybe he's on a budget."

He primped and mouthed something, but before he could finish I lipped for him to fuck off.

He sucked his teeth as he bumped his thick frame through the crowd and peacocked over toward the table, hand on crotch. Chiquita looked so scared I thought her Afro was going to shrivel up. When he hovered over our table, he looked at both of us for a second, ran his hand over his wavy hair, then stuck his face up to my face and growled, "What's that mess you said?"

I stuck my face in his face and matched his rude wanna-be-starting-something tone. "You got a problem? Go for it."

He clucked his tongue then said, "Your momma so white, she make Michael Jackson look black. Your daddy so black he stunt-doubles for shadows."

Chiquita's voice splintered. "Listen, my brother, that's not even call—"

"Pah-leeze, you'd best to raise on up outta here with your corny-ass snaps," I said. "Your daddy so black, he gets *two* unemployment checks. Your momma so greedy, I bought her a bean bag and she tried to cook it."

There was a moment of silence. Then he leaned close to me, putting his nose on mine. We laughed. He gave me a hug and kissed the side of my face.

He said, "What the hell you doing down here, Black?"

"Same thang as you, Brown."

"Where Red at?"

"Ain't my day to watch her." I told him she had to work and when I went by Walter wouldn't answer the door. "Guess she sitting around the house tonight painting her toenails and looking at them damn stale black-and-white movies."

"Them movies ain't stale. The Hitchcock stuff is dope."

"Not on a Saturday night."

"I know that's right." His face brightened up. "Havin' a good time?"

"Kinda sorta but not really. Just got here. And where is your damn shirt?"

"Damn, you sound like Moms." He nodded at my clothes. "You look fresh."

"A little something-something I threw together." I scooted over so he could sit down with me. "What you been up to?"

"Work." He picked some lint out of my bobbed hair. "Flex'n, babe. Chillin' mack-ah-dosh-us-lee."

"More like hiding out. Why ain't you called nobody?" I kissed the side of his face, then wiped my chocolate lipstick off. "Oh, Chiquita, this is my crazy brother, Brown. I mean Thaddeus."

When I looked over Chiquita's mouth was wide open; she was still tripping and gripping her purse like she was ready to break out of there quick-fast-and-in-a-hurry. She patted her heart, let out one of those sighs, relaxed and started fanning her face.

Chiquita said, "Grrrl, y'all had me going. I was about to put on my wings and bone up out of here. Nice to meet you."

"What's up, fox?" He shook Chiquita's hand.

"It's you," Chiquita said. Sistuh still had an uneasy grin plastered on her face.

"I got y'all on my tab," Brown said. "Wanna dance?"

Chiquita said, "Yeah, but not on this slow song. Later?"

" 'Bet."

While he cut his eyes at Chiquita, he asked me if I'd talked to Moms or Pops, wanted to know if Walter was bothering Red, told Chiquita she looked fly and it was nice to meet her, then walked back over to his spot next to the dance floor.

"You guys look different," Chiquita said. "He's rough."

"He's rough on the outside, will go off on you in a minute, but he's really a pussycat. He works at FedEx in LA doing the ramp-agent thing, but now he wants to be a cop or something."

"Why?"

"Hell if I know. Probably so they'll stop pulling him over for no reason."

She laughed. "Must be nice to have a brother who treats you like a friend."

"We take care of each other. You have brothers?"

"Only child. I have a coupla cousins that are my play brothers and sisters. Most of my family's still in Atlanta."

"Your mother and father?"

"Both dead. Car accident."

"Sorry to hear that."

"I grew up with Big Momma and Big Daddy. Both of my grandparents had strokes. He died fifteen years ago. She died about eleven."

"Who took care of you after that?"

"I ended up getting shipped around from relative to relative in Atlanta and ended up with my uncle Vernon. But nobody really took care of me. More like put up with me because I was family." She sighed. "Most of the time it's been just me, myself, and I."

"You have a roommate?"

"Not since my junior year in college."

"Best friend?"

She shook her head. "The one I had in high school stabbed me in the back and got with my lover."

And I knew that was what she called Raymond. I almost sounded jealous, but let it go before I said, "Lover?"

"Same as boyfriend. I just rather use that term because it has the word *love* in it. Not as in sex-love, but emotional. Any-who, he deserted me for her." She ran her hand over her hair and smiled. "Yep. Most of my life it's just been little old me against the world. Making bad choices in men and friends."

"Well, I find that hard to believe." I patted her hand and said a happy-go-lucky, "Looks like you did fine for yourself."

We stopped trying to have a conversation because the music that blended with all the mack-daddy conversation made it too hard to hear. A groove kicked in and took away the seriousness of our chitchat and we kicked back and table-danced. A gangsta rap mixed into the groove and Brown looked back at our table and motioned me to the dance floor. I shook my head. He flipped me off and grimaced. Acting as hard as he wanna be. I laughed, then touched Chiquita. "You mind dancing with my baby brother?"

She hesitated, then started to get up when Brown walked over to meet her. I smiled because this was the first time—other than to Red, Moms, and myself—I'd ever seen Brown be polite to a woman. His roughneck version of polite anyway. He's got this thing where he tries to overcompensate for growing up in a sheltered, biracial middle-class home by acting like he's hard core. He runs with hardheads and dates worse. He thinks being black means having plenty of attitude; I think having plenty of knowledge is what black is all about; Red thinks, black or white or whatever, being happy is all that matters. Moms don't give a shit because she ain't black; she just wants us to call her a couple of times a month and remember the other side of our family tree. Pops thinks we're all looney. Pops was the one that started us calling each other Brown, Red, and Black. He couldn't remember our names to save his life, so he'd call out for Moms to "Go get the Red one." The same with Brown and Black. If he had been home more often he would've gotten the names right. Might've even remembered a birthday or two, maybe even him and Moms's anniversary.

I waved at Chiquita but she didn't see me. She

looked like she was on a mental trip. Most of the night, even though we were tight, I wondered if Chiquita was thinking about the same thing that I couldn't get out of my mind: Raymond. I believe darkness made you do that, think about shit you didn't necessarily want to think about or deal with. And I knew Chiquita was cool and wasn't no fool, despite the circumstances we met under, but I was starting to wonder if I was kicking it with her for companionship or just to make sure neither one of us sneaked out and tipped back to visit Deputy Dawg. I mean I don't think I would, as a matter of fact I know I wouldn't, I don't think. I still remember his two-faced touch, but I couldn't imagine letting him feel me again. Not even a handshake. Nope, I wouldn't go back. I don't think.

Okay, most people have gone back to visit the dog pound for a conjugal visit a time or two, as I have myself. Because between me and you, back when I was twenty-five, after I threw the bricks through one of my ex's bedroom windows and that old-ass weave-wearing tramp he was with came flying out of his apartment half-naked, screeching like a bat leaving a cave, I did let him talk me into spending the night with him. Okay, I was stupid, but I was dick-whipped and he gave me forty more lashes to prove it. But hey, that's between me and you, so if I hear my business again, I'll know who told and that's your ass. And I know for a fact I ain't the only one that done did some ignorant shit like that. I watch Ricki Lake.

And still, I looked at Chiquita and couldn't help but to see her and Raymond between the sheets that I bought him for his birthday last month, rolling around, her Afro sheen staining the pillow cases, them pushing and pulling, straight up going at it like starving Ethiopians at a last-chance buffet.

And the thought of it made me wonder if what I gave him in bed wasn't good enough. I mean I hoped the shit I let him do to me and the things I did to him were way above average. I guess my jealousy and self-doubt were mixing into one hurtful song of pain, sorta like the music I was listening to. No matter how upbeat it sounded, it was still melancholy to me.

Chiquita was out there, looking at her fingernails, half dancing with Brown. And when she wasn't looking and talking and smiling and laughing, she drifted off and had that distant thinking-about-somebody-else look in her nonblinking eyes. The one you get when you're so wrapped around somebody that as long as they said they were sorry you would forgive a heinous act or two or three. That same zombie look I couldn't scrub off my ebony skin after me and my last boyfriend, what's-his-face, broke up. But I was stronger then, used to the pain that I'd never get used to, so I was able to fight the feelings and held on to that look until it faded.

Then I wondered if that was why she was trying

to encourage me to talk to Michael, you know, to get me away from Raymond for selfish reasons. Maybe that was why she stayed in town. She claimed she was too tired to drive, but the way she was energetically marching her svelte ass through every shop in the mall for three hours seemed to contradict the weary words on her lips. Maybe it's just me. Could be in the back of my mind I was hoping she met somebody worth meeting. Hell, at this point, even my brother would be a worthy sacrifice to calm my mind.

Had my life come to this?

But Brown went for the roughneck Yo-Yo type. Sistuhs with thick golden dookie braids and thicker attitudes, women that scratched their crotches and adjusted their tits while they spat out non-sequitur broken English. Chiquita and Brown were dancing, but they both seemed to be looking around at other people. Each had their own groove. I'm no chemist, but like they say, oil and water don't mix.

For a long moment, I wished I had kept Michael's business card. At least I could've gotten a free picture out of the deal. So he's water under the bridge. And with my luck if I did walk back over there and run up on him, he'd probably be sitting around laughing and eating yogurt cones with the wife and the 2.5 children he forgot to tell me about. That, a station wagon, and an ugly Chihuahua.

But I still did have the guy from the personals' number in my purse. So I contemplated giving him a call before it got too late, maybe see if he'd drop by the club for some face-to-face parley. After all this was a very nice public, crowded place to meet somebody. Especially a faceless brotha who didn't think that looks were important. I know what I said over the phone about looks not mattering, but I didn't want to seem shallow, so I lied, so sue me. At least this way if I didn't like him, I had my own flesh-and-blood bodyguard. If I looked half-bored or uninterested, or he was ugly, overprotective Brown would definitely snatch him up and out of my face.

28 / **INDA**

"**I** had just about given up on you."

"I'm surprised you're still out here," I said, then made like I couldn't remember his name, just to throw conversation back in his court. "Michael, right?"

"Right," he said. "What's your name?"

"Sooo." I played him off then adjusted my leather jacket and took a seat in his jasmine-colored director's chair. He sat facing me in a scarlet chair that was a little older, faded. "I still get my freebie or has the offer expired?"

He put a place marker that had a picture of Robin Givens covering her bare chest in his paperback book and dropped it into his dirty off-white bag of supplies. "Still good."

"Just don't make my head too big. Make my bob a little longer."

He laughed. "You want to do it?"

"Nope. I'll let you do it."

Before I knew it, I had found myself strolling out of the club to catch a breath of fresh air. Chiquita had moved on with her dancing groove. She tried to break free and muscle her way through the too-crowded room, but before she could ever make it back to the table, she was drafted back out for dance after dance. It was a bit too packed for the kid, so I was fanning myself and turning down dance after dance. Brown was walking around with a soda in hand, booty watching and on the prowl. So I decided to have the waitress give Chiquita a note that I was stepping out for some fresh air that hadn't been breathed on by everybody and their momma. I know it was too chilly out, because my nipples told me, so I grabbed my jacket out of the car and went for a solo starlit, moonlight stroll down the boardwalk of broken dreams to cool off and air out. Even though it was cold, I still loved the light breeze. The salty Long Beach crispy fresh ocean air was much more pleasant than the everlasting cow-dung aroma of a culturally dehydrated Chino.

I went to the phone next to the restored carousel and tried to call Wiley. He wasn't home, but I left a message anyway. He was probably out on a personal ad date. Which was better than sitting home on a beautiful night. I saw some of the gift and T-shirt shops were just closing up, the smell of cotton candy wafted over and made my stomach growl, reminding me that all I had eaten was a damn salad, so I hurried down and bought a couple of candy bars. Then I saw Michael was still sitting out on the more well lit side of the docks, bundled up in his hooded jacket with a scarf around his neck looking like a black Eskimo, by himself under one of the streetlights, reading one of those detective-mystery novels by the brotha Walter Mosley. Which reminded me of Red's Terry McMillan novel that I still hadn't finished as of yet. I like a brotha who reads. Especially a brotha who reads something written by a brotha who writes. Trust me, girlfriend, if you walk into a man's crib and he doesn't own any books, run out. Newspapers don't count because, although I love me some sports, the sports section ain't exactly on the list for winning a Nobel Prize. Trust me. Don't even wait for the shallow side to pop up. Anyway, back to the man in my face.

I asked, "Slow night?"

"Yeah. A bit."

I shifted around and tried to remember which was my good side. "Why aren't you at the club?"

"You can't shift around and change sides when I start."

"Sorry. You don't go out?"

"I like to party." Michael hunched his shoulders. "I was going to change and go in, but I'm not much on dancing when it's that crowded. Why'd you leave the club?"

"Too crowded. Too hot. Too loud. Too boring."

"Too bad."

We laughed. That one chuckle brought my wall down a little.

A few seconds later he cleared his throat and asked, "All dressed up and no date tonight, Miss Thang?"

"Nope. No date for you, Mr. Thang?"

"Nah." He tilted his head. "Well, I had hoped I would've had one tonight, but I guess it's another reading night for me."

"Girlfriend?"

"Actually, no. Somebody who's too busy, I guess."

"She must've had somebody else on the menu."

"I suppose. Hold your head this way so I can see your profile. You're moving around too much."

"Sorry, Rembrandt, but it's a tad bit chilly out here."

"You're feisty."

"Sorry. Didn't mean to offend you."

"Feisty's good. You have character."

"Scares most brothas off."

He asked me my name again, and again I acted like I didn't hear him and started talking about something else. I thought he was going to do one of those quick, two-minute sketches, but he had taken out some more colors, one of which just about matched my flesh tone of a smooth damn-near-perfect much-too-proud black. He looked in my eyes, stalled for a second and then when I looked directly at him, he slid an abbreviated version of that "impressed" look and went back to creating. Then he looked at my lips and licked his own lips and grinned.

"What was that all about?" I asked.

He sorta blushed. "What?"

I didn't answer. He looked at my chin, my hair. He said a soft, "Pretty."

"Thanks." That one sweet word took away so much of my hostility. I felt my face soften and I sorta went into a girly Inda-moment. "You tell all your customers that?"

"Only the ones that pay."

He finished about twenty minutes later. We talked off and on, mostly about nothing. He kept giving me that look Chiquita told me about, off and on. I guess his wandering eyes and generic words were what kept me warm. The drawing was real good, a lot better than I thought it would be because I actually thought it looked like me. It looked like too much work and too much perfection to be a freebie, so I broke out the wallet and tried to give him a donation, but he refused. He started closing down shop, so I asked if I could help him carry some of his stuff down to his car or wherever he was going before I went back to the club. He said no, that he didn't bring that much and could handle it. I was just sorta standing there, holding my picture and waiting for him to pack up, I suppose. He looked at me and that same nervous look came over his face. This time it made me nervous. Maybe because it was that look he had when it seemed like he'd gathered all his strength to walk back up the spiral stairs to our table. And this time I didn't have a girlfriend next to me to help me joke it off. It was just the two of us, under a streetlight, the stars and the moon, looking at each other while the contradicting lights made our shadows overlap. I was too nervous.

"Well . . ." I adjusted my already adjusted coat. "Thanks."

"Still not telling your name?"

I smiled but didn't answer. Michael walked over to me and extended his hand. When I reached out to shake his hand, he held my hand a little longer than usual. And it was nice. Well, like I said, the stars, the moon, the air, our shadows, the need for an agreeable moment in my life—I guess what I'm trying to say is I let him kiss me. Either that or I kissed him. I'm not sure if he was just going to kiss the side of my face, or if I leaned to kiss the side of his face, or what, but the next thing I knew we were kissing. Not holding each other tight or rubbing all over each other, just slow kissing. And I can tell you, ain't nothing like a brotha who knows how to kiss a woman the way she wants to be kissed. He kissed me how I deserved to be kissed. He slow moved his candy-apple-tasting tongue around my Butterfinger-tasting mouth and made me imagine he was kissing my neck, my back, got me to thinking about other thangs, if you know what I mean. It got too deep for me, so I eased back and wiped my lipstick from his face.

"You molest all your customers?"

He said, "Sorry about that."

I smiled. "That's okay."

Then we kissed again. Or rather I kissed him. What the hell. As far as I know, you only live once.

After a couple of more kisses, I told him that I had

left his business card at the table. He laughed, then he gave me another one. Much to my surprise, after a chemistry kiss like that, he didn't even bother to ask for my number. I guess after I didn't bother to tell the brotha my name, he probably figured the seven digits—or I should say eleven since it's a toll call—were out of the question. He looked like his pursuit of me was over. I guess if you play hard to get sometimes you don't get got. I finger-waved and said an awkward, "Take care."

"Want me to walk you back to the club?"

I shook my head. "That's all right. You've got too much stuff to be dragging."

He began walking backwards as he said his sweet goodbyes. And I'll tell you something weird—it felt like we were breaking up or getting divorced and I didn't even know him.

"Hope to hear from you," he said. "If I don't, it was nice meeting you."

He walked a few feet down the boardwalk. Then I realized that my loyalty to dog-ass-no-good-low-life-Raymond over the past months—even though it wasn't the best relationship in the world, actually after what I found out today it was a null relationship—had kept me from allowing myself to even keep a half-decent brotha's number for over five minutes. That was probably why I kept finding flaws in every brotha who seemed genuinely interested in what I had to offer.

I tried to be cool and not sound anxious. "I'm single."

He grinned. "Me, too."

"Very?"

"Very."

"Interested?"

"Very."

"You're here every day?"

"Most evenings. After five. Earlier on weekends."

"Michael," I yelled. "My name is Inda."

He sorta slowed his stroll, tilted his head like he barely heard me, stopped walking, and his expression changed. He put down his stuff and walked back to me. And, of course, I moved my picture and got my body ready to be kissed again. But he stood in front of me and gave me that look again. This time it was brighter and made me more nervous.

"Inda?"

"Yeah."

He shook his head and laughed a little.

I said, "What?"

He grinned and said, "Linda without the *L*?"

"Yeah."

"I'm Wiley. Michael Wiley."

29 / CHIQUITA

Even from the other side of the heavy bathroom doors the Naughty By Nature music was loud enough to make a line of sweat-faced sistahs keep up with the beat as they came swaying inside, finger-popping and bobbing their heads. Everybody's heels click-clopped with the rhythm on the checkerboard tile. Whenever the door opened I could see the brothers that had stationed themselves outside in the narrow hall by the pay phones. They struck smooth ebony man poses on the wall, probably running their age-old pickup lines and waiting for another Miss Stupid. When I passed by, a couple of the vultures thought my name was "Pssst."

I eased toward an empty stall while the grinning sistahs kept on redoing their faces and competing with each other for floor space. I found some counter space next to a tan-colored sistah in a skin-tight jean dress and fishnet hose. I was sandwiched between her and another sistah, who kept adjusting her micro-short dress for maximum cleavage.

One of the women looked familiar, but I figured I'd seen her in a rap video or something. Plus in this part of California it wasn't too unusual to run across a big name or two at a nightclub. I'd run into Wesley Snipes at Gotham, a pool hall on the Third Street promenade in Santa Monica, and had seen Alfre Woodard on Melrose coming out of Spike Lee's store and getting into a Benz. I thought I'd even seen Denzel driving a Jeep down La Brea in Hollywood. All of those places and people I'd seen with Raymond by my side, telling me how much he cared for me.

I went into a stall and closed my eyes. All I could see was Raymond in bed with that girl. Then when she raised up, the first thing I saw was a ring on her finger. I realized who the girl was. That tone was the same I'd heard over his c-phone. The girl that he said was nobody. If he'd fuck a *nobody*, then he'd fuck *everybody*. Then I felt the pain on my face from where he hit me. And in my mind I saw it again, saw it clear, saw that he'd done it on purpose. I knew about Gina weeks ago. She had a bad habit of mailing little notes and he had a bad habit of keeping them. He played it off and said it was his ex still hoping for a second chance. But that didn't ring true. Plus, I had stayed at his place one day last month so a plumber could unclog Raymond's doggone toilet. I was practically standing right next to Mr. Flirty Plumber when he pulled a tampon out of the plumbing. He looked at me like it was mine. I just shook my head because I'd never be that tacky. That was when I looked around and found the pictures and a note from the week before thanking him for the "good night and better morning." All of that was tucked on the top shelf of his closet under some sweaters. I didn't say anything because as long as it wasn't in my face, it was cool. If it was nothing it would go away with time. And I stayed because I knew that since he didn't really want me on that level, wouldn't offer me that ring that I really didn't want, I was safe with him.

But I had to stop playing that game. Had to stop playing myself, and want more for myself. After meeting Inda and talking to her and feeling like I was shortchanging myself, both in the education and relationship department, well, that made me want more for myself. She was and is one strong sistah. And she talked about her folks with a passion. I'd bet Inda's younger sister was just as level-headed and cool and calm and collected and together as Inda was. The way Inda's and her brother vibed I'd bet they were a real decent family. The kind I always wished that I had.

But even with me wanting to be a better me, the hurt and the hate that I always kept locked up inside me, sometimes I was scared that it would kill me from the inside. A few times I wondered if I'd die all by myself with nobody at my side and nobody who cared. Maybe that's the way I wanted it. Because then nobody would know about my mother.

All of a sudden the anxiety got too heavy and I had to pee real bad. My head was spinning, so when I finished I sat on the toilet, quiet and glaring at my empty hands until somebody tapped on the metal door to see if it was occupied.

When I came back out of the stall a crowd was still in front of the black-topped counter, arguing and painting their faces. I washed my hands and slipped out without fixing my face. Just when I made it back to the table, Raymond and his lover girl were coming into the club, holding hands like they were walking down the aisle. She was his fiancé. I was his fool.

So many feelings came up as thick as vomit. Feelings that I had to swallow. It felt like everybody knew. And I was ashamed for what I had been doing to myself. And embarrassed because I felt so stupid to let myself be abused by him.

His lover girl walked away. Then he glanced around the room. Smiled and winked at a couple of sistahs and the two white women at the bar. I bet he did that same mess when we went out together.

He saw me and his face jerked. Then he grinned and nodded.

I wanted to leave. But I went to him.

30 / INDA

After twenty more minutes of both of us talking and blushing, then slow-kissing a real long time like we were trying to get into the *Guinness Book of World Records,* we made strong promises that we'd try to get together tomorrow before I left Long Beach. I smiled my way back to the club. When the brotha told me that I was the woman he'd been waiting to hear from all day, I told him I didn't believe him, but that sweet sound in his nice baritone voice told me different. Then I called and tried to check my messages, but I couldn't because the stupid machine was new and I couldn't remember the factory code. But the warmth and sweetness of his words told me he wasn't lying. He said he had already called twice to tell me that he'd really like to meet with me. He said he called after two, so his first call was about five minutes after I finally left home. But when I didn't get back to him all day, he thought he'd blown his chance.

Then he said, "I'd really like to go on a date with you, if you don't mind. And a nice long walk."

"A movie?"

"That's fine, but movies are sort of impersonal.

Let's go out somewhere where we can sit around and talk and get to know each other. Then we can walk on the beach."

I said an excited, "Sounds good."

Being the prepared woman that I am, I did a *tahdow* and gave him my business card.

He said, " 'Children's Social Worker.' Nice."

"Thank you."

Then he gave me a different off-white business card. The first one he'd given me back at the restaurant said "Portraits by Michael V." This one said:

San Gabriel Valley Hearing Center
Michael V. Wiley
M.S., CCC-A
Licensed Audiologist
and
Hearing-Aid Dispenser

"Thought you were an artist?"

"Part-time. It relaxes me. And it's my dream deferred."

And it may sound shallow, but I had to do all I could not to run down the boardwalk and start turning cartwheels and doing splits. 'Cause let me tell you, moments like that with a nice-looking brotha sporting so much damn potential makes a sistuh's day. I was floating my panty-wet self back through the too-cold night air, nose dripping, lipstick smeared all around my damn mouth, and grinning so hard my damn face hurt. And you know what? I didn't even care. I just kept my Kool-Aid smile and went back to my car and dropped off my beautiful picture and took my jacket off before I bounced back into the sweaty, smoky club—rejuvenated. I felt a groove coming on so strong I wanted to butterfly until the sweepers came in.

I didn't realize I'd been outside almost an hour until I looked at my watch. I just hoped Chiquita didn't think I left her stranded. But when I slid outside, Party Woman didn't look like she needed company or a babysitter. Her cute ass was probably sitting up with a table full of men and phone numbers by now.

The club was still packed, the temperature was up a notch or two, music still thumping out a serious SWV groove. My heart damn near stopped and my throat lumped when I saw Raymond standing by the bar, dressed in gold pants and a colorful leather jacket. Gina was at his side, grinning up a storm and holding him so tight they looked like Siamese twins. At first I didn't recognize her because she'd made herself up and put her hair up in a bun. Plus last time I saw her she was butt-naked in my Betty Boop. Poor woman had gotten herself together the best she could and was wearing a white linen jacket over a short black dress and dark-dark hose. Raymond looked at me, then turned away like we'd never met. All I can say was it hurt. Real bad, it hurt. All the nights I'd let him be alive inside of me, the times I drove my dumb ass forty-some-odd miles, all the way from my apartment to bring him a can of chicken soup because he didn't feel good, had boiled down to this?

Just that quick he'd erased anything that was positive, that hopeful feeling Michael had given. All the euphoria just vanished. My 'tude was back.

I couldn't stand the sight so I bumbled in the opposite direction and looked around for Chiquita, and when I didn't see her I looked for Brown. He was out on the floor dancing with a small girl who had a very short skirt, a large butt, and bigger breasts. After I pushed my way down through the crowd, I politely told Brown's dance buddy that he was my brother and I needed to ask him something. She had a 'tude, but after Brown said I was his big sister, she looked me up and down, saw we had the same itty-bitty nose and shape of the head, then smiled and kept on a-grooving.

I asked Brown, "Where's Chiquita?"

"Who?"

"Girl I was with."

"Hotel."

"When?"

"Ten minutes ago."

Just then the music changed to a slow Michael Jackson song, the lights went down a notch or two, and the DJ called all "lovers in the house" to make way to the dance floor for the bump and grind. Some people started to walk away dabbing their sweaty faces and necks, then more couples came out on the floor. As I tried to make my way back up, Raymond and Gina walked right into me and literally bumped me back into three or four people. From the look in her eyes and the way she had scrunched her mouth, I could tell Gina knew who I was from jump street and was trying to make a point. Raymond looked at me, then smirked.

I said, "Excuse you."

He looked at me like I was Boo-Boo the fool. That did it. I hit him in the eye or nose or something. I didn't remember hitting him, I just saw his head yank and my hands coming back. I think my diamond ring cut his face. That other side of me had broke free. The next thing I knew Gina had jumped in my face, screaming and cursing, accusing me of following them down to the club, threatening to kick my ass, yelling at me for messing with her man.

"What?" I said, yelling over the music.

"You heard me, bitch! Don't be running your hoe-ish ass up on my man! He told me all about you."

"You'd best to get your finger out of my face."

"I ain't gotta do a damn thing."

Little Miss Indignant got her uncouth ass all up in my face and started talking about what she was going to do to me. That's when I pushed her backwards, because Inda don't play that. Her arms went wild, I think she was trying to hit me, but she lost her balance, spun around on her four-inch hoe-heels, and fell dead on her flat ass. The music came to an abrupt halt and the lights came on. Laughter filled the room over the DJ's calls to security. After talking so much shit, she looked so stupid sprawled out with her coochie in the air. Half the crowd was hanging over the rails watching us make a spectacle of ourselves; the other half had rushed down on the floor for ringside seats, because you know my people love to watch a fight. I take enough verbal abuse from clients at work, I'd be damned if I got pushed around by some ignorant bitch off the clock. I hated calling the sistuh a bitch, but if it walks like a duck and sounds like a duck, then, hey, it's a bitch. I felt so much hate in my veins for Gina, hate because she was so stupid. I hated the way I felt because I didn't even know her, but, Lord knows, I can't stand a stupid sistuh with that idiotic men-will-be-men attitude. She's getting run over and she's too stupid to look down at the tread marks on her damn near-flat chest.

Raymond ran over and helped her up. As soon as she got up, she slipped on a wet spot on the floor and fell right back down. Coochie back in the air. More laughter. She put her face in her hands, trying to hide. Raymond tried to help her up again, but she jerked away then swung at him.

Gina wailed, "WHY YOU HAVE TO SLEEP WITH HER? I'M TIRED OF YOUR SHIT! GET YOUR HANDS OFF ME! MOVE! NIGGER, MOVE!"

And of course, everybody and their momma heard. Raymond looked flushed. Gina foundered like a trout out of water, spinning in circles, finally finding her way to her feet. She shoved Raymond away from her and stormed around me, the long way. Raymond said something flippant, directed at me of course. At least he tried, but before he got to a good adjective, Brown had grabbed him by his collar and jerked him up off his feet like he was a rag doll. Raymond landed on his ass, talking much shit. Too much. That was until he looked up and saw it was Brown standing over him, flexing his muscles.

" 'Sup, Raymond?"

"Thaddeus?"

"Fool, why you dogging my big sister like that?"

"Brown. Let's go—" I said.

"Black, chill. I got it."

Raymond sprung up and tried to back away from Brown, surrendering with his hands up, wobbling because he was weak at the knees. When he backed away from Brown, he backed into me. That's when I started punching him in the back of the head. I didn't mean to do it, but I guess my heart and hands were on their own. He jerked around and before I knew it, Brown had his hands around Raymond's neck. Three heavyset brothas pulled Brown off. Not really pulled, because he had shoved all of them off as easy as he'd manhandled Raymond. Brown smiled, let Raymond go, and walked toward the door. Raymond was laid out on the floor trying to remember how to breathe. He looked up at me, like he wanted me to help. What really hurt the most was that part of me that wanted to make sure he wasn't hurt too bad. That damn caring part. I was madder at myself than I was at him.

Brown said, "C'mon, Black. Get'cha coat. We outta here."

I was too busy trying to catch my breath and straighten out my clothes to move.

All of this drama had taken less than one intense minute.

Somebody in a suit, probably from security, finally broke through the thick, nosey crowd. He grabbed my arm and slowly led me toward the front door. Some people snickered, some applauded, some raised glasses, some looked bored because they'd seen better fights, but most of the true brothas looked disgusted and every real sistuh had folded her arms and shook her head and gave me that *did-you-hafta-go-there?* look.

31 / **VALERIE**

Two A.M.

Sunday morning.

The time when Chino Hills slept.

The time when Valerie was wide awake. Stalking.

The house was dark when Valerie eased in through the back sliding-glass door. The garage door's whirring and rattling open would've made too much noise. When she tiptoed around the corner and crept into the den, Walter was laid out on the leather sofa, asleep in jeans and a button-down-collar shirt. The remote had fallen on the floor. The television was off, so that meant he probably had it on the timer. Empty beer cans and chips filled the end table next to him.

She looked at him and wondered what she had seen in him in the first place. Now she saw him differently. He was unforgivably evil. Whatever it was about him that had made her love him so much for so long wasn't there. Maybe it was there, but had been numbed by his reprehensible words.

After she put the can on the floor, she moved anything she might trip on and made sure she had a clear escape path to the front. When she came back, she stood and glared at him. Walter didn't move a muscle.

With patient, short, silent movements she thoroughly soaked the carpet around him to the point where her feet made a light sloshing sound when she walked. Then Valerie made a thin trail leading to the door. She barely turned the light on, using the rheostat on the wall to gradually bring the lights up, instead of dealing with the lamp that *clicked* on the end table. Slowly, she turned the lights up just enough so she wouldn't stumble over anything as she fled. It was quiet. She took a large plastic cup from the cabinet and stood over him, practicing the motion it would take to splatter his face. Then she changed her mind. She wouldn't throw it in his face, she wanted him to see the pain. She'd take time and aim accurately at his chest and genitals.

Walter was breathing hard. She thought he looked like he was dreaming his last dream. Anything after this would be a nightmare. She bumped the can and made a little noise to test the depth of his slumber. He stayed sound asleep and ignorant.

Valerie filled two Big-Gulp cups and stood over him. But she had to back off. She had bought a cigarette lighter that she planned to throw. Suddenly she realized that it wouldn't work. The problem was, when she let go of the lighter, the flame would go out. She needed matches. No problem.

The sole of her left shoe squeaked slightly when she stepped off the carpeted area onto the wooden floor, so she hopped on the ball of her right foot. She quickly slid around the corner into the kitchen and found the big box of wooden, long-stemmed matches they used for lighting the fireplace. Reliable fuel that Walter had bought.

When Valerie came back, Walter still hadn't moved.

She carefully threw the first plastic cup and everything wasted on his chest, crotch, and legs. As he struggled awake and tried to sit up, bewildered, the second cup landed another bull's-eye between his legs. "Hey, Whaaat the fuuuck?"

She brought the lights up. He cut short his scream and sobered when he saw Valerie standing close to him, dressed in black running shoes, black jeans, black leather gloves, black sweatshirt, and a black baseball cap turned backwards on her head. He looked down and saw the fire-engine-red metal gas container at her feet, matches in her hand. More important, he clearly saw the look in her eyes. He inhaled the fumes and gagged as panic quickly surfaced on his face.

"What, what, hey, what the hell are you doing?"

"You don't *like* me so it don't matter. This *dumb-ass uneducated bitch* is about to fuck you up for life. You burned me." Valerie struck a match. "Now I'm going to burn your ass."

32 / **INDA**

"I'm not playing with you!"

I backed up. "And I'm not playing with you."

It was the middle of the damn night. Chiquita had her fists balled up and looked like she wanted to jump off into my shit. She'd half chased me around her hotel room, tussling over her damn car keys. I tried to lock myself in her bathroom, but she cut me off. I shut my big mouth and darted as far away from her as I could.

"Chiquita, you've had a bit too much to drink."

"I drink as much as I want. Now please, give me my keys."

When I got over to her room, she was sitting up with three empty shot glasses of straight Jack Daniel's she had bought downstairs. The poor child doesn't really drink, but after whatever Raymond did to her at the club, she stomped down to the hotel bar and got the only strong alcohol she knew about.

Her hotel room was a mess. She'd had a fit and snatched the covers off the bed and tried to turn the mattresses over. Everything that wasn't nailed down had been thrown at the wall, including the Bible.

She saw Raymond when he rolled into the club

with Gina. When Miss Gina went to the ladies' room, her heart dragged her over to Raymond because she wanted to know what she had done to deserve being mistreated like that.

"What he say?"

Chiquita said, "All he did was say—"

I waited for her to finish. Her eyes watered. My voice softened. "What he say?"

"He laughed like I was crazy. 'It's a dick thang.' "

"That's it?" It felt like that answer was for me, too.

Chiquita didn't answer. But right after that she started crying and sort of staggered over to her purse, pulled her keys out, and cried that she was going back after that motherfucker. "I'm tired of being treated like this. Why he have to mess over me like that?"

And you know I wanted to grab a rope and gas up for the lynching, too. But I held her. "It ain't worth it. Let him go on about his business. He'll get his."

That's when I wrestled the keys from her. And I do mean wrestled because we were tussling like it was the opening match to Hulk Hogan and Wrestlemania. 'Cause let me tell you, sistuhs got a grip. We stumbled and fell across the mattress she'd already pulled off the bed and rolled around on the floor like two gunslingers in a cowboy movie.

"GIVE-ME-MY-GODDAMN-KEYS-INDA-I'M-NOT-PLAYING-WITH-YOU!"

"SIT-YOUR-NARROW-ASS-DOWN-AND-STOP-MAKING-A-FOOL-OF-YOURSELF!"

Now we were standing in the room, both our heads were messed up inside and out, our mascara was running from the sweat of our fight, and, to make it worse, she was smaller than I was, but she got that serious adrenaline rush so sistuh-girlfriend's a helluva lot stronger. Either that or I was just plain physically and mentally exhausted from dealing with anything that had something to do with that nothing Raymond. That's why I was in a corner with a death grip on those stupid keys, hoping this wide-eyed sistuh with her clothes half on ain't half as psycho as she looked, because, Lawd knows, I was two seconds from giving her the car keys and letting her go on about her way.

We stared at each other. A second later she blinked her eyes, then wiped her face. We didn't look at each other or say anything for a while. Just concentrated on catching our breaths.

"Inda?"

"What?"

Chiquita walked over to the window and looked out in the direction of the *Queen Mary*. She sounded like somebody's child when she said, "I'm sorry for acting so stupid."

I exhaled. "That's okay."

"I'm a fool."

"Nah-uh."

"I need a hug and a friend."

When I walked over and put my arms around her,

she touched my hand with her hand. I said, "You scared me for a minute."

"Scared myself."

I rubbed her head. "Better?"

She sniffled. "Thanks."

"No problem."

A few minutes later I handed her the car keys.

"How do you handle it so well?"

I hunched my shoulders. "After so much pain, I guess you go numb."

Chiquita laughed as she cried, joking about baking him an Ex-Lax cake or keying his car. I joked about throwing bricks through his bedroom window.

"So." She sort of laughed, then said, "I got a narrow ass, huh?"

"Girl, hush."

Chiquita caught me off guard when she closed her eyes and started humming something that sounded like a blues song. Sistuh had one of those straight up, backwoods gravelly voices. She waved her hand the way sistuhs did when they were having a certified Lawd-haf-murcy moment. " 'The way I use'ta luv ya' bay-baaaay.' That's how I hate your black ass now."

She finished and took a deep breath.

I asked, "Who's that?"

"I think it's B. B. King. I used to hear Big Momma play that song, but I never knew what it meant. Now I know."

I told her what happened at the club after she left. Told her how Brown stepped in and took up my slack.

"Your brother did that? He's kinda raw."

"Not kinda. Definitely. Just like our pops."

We calmed a bit, straightened out the room the best we could, then sistuh-girlfriend walked me up the hall to my room. Brown was lying across one of the double beds—vest off, shoes on—looking at a movie channel. Right up under the TV like he used to be when he was a kid. Knowing him it was probably a stupid porno that I'd have to pay for when I checked out.

"Damn." Brown asked and chuckled, "You ah'-right? Y'all look tore up from the floor up."

Chiquita looked surprised to see him, then a little bit ashamed. She used her hand to smooth her dress. "I'm cool."

"We're all right." I stretched. "I'll tell the front desk to send up some more blankets and you can stay if you want."

"Nah." Brown hopped up and grabbed his vest. "I got personal thangs to do in the morning. Need to be home in LA."

"What kind of *personal thangs?*"

"Wash my ride. Laundry. Food shopping. Pay my bills kinda thangs. I got my own responsibilities."

"When you coming out the way? I need you to clean out my storage space and move the heavy stuff so I can have a yard sale."

"Damn, why you want me to come all the way out there? It's so hot out there I saw the Devil going into a mall to cool off."

I laughed. "Make you dinner."

"Oh, you cooking now?"

"Off and on. I'll get Red to come over and throw down."

"Do my laundry. I'll cook. I can burn better than botha y'all put together."

Chiquita walked over, yawned and gave me a tight hug. She kissed the side of my face and whispered, "Thanks." Then she gave me back her keys, winked, and walked out. Two minutes later Brown was gone and I was left to myself. Lord knows, I didn't want to be alone. Not tonight, anyway.

I stood in my window and looked out at the ocean for a few minutes. After I showered I got a bucket of ice and soaked my sprained wrist. Then I decided to call and let Michael know how I felt about what he did to me tonight. Had wicked thoughts about sneaking out and meeting him somewhere. He answered on the second ring.

I said, "I just called to thank you for the nice evening."

"Thank you, too. Made my day."

"Okay, Michael Wiley."

"Okay, Inda Johnson."

I smiled. "Talk to you in the morning."

Sleep still wasn't my friend and I almost called Red. But, knowing her, she'd been knocked out with the setting of the sun.

33 / **VALERIE**

"Now I'm going to burn your ass."

When Valerie struck the match, riot-sized flames grew and danced in her face. She had never felt so much hate for anyone, ever. All the love she had accumulated over the years had done a complete 180-degree turn. It showed in her face as she stroked the match across the sandpapery strip.

When it lit, as the flame rose in her face, she saw Walter's eyes damn near pop out of his face as he struggled to find his balance. "*Don't!*" Walter clumsily jumped toward her, but his out-of-shape potbelly fell short when he lost his footing, then slipped on the soggy carpet and flopped on his face, grabbed his nose, then flopped over on his back. Again, his eyes widened with surprise at the carpet's wetness. He looked up at Valerie and the match. No matter which way he squirmed to get away, it was soaked. The more he moved, the wetter he got. When he realized he didn't have an out and looked up with a quivering lip, Valerie had already moved closer. As he reached for her leg, she flipped the fiery match right at him. It landed on his crotch. He screamed, a loud, ear-piercing wail.

Thirty seconds of flipping, fanning, blowing, and crying later, he realized he wasn't on fire. He was in the middle of puddles of mostly water. Valerie had watered down some nonflammable fluids, but not enough to kill the petroleum-like stench.

She'd become so despondent earlier, she considered a dramatic murder-suicide. Then she figured, why should she do something crazy like that? She was hurt, not insane. Then she thought about just doing him. Giving her husband the hell he'd given her. Minutes later, she rationalized he wasn't worth her doing a minute in jail. He'd taken six years of her life, why should she lose more? Her killing him would be his victory.

Valerie picked up the gas can and pointed at the skull and crossbones on it, indicating her seriousness with the definition in her voice. "Next time, you won't be so lucky. Because I don't *like* you."

Walter was rattled, and bumbled an ignorant, "What's wrong with you?"

"Glad you remembered how to talk."

His words trembled. "What's your fucking problem?"

"I want you and all your stuff out of my house by Tuesday. Take all you can take, I don't care. Take the paint off the walls. Rip up the damn carpet. Just leave."

"What?" Walter slid backwards, keeping his unbelieving eyes on the gas can. His fearful movements suggested he attributed his not being on fire to a fluke.

"You can take all the furniture *you* bought, all the stereos *you* bought. I don't care. This *uneducated minimum wage*," she started, then growled a bitter, "Just leave. You don't know how close you came to me messing you up. I just wanted to know if I could do it. I can and I will."

"What's your problem, girl?"

She yanked her hat off and threw it at him. "I CUT OFF ALL MY HAIR! THAT'S MY PROBLEM! DO YOU KNOW HOW LONG IT TAKES THIS SHIT TO GROW BACK? HUH? DO YOU? I DON'T EVEN *LIKE* HALLE BERRY!"

Walter's mouth fell open and let out a stupefied, "What?"

She rambled a vicious, "I want you to sign a quit-claim deed on *my* house. I want your name taken off. I get *my* house, you get *your* divorce. If you don't leave, sleep with *both* eyes open."

Before he could take a step forward, she took the cigarette lighter out of her shirt pocket and lit it several times. Walter jumped back and kept his distance, but yelled how he was going to call the police and have her arrested and locked away.

"For what? It's not against the law to pour shit on your filthy husband."

When she opened the front door and stepped into the peaceful serenity of the tree-lined bedroom community, Walter was right behind her, huffing about how she was delirious, how she needed help.

"Your problem is, you can't take rejection."

"But I will take my house. Be gone when I come back."

"No. Don't you *ever* come back here."

"I'll burn my house down before I give it to you. *With or without you in it.*"

He hemmed and hawed, choked on his words, but had no significant rebuttal.

Valerie tried to slow her breathing and control her erratic movements as she jammed the container in the backseat of her still-running getaway car. She'd left her car parked on the street facing the route to the 71 expressway with the driver's door wide open, just in case. She took her gloves off and threw them in with the lighter before she wiped her sweaty hands on her shirt.

She wondered, with what she'd done, what could he do? She had thought that he'd get violent. Her defensive plan was simple—kick, scratch, bleed, scream, spit, piss, bite, and run as fast as she could. And if she had made it through the ordeal and some-how miraculously gotten away, she was going to call her family. From a pay phone or from the hospital. It didn't matter.

But Walter still looked too shaken, standing there all wet, barefoot, and sweaty-faced as he stuttered his curses. He snatched his shirt off and threw it on the ground. His eyes squinted as he choked on the vapors. The more he bumbled, the more arrogant she became. Walter mouthed off threats, but kept his distance and looked like he didn't know what to do. Maybe because he'd never seen her like this. Maybe because she'd never felt like this. Just like he'd been holding back his hostility, she'd been banking her resentment of his rejections. Now she'd written him the first check.

When she got in the car, she rolled down the window and shouted, "Tuesday. Be gone one way or the other."

When she got around the corner, she stopped, turned off her lights, then came back just far enough to see the front of her house. She turned around and drove back because if she backed up, the brake lights and the sound of the engine in reverse would be a giveaway. Another smart move for an uneducated bitch, she thought.

She was trembling from head to toe. Her out-of-shape arm was tired from lugging the container in and out of the house. Her back cramped a little. Sweat ran off her face. Her eyes watered and her head hurt worse than it ever did. Massaging her temples only made the pain worse. She repeatedly slammed her fists into the steering wheel, mad because she'd told herself that she could do it and not cry. But she did it by herself and that had to count for something. A very hollow something. And she didn't weaken and shed tears in front of

Walter. That had to count for more. A whole lot more.

Everything she'd just done was blurred and already seemed like a dream. She wondered if she'd done too much or not enough. A few minutes later, two squad cars drove around the corner with the sirens off and the lights flashing. Both pulled into her driveway. Their flashing lights lit up the streets as Walter rushed out to greet them. He'd changed clothes. Lights came on in neighbors' houses. Moments later, a few people stepped out on their porches, a few more out on their lawns, a few more walked down and stood across from her house. The man her next-door neighbor Charlotte was with earlier came out of Charlotte's house in jeans and no shirt. All by himself.

When Walter rushed the officers inside the house, Valerie started her car, made a silent U-turn, and slowly drove almost two hundred yards before she turned her headlights on. As she sped up and took the back streets out, headed up Pipeline toward the 71, she knew it wasn't a dream. She couldn't go back and she couldn't go forward. The first place they'd look would be Inda's. The second would be her brother's. Right now she couldn't face her parents. She had nobody and nowhere to go.

A few miles away she stopped and opened her glove compartment and took out the map she'd gotten from AAA. She traced a route with a yellow highlighter, marked a trail through the San Fernando

Valley toward Canada. Then she looked up at the North Star. That was what she followed.

Miles later she got off of the 210 freeway in Pasadena and sped back the way she had come. Enraged.

She had unfinished business.

34 / **INDA**

I slept hard as a pet rock and woke up about nine. My damn wrist was stiff as hell. After I cleaned myself up, I called Chiquita's room, but the operator said her calls were being held. I asked them to confirm whether she'd already checked out, but they said she hadn't come down to sign her charge slip. But she could've left the hotel keys on the table. Then I looked at her car keys on my dresser, but that didn't really mean much. She could've had a second set. And if she didn't, a taxi could get her to Raymond's bedroom in under ten minutes. I know how it works when the heart takes over the mind and gets you to doing all kinds of off-the-wall shit. Like starting a fight in a club. Since I had a stupid attack and slipped into a Ricki Lake moment, I'm sitting up here with a swollen, stiff wrist.

When I passed the elevator and got down to Chiquita's door, I heard the television on, piping out the Sunday morning service with Reverend Price.

All I could say was I was almost afraid to knock, because Deputy Dawg Raymond listened to Reverend Price every now and then, especially when he stayed at my place and we didn't get out of bed in time to drive into Los Angeles for the ten o'clock service.

My mouth dropped open wide enough to count my fillings when Brown answered her door in his underwear.

I said, "Thought you went home?"

"Morning to you too."

And I know he put his green boxer drawers on to answer the door because he sleeps booty-naked, regardless of where he is or who he's with. His clothes and the clothes Chiquita had on last night were all mixed around the room, like somebody had a late-night game of strip poker with a side order of hide'n-go-get-it. I looked surprised, probably because I was surprised. More like in shock.

He lay across the bed. "I shoulda went to church today."

I heard gritty singing. The shower was running, so I asked a bona fide stupid question to see if Brown would volunteer some information about what was going on. "Where's Chiquita?"

He exhaled and looked ashamed. "You mad?"

I fake-smiled. "What you think?"

"Dag. You just like Moms. Just like her."

"You were here all night."

"Nuthin' happened."

"You lie like a rug."

"Straight up. Nuthin' happened."

"Don't you sound defensive."

"Stop looking at me like that. You act just like Moms."

After his elusive attitude shut me up, I sat in one of the chairs and watched Reverend Price. When Price is on, Brown shuts everybody out and listens like it's the last thing he'll ever hear. A few minutes later, the bathroom door opened and some serious streams of steam floated out. I felt the heat from the shower leading the way and I backed up because I'd just done my hair and Lord knows I didn't want it to flop before breakfast. Seconds later, Chiquita stuck her head out when I said "Amen" loud enough for her to know I was there. She stepped out of the bathroom with a towel wrapped around her. Looked like a light passion mark was on her neck. On the inside I was a little pissed for her using my brother and for my brother using her, but kept acting like this shit was as normal as the sun coming up. He knows what's up. She's a grown woman.

I pushed my face up into a cute smile and said, "Hey, girl."

She crooked her mouth, shifted a bit, and said, "Hey, Inda."

When she turned around, I followed her into the bathroom. My lips parted but I didn't say a word while she sprayed on deodorant and fixed up her face. I stood there, watching her mess up the ozone and hand wipe the steam from the mirror. She kept peeping back at me like she wanted me to say something first. I picked up her Afro comb and scratched my dry scalp. I said, "So, what's really going on?"

"You know how it is."

"No, how is it?"

"I needed somebody."

"You don't even know him."

She said, "We started talking."

"And?"

"He listened. And, y'know."

"Uh huh."

"It got late. He was kinda tired. Been drinking."

"Uh huh. I had a room. Right down the hall."

She gave me that sensitive look that asked me not to be so judgmental. "And I was a little lonely."

"Well, well." I grinned. "How you feel now?"

She broad-smiled. "Better. A load's gone. Lighter."

"You usually do after a good shit. At least I do."

We laughed that stupid, silly girlfriend laugh.

"You know, that's my baby brother. We fight like cats and dogs, but we look out for each other."

"I know. I liked that about you two when we were at the club. I wished I had that."

"I understand where your head's at, but I don't necessarily agree with what you did."

"I like him."

"Uh huh."

"From the moment he walked over to the table."

"I'm not saying a word. Not my business."

"Still my friend?" She pouted. "Please say yes."

"Yes. Damn, Chiquita, I don't know what to do about you."

"My eyebrows, so we can go."

I picked up the tweezers and helped her pluck her eyebrows. I said, "He's my brother, but he's a man. So, be careful."

She smiled. I finally gave in and kissed the side of her face. Something about her reminded me of Red, the uncontrollable grief and the sudden happiness. Plus they both have that idealistic, optimistic view of romance. Guess I'm jaded to the point of no return.

But it was more than that. All while we ate and shopped and cried yesterday, I had thought about it. Maybe I hoped she'd break the ice and bring it up first.

I didn't know her from Eve, so I didn't know how loose she was, if she was loose, or just hurt and latching onto the first emotion that came along. After she'd been with Raymond, not to mention that ghetto girl Gina had been with Raymond, and you already know that yours truly had been with Raymond just last weekend—I just hoped Chiquita used some common sense and put some spermicide and sheepskin in between her and my baby brother. Because, like I said, even though I might not have said it yet, I damn sure had been thinking about the possibility of contracting an STD, thinking about that mess nonstop. Which might have been part of the reason I was so hesitant about taking Michael's number. Emotional, but mostly physical timing. That little concern, plus the fact that Inda ain't one to be hopping from horse to horse without a thought about who rode it last. Plus I like to have some grieving period in between jacked-up relationships. I love the comfort of a man, because, like I said, I am a woman, dammit, but this sistuh is not and will not ever be co-dependent to the point of screwing for convenience. Or revenge. Because when you do the latter, the only one who gets fucked is you.

But my main health concern was for me, my Afro sistuh, and my blood brother. Raymond had been hoeing around. And you know if we knew about three sistuhs there were probably three more who we hadn't run into yet. Anyway, me and girlfriend Chiquita could have whatever he had picked up and was dishing around.

35 / CHIQUITA

Last night when I was waiting for the elevator, Brown stepped out of Inda's room. He called my name and smiled at me. I yawned. He yawned. With us being alone, I felt very uneasy.

Not knowing what to say, I gave him that phony 'bye-'bye airline grin we attendants give passengers as they exit the plane. "Your name is Thaddeus?"

"Yeah. But call me Brown. Your name is Chiquita?" He smiled. "Like the banana?"

"Yeah. Like the, uh, banana. Yeah."

"That's Spanish for petite or small. You part Mexican?"

I laughed. "Not that I know of, but you never know. Mama's baby, Papa's maybe."

"Bet you got teased a lot growing up."

"Yep. Sure did. Either 'Quita, Quita, chicken eater' or they'd sing that stupid banana song."

We started talking while he held the elevator door open with his foot, ended up talking over thirty minutes, so I invited him over for a few more minutes of chitchat. Company to last until I was tired enough to sleep the night through. I lay across the bed because I was too tipsy and he sat in the chair and we talked.

After the alcohol took over and I started babbling, I told him how I met Inda. About Raymond. Rapped on all that bullstuff. I thought he'd think I was crazy. But instead, he listened, shook his head, chuckled, then started telling me about some of his problems. How he never felt like he measured up to the rest of the family, about growing up with mixed parents that had an off-and-on relationship. I didn't know that their mother was white. And that made Inda and her brother more interesting. But even then, I didn't think that what he was saying was what was really on his mind.

Brown yawned and his eyes were starting to look bloodshot. When he told me he'd had a couple of drinks at the club, I told him he could lie down and take a nap until he felt good enough to make his long drive. If he wanted. I didn't really want him to, I just would've felt bad if I didn't offer and something happened to him.

He turned down my offer, but got to the door and hesitated. Brown rubbed his eyes and said, "I probably should. The Long Beach PD ain't no joke with a brother this time of night."

"Are they worse than the LAPD?"

"Only on days of the week that end in the letter Y."

We laughed and yawned.

He lay on the far side of the bed, I stayed on mine. I think he was asleep before his head hit the pillow. It took me a while to close my eyes.

I woke in the middle of the night and he was standing in the window looking out toward the ocean. He was crying. Not hard, just a couple of tears that made his face seem so boyish. His sad face looked all of six.

I asked, "What's wrong?"

He shook his head. "Nothing. I just cry in my sleep every now and then. Didn't think it would hit me tonight."

"Why?"

"Life."

"What?"

"Be thanking about thangs."

"Like?"

"Gwen."

Brown had met Gwen a couple of months before at an R&B club, Pinkies, in Moreno Valley, about an hour east of where Inda lived. A few days later, she'd come out and spent the weekend with him. Days after that Gwen's sister called him from Riverside. She'd had a stroke. A day later she was dead.

Since my grandparents died, I've been real sensitive to the stroke issue. I've seen what it does to people, how it took the life out of strong people and left nothing. I watched two strong people become more dependent than newborn babies. They looked right at me and didn't know who I was. Then I watched them get worse, deteriorate, and die. And there was nothing I could do but pray. And even then I didn't know what I was praying for. If I wanted them to be taken away so they'd feel better, or if I wanted them here so I wouldn't be left alone.

His voice lowered. "Gwen died just like that."

I put my arms around him. "How old was she?"

"Twenty-three." He wiped his face. "Went to bed one night and didn't wake up the next day. She had a two-year-old boy. It was kinda rough on me, looking down in a coffin that had somebody in it you was with, laughing, partying with, and loving less than a week before. Makes you thank about thangs in a different way. Appreciate family. Makes you wonder what's important."

"That's so sad."

"People die and you never get a chance to talk to them again. No matter what you wanted to say, it's a done deal."

"Inda didn't tell me."

"They don't know. Keep it to myself."

I didn't say anything. I'd keep it to myself. I knew what it was like to hold on to something troubling and keep it inside.

"I guess that's why I ain't been coming 'round my sisters like I should." He grinned. "Since Pops ain't around like he should be, I have to look out for those knuckleheads. Guess I been off meditating and thanking about straightening out my life."

Brown sounded more mature than he looked. I'd never seen a man so big and strong look so vulnerable. I didn't bother to ask him any questions, because I was afraid that my own dilemma I'd kept inside might slip out at a tempting moment like the one we were living inside. I just listened to what was on his mind. Then he asked, "What's your pain?"

His words startled me deep inside like he had read my thoughts. Maybe something was showing on my face. "What do you mean?"

"Everybody has some kind of a pain. What's yours?"

"I don't have any pain."

"Good."

Then I moved near him, close enough to stop the words. I kissed him, wanted him, and we started taking our clothes off. While I ran my hands over his chest he lightly sucked on my neck. Even though I bruise easily, I didn't stop him. We had got into the bed, got ready for the dance that I think we both needed to make us forget about the sad music life was playing, then he rolled over.

I asked, "What's wrong?"

"Let's not. We don't need that right now, Fox."

"Okay."

"That won't fix nothing. It'll just complicate thangs. Wake up in the morning kicking yourself."

I felt foolish. Too damn naked. But I smiled. "Thanks."

"Don't get me wrong, you're all that. Plus you're my sister's friend. It wouldn't be right. Not now, anyway."

"And you're my friend's brother."

"I'm sorry. I mean, I was looking at you, thanking

about how sweet you looked, but you know. Your body's tight but I didn't want it to jump off like this. Maybe I should head on home."

I looked at my hands. "That's okay. I don't mind. You can stay."

I said I didn't mind, but for the second time that day, I think I felt abandoned. Like Chiquita wasn't enough. But I knew he was right. So the rejection felt good. I guess I was used to getting acceptance by leading with my body. These breasts, these hips, this vagina had been used and misled so much. Mostly by my own device because I knew the weakness of men. And for once I knew and admitted the weakness of me. Then I felt bad because I wondered what he thought about me for offering myself to him to momentarily calm his problems, for allowing myself to accept him to superficially calm mine. I know I'm a good person. A little confused at times, a little messed on the inside, but not any more confused or messed up than anybody else. Everybody's got a problem. A different kind of problem that makes us all look at and do things a little differently.

Brown said, "Hard being a man. We ain't suppose to feel thangs. At least not too much and not too long."

"Who said that?"

"Society."

"Why you feel that way?"

He didn't answer.

I said, "Hard being a woman, too. We're supposed to feel everything."

When he got quiet, I was going to put my gown on and sleep on the floor or go down to Inda's room, but before I could move he snuggled up close to me and made me feel safe. I wasn't used to the caring or the tears. Maybe I wasn't used to a man touching me like that just because.

I said, "My folks."

"What about them?"

In the time it took me to say those two words, I was almost to tears. "That's my pain."

"Why?"

"I don't know who my father is. Or was. I think that's why I do some of the things I do. When you don't have somebody to guide you you end up going in all directions. Doing fucked-up shit."

"Wanna talk about it?"

"I never have. I don't know how to." I closed my eyes. "And I don't want to. Let me keep it to myself for a while."

Then the phone rang. I thought it might be Inda calling, but when I answered the first thing the voice said was, "I love you. Look, why don't you come over so we can talk—"

I hung up. Just hearing his voice brought up so much of a different kind of pain. After I rang the desk and told them to hold my calls, I moved closer to Brown, but I didn't close my eyes. Even with them open they felt closed because I couldn't see anything.

But I could hear coarse breathing. My own troubled breath. I could tell Brown was awake too. His dreams must've had him too rattled to sleep. He was holding on to me like he was trying to steal some of the pain that was swelling in my heart. And we rocked each other.

He whispered, "It'll be all right."

I told him the same.

36 / INDA

After we checked out, I rode up to Thrifty's Drug Store and bought a wrist support. My wrist didn't hurt too bad, I could flex it, but it was tender, and since I'd sprung it playing softball in the summer, I didn't want to take any chances. Anyway, we convoyed like we were the first leg of the Underground Railroad. Chiquita followed me, Brown followed Chiquita. So that meant I was up front leading the way like Harriet Tubman. And let me tell you, I could feel the Sunday-morning positive vibes coming from all of our cars.

Michael met us for a Sunday champagne brunch a few miles down the way in the part they called Belmont Shores. A nice sedate part of Long Beach that was far enough away from Deputy Dawgville for Chiquita and myself to forget about yesterday and last night, at least for a while. But that stupid grin on her face told me she didn't want to forget all of last night, because evidently something went right after all the wrong.

Chiquita had picked up some jeans on sale at Old Navy and a T-shirt yesterday. I had thrown on my same black jeans, white T-shirt, and a short-sleeved jean blouse with Charlie Brown on the pocket. And since we both had jackets to block out the early morning cool, we were good to go. The way Mr. Sunshine had a big happy smile and was beaming down, it took about fifteen minutes for it to burn away the low morning clouds. It was that kinda weather that was too hot for a coat but too cool not to have one on, so me and Chiquita draped our jackets over our shoulders so the nipples on our bosoms wouldn't be poking out across the tables.

After he sipped his orange juice, Brown said, "It's nice down here. I could kick it back here all day."

Chiquita took a sip of the champagne and smiled. "It's relaxing. Calm."

And after all the drama and calamity of yesterday, I knew exactly what she meant. But I had a word or two to say to Brown, who was looking a little tension-relieved himself, I might add.

I said, "Thought you had to rush home and wash your ride. Do your laundry. Go food shopping. Couldn't hang out with your sister because you had your *pay-bills kinda thangs* to do today. You know, take care of your own *responsibilities* all day today."

"Black. Chill."

Chiquita blushed.

We ignored Brown's complaining because he still had on the clothes he wore last night. He didn't want to be outside because he didn't feel too fresh. His linen was clinging to the smoke from the club. But we kept on our shades and sat out on the balcony in the sunshine and soaked up rays and lighthearted conversation. Chiquita was surprised to see me with "the cute painter from the restaurant."

"Thanks for the compliment." Michael winked at me and said, "Yeah. We ran into each other on the docks last night. Ain't that right, Linda-without-the-L."

I felt the naughty public kisses from last night and blushed.

"Cat's out the bag." Chiquita smiled. "Oh, that's where you tipped off to for all them hours."

"Miss Thang." I smirked and nodded at Brown. "And I know you didn't need my company."

So Michael and myself played it off and let them think we never had a word between us before the restaurant. Neither one of us said anything about the personals, because, you know. Ain't their business no-way. We sat around talking about family. Both of his parents were speech pathologists. I told him my pops worked for the FAA and my moms was an assistant principal.

The way Chiquita and Brown were holding hands off-and-on and feeding each other on-and-off, it looked like they'd been together awhile and she never knew anybody named Raymond. That distant look sistuh-girlfriend had been wearing all yesterday and half the night was long gone. After a couple'a hits of champagne, Michael loosened up and sat closer to me and started some mild flirting. And mild was nice and greatly appreciated because I really wasn't in the mood for anything intense so quick. And at that point, I didn't think I'd ever want intense for the rest of my days. Just a movie and dinner companion. Nothing more.

Anyway, after I assured him that my baby brother was safer than he looked, Michael turned up the flames hot enough to cremate anything negative Raymond or an ex-husband had left behind.

When we got ready to go, he leaned over and whispered in my ear, "I like you."

Those sweet words made me tingle. I smiled. "Like you, too."

my parents there year before last for their thirty-fifth wedding anniversary. They had a ball. You been on Beale Street?"

I sighed. "Yep. A time or two."

Brown said, "I wish I could go and see that hotel they killed Martin Luther King at."

I said, "The Lorraine Motel, I think. I grew up a few miles away on Kansas Street."

"I'd like to see the Civil Rights Museum." Brown nodded. "But I know me. Whew, I might be getting mad at the left side of my family."

"I know what you mean," Michael said. "I'd look at all that history, get mad, and start cussing out white folks."

"I know that's right." I laughed. "We'd do it in stereo."

And there it was again. That guilt that wouldn't go away no matter how much I padded it with alcohol, sex, and laughter. There was something I wanted to tell Inda. And after she'd been so good to me, I felt like I had to tell her. I owed her the truth. But she had been so busy looking at romance novels and talking to Michael while he flipped through the detective ones. We hadn't had a moment to be alone.

After we left the bookstore, Inda and Michael were walking behind Brown and me. The men were on the outside, protecting us in case a car jumped off the curb. That was what Inda said.

Brown said, "Yeah. Like we're car-proof."

Michael laughed.

A moment later I turned around and said, "I've got to potty."

Michael and Brown went inside a record store and Inda and I went inside a family seafood restaurant that had a surfers motif and Beach Boys music. The ladies' room was upstairs.

Maybe my expression changed or something because Inda said, "Chiquita, what's going on?"

"I'm tired of pretending I'm okay." My voice cracked. "I need a friend."

"What's wrong?"

"I lied to you about something."

"Okay." Her voice sounded worried. "What's up?"

"Between me and you?"

"Yeah." She took a slow breath. "This got something to do with Deputy Dawg?"

"I wish it was that easy." I shook my head. "This ain't got nothing to do with that bastard."

"What's wrong?"

My words were thick as mud. "My momma isn't dead."

Last winter I had gone looking for my mother. My personal expedition. I'd never lived with her and had only seen her a handful of times. I never knew why it was like that but it was. Big Momma and Big Daddy took care of me until they died. And my mother wasn't at either funeral. Then I stayed with other relatives. I got her address from a relative and flew back to Memphis to try to find some understanding, to make some kind of a family bond. And I was angry because I'd found out that all the time I was in Memphis as a child, she was there too. And she'd never called or came to see me since I was in pigtails.

When I got to South Memphis the weather was in the upper forties. Snow and ice was melting. The sky was bright blue. A beautiful day. Trees were naked and looked feeble, stood crooked like old people pointing at each other. Maybe they were snitching that I was on the way to bring up the past.

The narrow wooden house was next to an empty lot and didn't have an address out front. Next door was an empty spot filled with broken glass, liquor bottles, paper, old mattresses.

After I parked my rental car, I held my head high and strolled with purpose. Some serious purpose. But inside and out, I was stiff. I was numb but I sure felt every step.

Their house was a one-level with chipped green paint. A black man wearing forties-style baggy pants, a three-shades-of-brown butterfly collar shirt and a button-down was on the porch. His dark vinyl house shoes were barely on the tips of his white-socked feet. He sat out front like he was guarding his house, like it was the most important thing on the block. And I was so nervous I made my boots click-clack on the way up to the porch. Cleared my throat and hummed to keep from going crazy. After all that noise, when he didn't move, that frightened me.

"Excuse me." I was standing over him, shivering. "Sir?"

He was sitting in a rusty metal lawn chair, slumped over with his legs crossed. A chipped wooden cane was next to him. He looked like what happened when you took the soul out of somebody and left the shell behind. His breath steamed from his rubbery mouth like he was getting older right in my face.

"Good afternoon." I smiled my best smile. He glanced over my clothes, then frowned. My smile ran away. I was overdressed in a pinstriped suit, leather gloves, and a long leather coat. Perry Ellis perfume. But I felt naked.

"How are you doing today, sir?" I spoke in my kindest voice. "Does Miss Thompson live here?"

"Don't no Thompson live here."

"Raylette Thompson doesn't live here?"

"Who you?"

"I'm . . ." I choked. "I'm her daughter. Chiquita Thompson."

"Her name Wilson." He spat. "Been that a long time."

I pushed my cold hands deeper in my pockets and gripped my keys. I thought that maybe my senile-ailing-ignorant-funky-old-clothes-wearing-ain't-got-no-home-training-needs-to-be-slapped-stepdad would give me an asinine hello. It was my own fault for expecting kind words that said, "You're family, you're welcome."

He turned his head away and spat into a bent tin cup. "Bae-Bae, somebody here to see you."

I repeated, "Somebody?"

When I heard footsteps heading toward the front of the house, I wanted to jump off the porch, run back to my car, and speed to the airport. Maybe just hop on the interstate and head west until I gurgled in the Pacific.

He said, "Stop that racket."

I stopped hitting my hand against my leg, clanging my three silver bracelets. Something in the house dropped. The sound was close. When I looked behind me, it seemed like my car had moved farther away. Abandoning me.

Then there she was. We were separated by dirty mesh in a warped aluminum door. She stared, then held the door open with one hand, crossed the line without a smile. That made me want to cry. But I raised my wall higher. Returned that same gaze.

I said, "I'm Chiquita Lynn. I'm your daughter."

"You thank I wouldn't know my own child?"

My phony airline smile left. Nobody said a word. Like me, she'd brought resentment to the porch.

We stood, mother and daughter. Complete strangers. It hurt more when I admitted that I knew who she was, but I didn't know a doggone thing about her. And since I didn't know anything about her, I didn't have the slightest idea how to get the doggone reunion started. Her eyes lit up for a moment, she sort of smiled, then went back to that cold-blooded look.

Her brown eyes walked down my jacket, across my suit. She rubbed her hands across the leather. Then opened the jacket. Inspection of me all grown up. I didn't like it. Then she raised her eyes to mine. I had stopped breathing and went numb when she touched me. I said, "How are you doing?"

"My light bill is behind."

"I'm sorry, what?"

"My light bill behind."

It took me a few seconds of looking at her to understand what was going on. First impression from her, struggling Chiquita—who worked three jobs at the same time to put herself through college—looked like a check ready to be cashed.

I'd never pushed her away, at least not on purpose. Never. I'd just found out where she was and I had to beg my uncle Vernon for that information. I'd spent too many moments staring off into space, wondering if the phone would ring and they'd tell me a mother I didn't know was dead. But instead of a mother's love, I'd been given another slap. This one from reality.

I said, "I don't have any money."

Her lover man was ignoring us both, but he was

listening. Hoping for some doggone money. Lights were on all through the house. A radio or a television was playing in the back.

The words burned from my throat. "Who is my real daddy?"

The silence almost made me crazy. I wanted to know what she was thinking. She scratched her face. "Why you ask a fool thing like that?"

"Because I don't know."

"You know."

"You never told me."

"That why you here?"

"Yes."

"If you don't know you oughts to know."

I ran my hand across my hair. "Was Tommy Williams my daddy?"

Her lover man shifted in his chair and looked in the opposite direction. I shifted too. The way they reacted together, the way nobody answered, I wondered if I sounded stupid.

"Yeah," she said. "That your pappy."

She said it without expression. Didn't flex a single muscle in her face. We stood in silence. The wind blew papers down the streets. Dogs barked. I tried to read her face for a lie. But I didn't know her well enough to recognize it if it jumped out and bit me. I had to face the truth and quit fantasizing about some Brady Bunch kind of reunion.

Other people in my family said they thought he was my daddy. *Thought.* As far as I was concerned, it wouldn't count unless she said it to my face. She had to tell me who she had laid with.

Tommy Williams died in a car accident when I was a baby and never saw me. I didn't have any pictures. No number or address. Just the name I overheard when Big Momma was talking.

Since I said it first, I wondered if it counted, or did she play along to shut me up and shut me out. My fingers found their way down my side, opened my black purse and took out my wallet. When I gave her the sixty dollars I had, she took it out of my hand almost as fast as I could get it out.

She asked, "Why ain't you never called me Momma?"

"I didn't have your number."

"No. I mean, why ain't you never acknowledged me as your momma? You never say my name."

I tried not to sound like a bitter child. But that was who I was. Smile or frown, that was who I always was. "Why haven't you ever tried to contact me or wish me happy birthday or come to my high school graduation or come to my college graduation? What did I ever do to you?"

She didn't answer.

I hesitated. "Who was I named after?"

"What?"

"Who gave me my name?"

"Why?"

"Because it's important to me. People should know."

"Nurse at the hospital gave it to you."

"Black or white?"

"Some white lady."

Johnny grunted then grabbed his cane and struggled to his feet. She handed him the money. He went inside. He shuffled to the back part of the house and closed a door.

"Why didn't you ever call Big Momma's house to see about me?"

"You come to my home to chastise me?"

"No, Miss Wilson." I softened my voice. "I came here because I'm your daughter. And I wanted you to be my mother."

She said a dry, "Good for you, Miss Thompson."

What hurt the most was that little girl inside of me I always hid. That sad girl in pigtails. The child who raised her skirt to get attention. The woman who kept meeting guys like Raymond and staying with them because that was where she felt safe. In a place with no real feeling or caring.

"Here's the phone number to the hotel I'm staying at."

"For what?"

I bit my lip and headed for the car. Hurried away. I didn't say good-bye. Inside the car, I looked in the rearview mirror and cut my hostile eyes at the mean woman who looked just like me. I had walked up on her porch and let her wound me.

I never wanted to get married because I didn't

want to give her a son-in-law. Since she'd never given me anything, I didn't ever want to give her something. Not even indirectly. And I'd told myself that if I ever got pregnant, I wouldn't keep it. I didn't want to lie to my child by saying that my mother had died.

Inda's asking about my parents yesterday, then Brown asking me what my pain was, had brought that up to the surface. Then Michael asking about Memphis. That was my doggone burden.

I told Inda a lot more than that, told her about the time my mother came and got me when I was about five or six. I watched my mother's drunk boyfriend come home and beat her and kick her under a dinner table over a few dollars. He beat her in front of me. Then I told Inda about when my mother wouldn't sign the papers so I could get Social Security from my daddy's dying. When my mother wouldn't sign, that made me think that that man wasn't my daddy. After that I felt like she had shut me out.

When I finished talking about the trauma, I held Inda's hand. I said, "That was why I said my momma was dead."

"Chiquita, no."

"I know this ain't exactly the right time to bring it up, I mean I know we're having a good day. Maybe the champagne got me buzzed, but I had to say what was wrong before we all went our separate ways.

Just wanted you to know in case we, you know, didn't run into each other."

I think I told her because she was still a stranger, somebody I could walk away from and still have my secrets to myself.

I said, "Forgive me for lying like that for no reason."

Inda couldn't answer. She nodded. And her face was filled with tears that told me what she felt. She wiped my eyes, held me closer and said, "You'll only have one mother, Chiquita."

"You and your momma get along good, huh?"

"Hell, no. Hell, who does? But she's my moms." She chuckled. "Don't let that ruin you. You're a nice young lady."

"Just like you?"

Inda smiled a little. "Just like me."

"Divas?"

"Straight up." Inda held my hand. "But seriously, Chiquita, all of that past pain has been given too much power. I deal with children and parents like that every day at work."

Before she could say anything else, I heard somebody charging up the stairs. At first I thought it was one of the waitresses or waiters, because the kitchen was down the hall. Then there was a knock on the bathroom door, and Brown's voice called out, "Black, you in there?"

"Yeah. We're coming."

His tone was forceful and scary. Urgent. "It's an emergency."

"What?"

"Red's missing. She tried to kill Walter and ran away."

38 / INDA

I rushed out into the hallway with Chiquita in tow, both of us dabbing our eyes with tissue. "What the hell you mean Red's missing and tried to kill Walter?"

Brown looked rattled when he saw our wet faces. Michael, too. I was trying to figure out what the hell Brown was babbling about, because when he gets upset he talks a tad bit too fast for the kid. And when his face gets that stern he looks just like his daddy, three shades removed. Especially since they both have the same height and thick build, but Pops has a bit of a sixty-year-old tummy and doesn't have an arrogant strut.

Brown recouped and said, "Something went down between her and Walter and she tried to kill him last night."

"That don't sound like Red."

"Who you telling."

"What she do?"

"I'm not knowing. Moms was talking at a thousand miles an hour and all I made out was something about Red burning down their house. I tried to ring Moms back but all I got was her machine."

"Who did you talk to?"

"Nobody. I checked my machine a minute ago and Moms had called damn near every minute since three this morning. The police called my crib and left a message. Sounds like they had been after Red all night and this morning."

"Police after Red?" And let me tell you, my mind went blank. This was too much to digest in a second or two. Actually I was waiting for my baby brother to crack a smile and break out a string of your-momma jokes. But with each second, his light-brown eyes just got filled with worry. I asked, "Did Red call you?"

"Naw. I mean yeah. Naw. I mean I called Red's crib but the phone just rang. Check your machine. She would've called you before she called me."

"Well, I don't know the code to my machine."

"What you mean you don't know the code?"

"I mean I don't know the code."

Lawd-haf-murcy. If it ain't one goddamn thing, it's another goddamn thing. I hadn't even finished drying my tears from what Chiquita had told me, and now it sounded like Red had flipped the script and lost her mind. In less than a minute, my new girlfriend was a motherless child and my roughneck brother was telling me that my angelic sister had turned into a fugitive in line to get on *America's Most Wanted*.

Brown said, "You don't think she'd do nothing to herself?"

I looked at him. "Why you asking something crazy like that?"

He shrugged. "Just worried, that's all."

First I thought about her moods. That depression that came and went like the tide rolling in and out. Then I remembered how she was when she picked me up in Long Beach yesterday morning after I'd walked out on Raymond. Put-offish and distant. Bitchy. And let me tell you, my mind got so cramped with bad feelings that nothing made any sense. All I could do was say, "Let's go."

When I rushed to a pay phone and buzzed Red's house, the phone rang and rang. Moms wasn't home and I got Pops's answering machine. Everybody was missing early on a Sunday afternoon.

"Inda." Michael came up to me. "Anything I can do?"

"No. But thanks." We all headed for the stairs. "I'm sorry we've got to rush off like this."

He gave me a hug and said, "Call me and let me know."

"Thanks, Michael."

Then there was Chiquita. The child looked so lost. So alone. Outside, I gave her one of my cards so she could call me. It felt like it was hard to say good-bye to her, especially a minute after she'd reached out and needed me like a sistuh needs a sistuh. The girl had opened a wound and I was about to run off and let her bleed herself to death. We knew about people being estranged from their parents, because when Moms and Pops got married and had us, Pops's side of the family had a fit. I was about to graduate from high school before they got back together and all of us got to meet.

But right now Red had got her narrow ass in some kind of trouble and had a wound that needed to be checked on and cauterized. And Chiquita would be all right for the moment. Either way, I had to go take care of my own blood first. We could talk after the dust had settled on the other side of town.

"Chiquita," I said. "Make sure you call me."

"Okay." Chiquita gave Brown a one-armed hug. He kissed her lips. She looked surprised. I was too upset to have any more surprises, so I just banked that one for later.

After we ran to the cars and started to pull out of the parking lot, Michael blew his horn and headed toward Pacific Coast Highway. Brown was leading the way toward the freeway and zipped through the light before I could make it. A police car was in the intersection so I had to stop or get a ticket and spend another weekend in traffic school. Chiquita blew her horn and pulled up at the light next to me. We'd crossed PCH and I thought she was about to tell me good-bye again because the next entrance was the crossroads to entrance for the 605 north and 405 south. The 405 would take her back to the sanity of San Diego in an hour and some change.

"Inda." She raised her shades and yelled, "I'm following you."

"I'm sure everything is fine." And I knew I was lying my ass off. My shades hid my eyes and kept the truth inside. "You don't have to. We live almost an hour from here."

"Don't matter. I want to make sure you're okay." She nodded. And she looked as scared as I felt. "I'm following you."

39 / **INDA**

Talk about a sistuh getting the memo a tad bit late. Moms and Pops were already in town and pulled up at Red's crib right when we did. I think they'd already been there a while and were just getting back. Both of them hopped out of a rental car before it quit rolling. Moms fanned her face. Her nose turned up because I know she smelled the ripe cow dung drifting from the east.

After the police had called Moms, she called Pops, then he drove thirty minutes from San Francisco to Oakland and hopped on a nonstop south to Ontario International. Moms zoomed to San Diego International Airport and hopped on a nonstop north from San Diego. Pops's flight was a little over an hour and Moms's was less than that, and they hooked up at the airport and drove here together. Probably working each other's nerves all the way.

And would you believe neighbors were out right then, in the broad of day, peeping down the street, but not coming a step in our direction. They were gawking at us like we were either the Manson family looking for trouble or lepers looking for victims.

Pops hadn't shaven and was dressed in loose jeans,

cross-trainers, and a gray polo shirt. He hugged me and said, "Hey, baby-cakes."

"Hey, Pops."

He whispered in my ear, "You got Roscoe?"

"In the car."

"What happened to your wrist?"

"Sprung it in a fight."

"Inda." He could remember my name when he was pissed off. "You and that damn brother of yours."

"Dag. She started it."

"And you had to finish it."

"You know me."

"Just like my mother used to be."

"Momma Lorraine was nice. God bless her sweet little soul."

"She fooled you too."

Nothing on my Pops had been ironed worth a damn. When he took his fedora off it looked like his wooly hair had been hit with another coat of black dye since the last time I saw him. His shirt was unbuttoned so the hairs on his chest stuck out like jungle weeds.

Pops went over to my brother and asked, "What the hell is going on, Brown?"

That was part of Pops's man thing, thinking a woman wouldn't know or be able to drop down the details. My baby brother shrugged. "We just got your messages. Don't know yet."

"Inda." That was my super-tanned moms hurrying

down the driveway toward my car. Chiquita had parked on the street and was walking up Garden Court behind me. "I was starting to get worried about you too. After I couldn't reach anybody I thought all sorts of things."

And let me tell, even though I was a woman of thirty-something, and a tad bit on the attitude side of life, I was damn happy to see my fifty-year-old mother. I said, "Hey, Moms."

"What the hell is going on?" she snapped, and her ponytail bounced off her butt. "They told me the house had been burned down."

"You don't have to sound disappointed."

"Don't start with me, Inda. Where's your little sister?"

"Why you shouting at me?"

"I'm not shouting."

"I don't know where your grown child is."

"You live right around the corner from her and you don't know?" She tiptoed two inches and hugged me and almost pulled me over. Before I got my balance back she was talking too fast. "You haven't heard from her?"

"Not since yesterday morning. You ask Walter what happened?"

"He's not here."

I asked, "Where is he?"

"How the hell would I know?"

"Moms, chill and take your fingernail out your

mouth." I looked at my watch. Almost three. "Maybe he's at work."

"We just went by the dealership. He's not there and they hadn't heard from him since he left work yesterday evening."

Chiquita asked, "You have his folks' phone numbers?"

"Moms, this is Chiquita. Friend of mine. And Brown's." They said hi. After a deep breath I said, "I think I might have his mother's and brother's numbers back at my place."

Moms took her jean jacket off and adjusted her red and gold sundress. A web of lines were in her forehead and crow's-feet were in the corners of her eyes. Her makeup was hardly on and the woman hadn't done anything to her brunette-turning-gray hair but pulled it back in a ponytail and thrown a Chargers baseball cap over it. And for Moms not to be dressed head to toe meant she was beyond worried.

"I called you all night. I wanted you to come over here and tell me what was going on. When they said the house burned down, and I couldn't reach you or Thaddeus, I thought all of you might have been in the damn house when it caught on fire." Moms was getting damn snappy and I was about ready to walk away. Made a sistuh want to go clean her room to get some fresh air. Maybe just slip three or four Sominex in her coffee. She asked, "Where were you?"

"Will you lighten up?" Damn, I felt guilty for being the oldest. "I was in Long Beach."

"Running the streets all night? That's why you couldn't be around when somebody needed you."

"Moms, how was I supposed to know—"

"I figured you were down at that Raymond's house for the weekend. That's why nobody can ever catch up with you."

"Eh, Moms. I'm here now, okay? So chill with the madness."

That made me look at Chiquita because I felt uncomfortable with Deputy Dawg's name being brought up in an intimate way at a bad moment. Chiquita adjusted her stance and looked away like she wasn't listening. Then she strolled up the drive toward Brown. That was the first time I noticed the sadness in her face. Behind all them smiles and being bubbly, there was some serious pain.

Before we could make it to the house, Red's next-door neighbor, Charlotte, stepped out her own door and came over. She was in her CSUDH sweats and dark blue house shoes. No makeup. Two cars were in her driveway.

Charlotte called out, "Inda, is everything all right?"

"Hell no." Then I asked, "What happened over here, Charlotte?"

She blew air like it was some serious emotion that had been let loose. "Grrrl, come over here in the shade."

Wanna talk about drama? Police cars, ambulances, and fire trucks, oh my, for two hours, in the middle of the night, all with lights twirling and lighting up the neighborhood like rainbows chasing rainbows. Then damn near all of the neighborhood was standing outside for another hour after that like they were waiting for the second show to begin.

A brotha had pulled up and was sitting on top of a new 300ZX. A bright banana-yellow car with the T-tops off. I'd seen him around before. Somewhere. So I guess the few African-Americans for miles around had networked the news and would be carpooling and riding around here for the show.

Charlotte nodded toward the brotha. "Who is that? He's been out here being a looky-loo for the last hour or so."

I joked, "Thought it might've been your ex, Clarence."

"Grrrl, please. I had him thrown in jail yesterday for violating the restraining order."

The brotha in the yellow ride drove away. Nothing was happening worth watching, so I guess he moved on. Before he left a couple of other people slowed and gawked as they passed by. This should be a full-blown parade by dinnertime.

We were all standing around trying to think of where Red might've gone. The closest relative was Moms's stepbrother what's-his-face in Vegas. All of Pops's side of the family was back in Chicago. And this didn't feel right. If she'd done something to Walter, with the way he'd been acting, ain't no telling what he would've done to her. I didn't want to say that thought out loud with everybody already on the edge. But I had a feeling that it was time to dust off my .380 and go on a scavenger hunt.

"This might be all day," I said. "Chiquita, you don't have to stay."

"I'm fine. I just want you to calm down and keep your head straight. You can't help your family if you're not thinking right."

I smiled a tight smile. Chiquita was an angel. I said, "Thanks."

"Maybe I can help in some kinda way."

"Just hold my hand and keep me from tripping too hard."

"I'll do what I can. I owe you that from last night at the hotel when you saved me from doing something stupid."

Moms walked over to talk to a couple of the neighbors. By then a couple of young Asian and white people who lived across the street had come over and said the same thing that Charlotte had already told us. Brown and Pops had peeped in all the front windows, checked to see if any were unlocked. Brown had unbuttoned his vest and was sweating down his chest and neck. He ripped his pant leg when he jumped the iron gate and went to look in through the back patio door. The blinds were drawn and he couldn't see inside. I called from next door and Moms said she could hear the phone ring, but nobody picked up.

Moms asked Charlotte, "Did my daughter get hurt?"

"I don't know, Mrs. Johnson. I got here after it was over," Charlotte said. She had a couple of pieces of luggage under her hazel eyes. "My friend stayed over last night while I went to work, and when I got home this morning he told me all about it. But he did say there was an ambulance out here for a while. I'll run inside and call a friend and have her check the hospitals. What's Walter's last name?"

Moms wiped the sweat off her nose and said, "Sinclair."

I wiped the sweat off mine, fanned my blouse and said, "Maiden name Johnson."

"Inda." That was Chiquita walking away from Brown and interrupting my train of thought.

In my mind I had fingers around Walter's neck. If he was burned, I'd scrape his ass like toast first, then choke him.

Chiquita put my hand in her hand. "You probably should go home and check your machine to see if your sister called you this morning or something."

"You're right."

Moms grabbed her jacket and purse out of the rental car. She yelled back to Pops, "Babe, I'm going over to Inda's to check and see if Valerie went over there."

"Okay, Babe. I'm gonna go down to the station with Brown. We'll meet back here."

"Just come by Inda's."

"Okay. I wanna find out what the damn problem is. Somebody know where my child at."

Chiquita hopped in the backseat of my Camry. Moms beat me to the car, hopped up front, and clicked her seat belt on, then made me stop cussing and put mine on. Pops and Brown went over to the rental car like the Dynamic Duo heading toward the Batmobile, then took off like they were on the way to the Bat-Cave.

But they still didn't leave faster than me. When I screeched away and turned the corner, people jumped out of the streets and Moms's seat belt locked tight around her chest. She gripped that oh-shit bar and held on. When I turned the second corner, in the rearview I saw Chiquita's purse and Afro fly from one side of the car to the other. I think her feet flipped over and went in the air. I was driving so fast I almost collided head-on with a big-ass U-Haul on the way out the maze of streets to Chino Hills Parkway. The truck was zooming so fast I thought it was about to tip over trying to miss me. Then I swerved and almost hit the two cars right behind the truck.

It took me two seconds to recognize the devil-eyed driver in the U-Haul. Walter motherfucking Sinclair. I screeched my brakes and made a U-turn.

40 / **INDA**

"**I** said I don't know where she is."

Walter hopped out of the cab of the U-Haul, slammed the truck door, and had the nerve to storm away. His brothers were behind him like they were his bodyguards. Neither one of them spoke to any of us.

Moms said, "Your wife is missing and you don't care?"

Walter waved us off.

I pushed my way through his brothers and asked, "What happened? You'd best to say something."

"She tried to kill me," he growled, "that's what happened."

Moms said, "How?"

I said, "And just why would she try to hurt you after you've been *so good* to her?"

"For no damn reason. Your sister's on something."

Walter was fuming, accusing, and babbling. Him and his brothers, Jonathan and Karl, both of whom were short as me but about as big as Walter, with serious Bozo-the-clown receding hairlines, were with him. And I don't have to tell you how many times both of the idiots had tried to get my number.

Walter mumbled, "Crazy-ass bitch tried to burn me and the damn house down."

I said, "What was that you just said?"

"What ain't what I said."

And that was when Chiquita did her job and held my arms at the elbows to keep me from rushing up in Walter's face, nails extended and teeth showing. And like I told you before, sistuh had a grip. I yelled, "What the fuck did you do to my sister?"

Moms said, "Inda, darling, no."

Pops said, "Inda, stop it. That won't do your sister any good."

Pops sounded like he was an ambassador at the UN negotiating for hostages. I took a breath and straightened my bra and T-shirt. Pops don't want a sistuh to get emotional, fine.

"Walter." Moms ran her hand over her head and calmly asked, "You want to calm down and tell me what happened between you and Valerie?"

"She's crazy, that's what happened."

Pops tried to talk to him, but Walter walked away and opened the garage door. Pops asked, "Mind if we come inside out of the heat?"

"Yeah. I mind. Why don't you get off my property."

And let me tell you, after that attempt at being civil didn't work, the conversation got a bit loud, the Inda-mouth cranking up and leading the way. What pissed me off was my parents were two inches away so I couldn't talk the way I really wanted to. When

Walter and his brothers started taking the furniture out of the house and wouldn't answer any questions, Moms started flipping out. Tears were jumping off her face. And that pissed everybody off, because you don't upset Moms and walk away like she ain't shit. Now Pops was holding her back. Then Brown stepped in between Pops and Walter. And you know Inda had to jump in between Pops and Walter. Then Chiquita had my damn arms at the elbows again. Then Moms jumped in front of me. The cycle continued.

Pretty soon everybody was shouting at each other. I said forget the dumb shit, adjusted my bra, wiped my brow, and went to my car to get the .380.

All the Community Watch neighbors were out watching their community's court jesters, everybody either had their arms folded or hands in pockets and were giving us that there-goes-the-neighborhood glare.

Chiquita was flapping her hands, following me, chewing her lip. She tried to cut me off. "What are you doing?"

"Looking for Roscoe."

"Who?"

"My .380."

The reason I had a gun was because some of the supervised visits between parents and children got out of hand from time to time, and some of my cases were in East LA and other not so nice boroughs with not so nice parents, so a sistuh needed to be more prepared than a Boy Scout. And right now I was ready to send my rude so-called brother-in-fucking-law on a Jimmy Hoffa camping trip and pack myself up and move into Sybil Brand with the rest of the felons. Maybe stay local and kick it at the Chino Correctional Facility for the next thirty-to-life.

Before I could reach under my seat, three police cars whizzed around the corner with the lights flashing and the sirens on.

41 / **VALERIE**

The night Valerie disappeared and left Walter soaked with chemicals, she drove north. Looked at the star of freedom and drove with it being her guide. Little money in her pockets. Tears in her eyes and no destination in mind. No destination in her heart. Just rode. In the slow lane doing somewhere between fifty and fifty-five. Toward Canada.

When she reached Pasadena, she got off the 210 at the Lake exit, turned around and went back the way she had come. Thirty minutes later she was there.

Valerie rang the doorbell twice before Daniel opened. He had on the same pj's she'd worn when she spent the night. When she walked in, he hugged her. "Where did you call from?"

"Grocery store around the corner. Lucky's."

"You're trembling. What's wrong?"

Valerie kissed him on his lips then slid her tongue deep into his mouth. After their first kiss, Daniel looked surprised and was about to say something, probably about the gasoline-like smell all over her clothes, but she cut him off. "Don't ask."

Daniel said he'd go down and move her car to his garaged parking and leave his yellow 300ZX in visitors' parking. When he came back up with her suit-cases, Valerie was sitting on top of his bed. Hands at her sides. Legs crossed. Nude. Big fluffy white towels were out. The shower was running, waiting for them. She stood and walked to Daniel. Again she kissed him as she took off his pajamas.

When he opened his mouth, "Valerie—"

She smiled and put her hand on his mouth. "Don't ask."

42 / **VALERIE**

When Valerie finally called Inda after eleven on Wednesday night, big sister was furious because Valerie had left a suicidal message on her machine and then disappeared. Nobody knew where Valerie had gone.

On Monday Valerie had flown to Palm Springs, gone by a bank, and withdrawn all the money in her and Walter's joint savings and checking, which came to about three thousand dollars. Walter had deposited his bonus. Before she left she'd gotten cash advances on all of their credit cards, three of them that had never been used—another seven thousand dollars. She kept three hundred dollars for herself and got money orders for the rest. She overnight-mailed them to Inda. She drew a smiley face on a piece of paper and wrote a note to Inda:

I'm okay. Luv you, Black.

Red

P.S. Scratch my booty.

Walter had added to the paranoia by calling everybody, including Valerie's job, and saying that Valerie was on drugs, that she had suddenly snapped for no reason and had tried to kill him.

On Sunday Inda said she had tried to file a missing persons but couldn't because, regardless of Valerie's habit of always checking in with somebody, she hadn't been missing long enough. Plus, she'd just had a wild domestic with her husband. A scene that the police said was crazy, but definitely not illegal.

Since Valerie hadn't called work, and Walter had called them first thing Tuesday ranting and raving for them to contact him when she showed up because he didn't have any way to get any money, the agency she worked for had phoned several times each day looking for her, trying to find out what had happened and asking what they could do to help.

Their mother was at Inda's pulling out her hair when Inda told her about the vague, irrational note and the money orders she got by Express Mail Tuesday morning. After Inda told her how much money it was, her mother said she thought Valerie had been kidnapped and the kidnappers made her write that note. But Inda reminded her that kidnappers don't send you money—you send them money.

Pops was in LA staying with Brown in case Valerie showed up there first. Baby Brother was "bringing some of his homies" down from LA to have a back-room talk with Walter when the sun went down. Inda had panicked and took the tape from her answering machine with the message and the note to the police.

Valerie yawned and said a serene, "Oh, yeah, I forgot about that message. Tell Moms and Pops I said hi, and deposit the money orders in your bank account until I need some cash. I'll need some of the money for a retainer fee."

"*Forgot!* Retainer fee? Where the hell are you?"

"Chilling."

"Valerie, talk to me now." Inda's words overlapped, "What's going on—"

Valerie dropped the phone into her naked lap, immediately absorbed by a bittersweet feeling. When she finally put the phone back up to her face, Inda was back on the line babbling her relief.

Without explanation, Valerie smiled and said an abrupt, "I'll be in touch."

Inda was still talking when Valerie hung up the phone.

Valerie looked over at the sleeping Daniel. The man who had fed her, bathed her, clothed her, satisfied her with so much affection. All done with tender kisses and kind words. So many kind words.

He was overcoming, so she knew she could overcome. With what she felt inside, it would take a long time. But it wouldn't take six years. Probably not even six months. One day at a time. She had nothing but herself, and that's all she felt she needed. That was more than enough.

She cuddled up inside of Daniel's warmth and went back to a welcome sleep.

43 / INDA

For the next couple of months, we all hung out, kicking it like the Six Musketeers—Red, Daniel, Brown, Chiquita, Michael, and myself. A few times in the middle of Oktoberfest, Charlotte and Nelson—that's her toned African-Man Investment Banker from the Ivory Coast—came out of the house long enough to go into LA to enjoy some festivities and swing by a few movies. All of the month we were kicking it at Magic Johnson's *bad*-ass theater in the Baldwin Hills Crenshaw Mall, hanging out at clubs and pool halls in Santa Monica, then hitting after-hours jazz at 5th Street Dick's in Leimert Park, making it seem like life and friendship and family was all it took to make everything right.

Off and on, I had asked Chiquita what she was going to do about the situation with her mother. She didn't know. Felt like she had closed up on that issue, so I let it go.

Right after I moved in with Valerie to help her with the bills, that was less than a month after she'd changed the locks on her doors and pocketed the key to her heart, me and my little sister went down to Chiquita's and spent a couple of weekends shopping and eating. It was a girl thang. Which was convenient because she lived across town from Moms's Mission Bay condo. Fifteen minutes away. After Red and I dropped by and picked up Moms, we swooped Chiquita up and did the mall thang, then dropped Moms off at her crib and hung out at the beach and Mission Bay and met some of Chiquita's friends.

Things kinda slacked off after that.

Red was busy getting her education groove on, studying night and day, trying to make up for lost time. Actually I think she was preparing herself because that cute guy Daniel would be leaving to go to graduate school pretty soon, so I think she was working on some form of a gradual detachment. I know because she started taking numbers from guys that flirted with her, and had the nerve to flirt and wink back, and, trust me, for her that was extreme behavior.

Daniel came by a couple of evenings a week to either take Red to the gym or go jogging over in Walnut Park. Then he'd stop in for a few and cook or maybe they would go out to a movie. Either way, Red would have him out of the house and be in her bed before ten p.m. Then she stopped spending as much time with the brotha she kept saying was "such a pretty man." The man was fine, handsome with nice caramel skin, a bit on the slim side, but pretty? Straight-up handsome, yes, pretty, I don't think so. Anyway, then she switched up and would just meet him out at the movies or dinner or whatever, wouldn't even let the brotha come over, and she would still be back home in a few hours, in her bed, reading light on, book in lap. She snuck out on a couple of lunch dates with a couple of other pretty nice guys she met. Me myself, I was rooting and waving a flag for Daniel. But then again, she'd been out trying to get her own independence and find herself.

I asked Red, "Why don't you let Daniel come over to the crib anymore?"

"It wouldn't feel right."

"Why?"

"Because."

"Go on."

"Too many memories in this house."

"Make some new ones."

She shook her head and blew air. "Makes me uncomfortable."

And that look on her face told me it was a lot more than that. "Walter bothering you?"

"Calling every day. Leaving messages. He wants to get back together."

"And?"

"I have to think about it."

"Excuse me? I know I didn't hear what I thought I just heard."

"I mean, he is my husband."

Well, Red and Chiquita got along just as good as Chiquita and myself. But still Red thought that me and Chiquita had an unusual friendship. Which we did. Maybe that's what made it special. That bond and that wild, hurtful weekend that neither one of us would ever forget. And after what Red had done and got away with, Chiquita was looking at her like she was some kind of folk hero.

Days after that Chiquita was supposed to come up and go to Knott's Berry Farm with us. She called Brown that Saturday morning, about thirty minutes *after* she was supposed to be here at Chino airport and said she couldn't make it. Left a message on his machine out in Los Angeles. Which was sorta whacked since we were all here waiting with tickets in hand. She said that she'd caught some kind of a bug, probably on one of her flights, and the medicine had her drowsy and not thinking straight.

After that, well at first it took her too many days to call me back when I phoned her. Then she didn't return any of my phone calls. Brown said he couldn't catch up with her either. And from the disappointed sound in his voice, I could tell he was really hooked on her and she had let him down. He called me almost every other day to see if I'd heard from her. If he was in love, he'd never admit it. But I knew he was because he's my baby brother and I know him better than I know myself.

And I really cared for that narrow-ass Mexican brown-skinned girl with the cute little Afro. I liked seeing that oil 'n water together. She had him sprung so bad he started to straighten up, attitude wise. Which was cool, because he's finally starting to get himself together. But you do that when somebody special comes into your life. He had passed all the tests, did good enough on the oral, physical, and background, so he thought he was a shoe-in for the police academy. He was back to working out almost every day, either running or training with the other hopefuls down at Dodger Stadium. With all the shit sprouting up in LA, I've got very mixed emotions about that police-shit, so I'll keep them to myself.

Anyway, I'd been out most of the evening and it was way after midnight when I pulled up in Red's garage. It was Saturday night and I'd gone to a play at LBCC with Michael. This was one of those evenings a sistuh should've spent the night and saved the drive for the morning, because after a while riding up and down the freeway starts to get old. But me and Michael hadn't crossed those lines of intimacy yet and I didn't want to put myself in a bad position. Trust me, Inda wants hers, but I don't hop man to man, without a full checkup in between. Not until I was sure that was what Inda wanted.

When I came in the house, Red woke up on the sofa, looked at the clock, grabbed her accounting book, and raced up the stairs. When I saw the cup of coffee and Diet Pepsi on the end table, I figured, knowing her, her weak bladder was acting up and she had to pee super bad. When the toilet flushed, I thought she'd come back down for a few and chit-chat, especially since neither one of us had to get up the next morning. But she didn't, so I guess she was still mad at me and the Inda-mouth. So I decided I'd go into my room and click on the tube and catch a few minutes of *Live at the Apollo*.

I was walking up the stairs, and as soon as I got in the hall I heard Red whimpering. Sounded like a baby crying. I thought damn, after all her estranged and soon-to-be-ex husband Walter had put her sensitive butt through over the last few months, she was probably up in her room, alone in the dark balled up into a knot, and pouting over her jigsaw puzzle of a life. Because I know my sister. She's the type that lives in a city called denial; if she don't say it, it ain't true. Which was why she still hadn't admitted Walter was a mistake from the get-go. Probably never would. And would you believe he started calling over here for the last few weeks, 24/7, sounding like a reborn man. All apologetic and polite and shit. He wanted to see her, alone. Offered to take her to the Bahamas and even get separate rooms. Just to talk. Trust me. Nobody goes to the Bahamas just to talk.

Last night I asked her what she was going to do, because Inda wants to know what she wants to know. She shrugged and said a heartbroken and confused, "Don't know yet."

"What you mean, don't know?"

"Don't know means I don't know."

"Why are you yelling at me?"

"Why you keep asking me that?"

"After what he did to you, how can you not know?"

"Inda, get the hell out of my face."

"I ain't in your face yet."

"Don't make me hit you."

"Ain't nothing in this room but space and opportunity."

"Let my arm go."

"Ouch. You broke my nail."

"Your momma."

"Your daddy."

"Don't walk away from me when I'm talking to you."

"Shut up."

"You are not going to have me move over here, then turn around and kick me to the curb without letting me know what's up."

And you know we had to have a long, drawn-out sister-sistuh fight. Name calling. Door slamming. Then we quit speaking to each other. And we were a little tense for a minute. Red knows how to carry a grudge. But it ain't my business who she lays with. And you know I felt bad for going off on my little sister.

All that to say that after Red ran upstairs a minute ago like she was still holding a grudge against me, I decided to dust my animosity for her ex off my shoulder and go comfort her for a bit. Sincerely apologize even though I won't mean it. Maybe listen to her heart and support whatever she did, no matter how wrong it was. Just grit my teeth and nod my head while I rubbed her back. After all, she had always been there for me and most of the time she was all I had. Brown's cool, but ain't nothing like a sister in your corner. And I still owed her from the night she came to Long Beach in the middle of the night and rescued me from Deputy Dawgville. Plus I felt bad for not inviting her to ride down to the play with me.

Anyway, when I trudged up the stairs, eased open her bedroom door, and flipped up the wall switch that turned on the soft lights on the rotating ceiling fan, she was booty-naked, spread-eagle with both her wrists in a paisley scarf, tied to her gold bed poles like she was a captured house slave. Her somewhat-of-a-boyfriend Daniel was in his birthday suit, face-down in the motherland working her like he was an Ethiopian at a last-chance buffet. Valerie's eyes bugged open, but she didn't stop her, ah, you know, her little, whimpering love talk to Daniel. I don't think the greedy bastard even noticed me. Either that or he had found the Colonel's secret recipe.

I shrieked, dropped my shoes and purse, and ran to my room and closed the door like I used to do when Moms had caught me tipping out after my bedtime. I thought about throwing a sheet over my head. But I just clamped my hand over my mouth and felt *real* stupid. I'd left so fast I didn't turn the light back off. About ten minutes later there were heavy footsteps in the hall, then an angry tap on my door.

"Come in."

Red stepped in wearing a satin housecoat and whispered, "Forgot how to knock?"

"Forget how to lock?"

She threw my pumps and purse on the floor. It looked like a wet towel was in her other hand. After we stared and snickered and blushed until both of our giddy faces started to hurt, I sang a naughty, "Didn't know you had company."

"Shhh. Quick." Red giggled and made a funny face of victory. "Loan me a couple of your jimmies."

"Loan?"

"Gimme."

I threw her the whole damn box of Magnums. Somebody might as well put 'em to use before the expiration date rolled around. "Thought you were home alone."

"I was downstairs and fell asleep doing home-work." Red looked embarrassed. "He was asleep when you came in. He worked twelve hours today."

"You must be the overtime."

"Hush your mouth."

I mimicked Red, "Oooh babeee it's yours, take it all, go baby-bee, go, yes baby, yes ahhhhh yesss."

"Shhhh!" She turned bone-red. "Did you want something?"

"Grrrl, you make me want to give in to Michael."

Red laughed and closed the door. But I was so

happy for my baby sister that I could puke. She had a good reason to change her sheets. I was still living on the celibate tip and had to change mine to blow time. Still sleeping alone at night.

And there was a patient man across town who wanted me so bad he paid for both of our tests, which came back negative, and was still waiting for the green light of glory from me. And you know after all the drama I'd been through, my light of passion was flashing a bright yellow—caution, caution, caution. As long as I was living in the past it might not ever change.

As soon as I heard Red's bedroom door close and lock, I walked across the room and locked my door. And I hated to admit it, but seeing that wicked shit they had going on got me kinda excited. After I grabbed a T-shirt to sleep in, I undressed and looked at myself in the mirror. At first I was checking myself, massaging circles in my breasts to make sure I didn't feel any lumps.

I held and softly squeezed my own breasts. My other hand lightly ran its fingers around my neck. Touched my own thighs. My hips. Butt. Ran my hand between my legs and felt the lovely sensation that told me I was a woman of needs. It had been a long time since a brotha laid eyes on this four-star package. A long time since my coffee had been stirred. I'd been saving myself from pain so long that I was depriving myself of pleasure.

Then I called Michael.

He answered on the first ring. "You made it home safe."

"Sorry it took so long to call. I was talking to Red."

"So you two are speaking again."

"Yeah."

"Good. How's she been?"

"Tied up." I giggled and yawned. "Thanks for the play."

"When can I see you again?"

"Soon. We need to talk about something first." What was funny was that I was about to ask him the same thing, when I could see him again. And again. I smiled and looked at the paisley scarf on my dresser. "If I make love to you, if I let you inside this body, if we cross that line and become lovers, you know that will change everything between us. It'll be more than a friendship. I'll get emotional and start expecting you to be there for me."

"That's what I'm hoping for."

"One-on-one. For and with nobody else."

His voice smiled. "That's what I'm hoping for."

And let me tell you, Inda got nervous after he said that.

He said, "When will I see you again?"

"Friday night. Saturday morning. Saturday night."

44 / INDA

And let me tell you, I thought Friday would never come. As soon as the clock struck five, I left my j-o-b in Pomona and rode down to Long Beach to meet Michael. Anticipating and nervous as hell. Hoping the love lasted and praying the Magnums fit and unrolled down to the serial number. I was going to him because he'd been driving out my way most of the time, plus traffic heading my way was a bitch during rush hour and a super-bitch on any given Friday, so I decided I'd do the drive for tonight. Plus he lived by the ocean. Alone. Hint, hint.

I was early so I stopped at Cerritos Mall to pick up a blouse. Maybe some nice lingerie and bath oils. When I passed by one of the shops, I had to do a double-take when I thought I saw Chiquita standing there, holding a boss green evening dress up in front of her like she was trying to size it up. I almost didn't recognize her because she'd permed her hair, dyed it black, and slicked it back in a very artistic, Essence model style. The sistuh looked beyond beautiful. Thin and slim with that little bit of a butt she had poking out with the joy of being a black woman.

"Chiquita?"

"Inda?" She smiled, put the dress back, and hurried over to me like I was the person she'd missed the most. We hugged like long-lost sisters, kissing the sides of each other's faces, laughing and holding each other and rocking side to side.

"I've missed you," I said and smiled at her new look. "Your hair is awesome."

"Thanks."

"Why didn't you call me and let me know you were coming up to see Brown?"

She smiled, then a funny look came up in her face. I looked to the other side of the store in the waiting area and saw Raymond looking over at us. I understood. I mean, I could've, should've, and would've turned around and stormed back out, but Chiquita lost her glow and held my hand a little tighter. And the feelings I had for the child had permanently moved into my heart. I just held my friend's hands a little tighter.

I asked, "You okay?"

She nodded. It's hard to talk with a mouth full of guilt.

"Brown misses you."

"How's he doing?"

"He thinks he did something wrong."

She shook her head, no. "How's he doing?"

"Call him sometimes."

She shook her head, no, then said, "Tell him I said hi."

I shook my head, no. "Call him sometimes. At least leave a message. Don't leave him hanging. Please?"

She bit her lip.

"He wanted to know if you ever went back to Memphis to handle your business?"

She said a low, "Not yet."

I didn't say anything. That was her business.

"I will one day."

Even though she was smiling, Chiquita kept that shamed, funny nonblinking look in her cute face. I think both of our eyes started to get watery. I wanted to rescue her, but you can't help somebody who don't want to be saved.

"Take care of yourself." It was so hard for me to say that to her because, you know, it's so damn final.

"You, too. Tell everybody I said hi."

I think we both sighed at the same time. I think hers was from the relief of not having to lie to me anymore, mine was because I knew she was okay, so far as being alive was concerned. And I knew that the next time we saw each other on the streets, if we ever did, we wouldn't speak, we'd walk on by like strangers. So I had to get my last few words in before we parted.

"You know I want to curse you out, don't you?"

She let my hand go. "Take care."

And that hurt me. Raymond got up and started to walk toward us. A real cocky stroll. I think he waited that long to make sure my brother wasn't with me. By the time he made it halfway, I told Chiquita to be safe and I was gone. I actually think I started running.

I'd totally forgotten what I came in the mall to buy. The mall wasn't near full, there was plenty of room, but I still tripped over a trash can and managed to bump into a few people while I was trying my best to get out of there. When I got to the exit and opened the door, Gina walked in. Dressed in a beige business suit and Hollywoodish sunglasses, strolling by herself. She caught the door with the hand that still sported an engagement ring. She looked right into my eyes, smiled, and spoke to me like she'd never seen me before in her life, then headed in the direction I saw Chiquita. I didn't even look back. Not my business. Even when I felt Gina suddenly remember who I was, snatch off her sunglasses and look back, I kept on moving. Even though I knew she was two steps from seeing Raymond and Chiquita, I headed to my car and left the mall. Like I said, not my business.

45 / **INDA**

Later on that night, I drove and parked out in front of Raymond's stucco apartment building, right behind Chiquita's Miata. I told myself I would let it go, but you know how Inda gets. My irresistible impulse had taken over before I could get comfortable at Michael's place. This was on my mind. So I told Michael I had to run to the store for some personal stuff, then drove over to the other side of Long Beach and parked on Cedar Street. I opened my trunk and took out the two red bricks I had picked up along the way. Then I stood in front of Deputy Dawg's dimly lit bedroom window with a brick clenched in each hand and thought about the time I bricked what's-his-face's apartment.

I walked around to Raymond's front door and gently set the bricks down so when the door opened, they'd knock over. He'd have to notice them. I just hoped that one day I'd get to the point where I didn't need any bricks in my life. I could throw garbage on his car, spray-paint WHORE on the windshield, but I really didn't see the point. When I got through, other than me getting funky from mixing in the garbage, not a damn thing would have changed. So I guess this and last month's therapeutic barrel-burning of every Hallmark card and gift he ever bought me were my ritual of letting go. But, then again, just because he wasn't mine, Raymond could be Chiquita's soul mate. Never know. And if he wasn't, it wasn't my business.

Sometimes you have to let people change and grow on their own, you have to back off and hope it turns out for the best. That's what I did with Red when she hooked up with Walter, just let her make her own mistake. She had to grow at her own painful pace.

Actually, even though I'd thought about it, I didn't come down here to see Raymond. Even though he still had my Betty Boop and owed me fifty dollars from awhile back, it didn't matter: fifty dollars and a T-shirt with the picture of a dumpy white woman on the front was a cheap price for freedom. And I wasn't here for him anyway. The love that had me out here wet-eyed and in pain was the love I felt for Chiquita. I didn't want to see my friend get hurt any more than she already had.

And would you believe Deputy Dawg still had the nerve to ring my phone a few days back? When I hung up in his face, he called back later and left messages asking me to meet him somewhere. As far as I'm concerned he was never really in my life and he had been out of my mind for weeks. He wasn't worth a thought. Five years from now he won't even matter. I just missed my innocent sistuh-friend who had the energetic smile and used to wear the cute Afro. I wrote a note and stuck it under Chiquita's windshield wiper, right next to the two tulips I bought her.

NO MATTER WHAT

NO MATTER WHO YOU'RE WITH

I'M STILL YOUR FRIEND

SISTUHS NEED TO STICK TOGETHER

BE STRONG, BE SAFE

BUT MOST OF ALL, BE CAREFUL.

46 / **CHIQUITA**

It had rained all night in Memphis. But it stopped right before I had parked out in front of my momma's house. I put the radio on AM and listened to Betty Wright singing about loving after the pain. And I kept smelling the two-day-old tulips and reading Inda's note because it was my affirmation of the moment. I kept reading and repeating out loud, "Sistuhs need to stick together."

Something about those words had became my strength. In my heart I knew that even if I didn't know her, my momma was a sister. Not that I wanted to blame myself, but weeks ago when I had talked to Brown about the first time I came out here uninvited, he thought I might've come off too strong. Too mad. I didn't know why, but him saying that sort of upset me. Maybe I wanted him to take my side and be against them.

"Now you know I'm down with you. But to be fair," he said, "I need to hear both sides of the story."

That was the day I was by his side when he drove out to the veterans' cemetery in Riverside, California, to make his peace and say his words over Gwen's grave. When he couldn't take my point of view, part of me felt betrayed, like he didn't really understand me. So I left and went back to the place I felt comfortable because there I felt nothing. Back to the same old bullstuff in Long Beach. And I didn't realize how much I missed Brown, how much I missed sassy Inda, until I saw her. And I could see in her eyes that I'd hurt her more than I would have ever imagined. She was always so invincible, so easy to move on, that I didn't think little old me would even be missed by her. She really cared about me. I know Brown did too because when I said I was afraid to come back to Memphis he had said, "I'll go back with you."

"You don't have to."

"I can jump-seat on a cargo and fly for free. We can meet at the airport back there in Memphis, rent a car. I'll wait out in the ride while you talk, or walk up to the door with you if you like. Whatever you need and feel comfortable with."

"Thanks, but no."

"I don't want you crying over the grave of somebody you didn't know."

"Thanks. But let me deal with it at my own pace."

"It's on you. Change your mind, my offer still stands."

"It's something I should do on my own."

He put his big arms around me. "Even Mike Tyson had people in his corner to help him out between rounds."

I laughed. "He got knocked out in Japan."

"That's not the point. Everybody needs help."

I laughed. "How would you know?"

"I needs a hand from time to time. Ain't ashamed to admit it either. Why you think Jesus had twelve homeboys? He needed some h-e-l-p."

I think the way they were as a family made me realize how much I wasn't a part of one. Since I didn't see where I fit in, I made myself a reason to leave. Didn't feel needed, or think it was necessary to try and find out if I really was wanted in their lives. I was still amazed at how they were that day when Valerie had come back home from hiding out, that was some days after she had disappeared and a few days after Inda had talked to her about what happened with Walter. I was back up there on my day off, helping Brown and his pops clean up the mess Walter had left behind. Then we heard somebody singing the Dinah Washington jazz song that was on the radio, the song called "Soft Winds." And the voice was loud, pretty and clear. Valerie walked in the house, went from person to person hugging, kissing, dancing, and singing. With sarcasm, relief, and love, everybody stopped cleaning up and applauded. Valerie had called the day before and told them she'd be back home that day. I would've thought that she would've been upset with the way her home had been left, but she nodded and smiled like it was the best doggone house she had ever seen.

"Well, well." Her father folded his arms across his

chest and said, "The dead has arisen. Wait until Mimi sees what you did to your hair."

As soon as she touched her head, Valerie's smile went away. I thought she was about to walk back out, but she rotated her neck and said, "Pops, can't you say something nice for a change?"

"You look like that girl what's-his-face Justice married."

Brown said, "No, she don't."

Inda said, "She wish."

Valerie tisked the same way Inda did and rolled her eyes.

Their father said, "But you look better."

Valerie smiled. "Thanks, Daddy."

Inda put her hands on the hips of her jean shorts and said, "Hello, Miss Firestarter. Smokey the Bear came by to have a chat with you."

"At least I'm not a Spider Woman climbing over walls."

"Lunatic."

"Psycho."

"Scratch my booty."

Their father said, "Girls. Knock it off."

I stood back and let them be them. After her father looked at her to make sure she didn't have any bruises, because nobody believed that her lover man hadn't touched her, Valerie and Inda hugged and rocked side to side. Hugged. Kissed. Then sat down and talked serious for a minute. Inda left to go get their mother from next door at Charlotte's house.

Their mother had allergies and the dust kept making her sneeze. Valerie came over and hugged me. "You must be Chiquita."

I smiled. "Yep, that's me."

"Brown told me all about you when I called him yesterday."

I cut my eyes at him and grinned. "What he say?"

"Said you're all that and a bag of chips."

"Red, chill," Brown said. Then asked her, "What you wanna do? Walter took all the furniture—"

"I see."

"—except the old stuff."

"Put some covers over what he left." Valerie grinned. "Throw a paint party. Call your friends, I'll call my friends at my old job, have Inda call all her ex-boyfriends—"

"Screw you."

"—and we'll get some beer and pizza and wine and whatever and paint the whole place."

I said, "I'll invite some girlfriends up from San Diego."

"That'll work. We can kick the fellows out and have a girls' night when we get through cleaning up."

"If my boys come out here and paint, and you got a house full of fine honeys"—Brown winked at me—"you know we ain't leaving before the noon the next day."

"Pops," Valerie said. "Loan me some money, cheap-skate."

"Black, your sister got a loose screw," Pops said. "I know Red ain't talking to me. You know how much a last-minute plane ticket cost me and your mother?"

Valerie stood behind him and threw her arms around his neck. "I'll need some help on getting money for carpet too."

"Dang," Brown said. "We'll have to pitch in for that."

"Yep." Valerie touched the walls and smiled. "Pops, get your baby girl some white gloss paint. And get some new locks while you're out. Brown, change the code on the garage-door opener and the house alarm too. And when Black gets back from next door tell her to start moving her stuff over here. All of her plants will make the place look nice again."

"Hold up," Brown said then came over and stood close to me. "Black didn't say nothing about moving over here."

"Who's moving over here to this tore-up place? Looks like a damn Section 8 crib." That was Inda's voice. Inda and her mother were walking in with angry faces. Their mother was in Spandex shorts and a big man's shirt. Inda said, "Moms, I told you I wasn't lying. Look at what your daughter did to herself."

Their mother looked at Valerie. First their mother's mouth dropped open, then she rolled her eyes and shook her head the same way her daughters did. I grinned and watched them do little-bitty things that told me they'd all lived together as a family. Habits that showed they were connected. Her mother hurried over and ran her hand over Valerie's head. "What the hell did you do to yourself?"

Before Valerie could answer her mother had walked back out.

"Moms, aren't you gonna ask me how I am?"

"Oh, I can see how you are."

Valerie ran after her mother. "Moms, don't be mad. You know I love you. Come sing with me."

"Give it up, Red," Inda said. "It's not gonna work this time."

A minute later, Brown made a quick food run. While the day ended we were sitting around on the scarred-up parquet floor, drinking bottled water, Brown and his father were drinking beer, eating Chinese food, and listening to their pops's radio. Their mother was still next door and sent a message that she wasn't speaking to Valerie until her hair grew back. But what their mother was really doing was, well, she had been to the Ivory Coast a few years ago and was talking with Charlotte's lover man about the country.

"Red," Inda said, "you must be crazy if you think I'd move over and smell *fresh* cow dung every morning."

"I'll give you the master bedroom with the two-door walk-in closet, shower big enough for two, and big round bathtub and vanity mirror, and you can decorate any way you want to."

Inda looked at Brown. "Get that truck ASAP."

I was too busy laughing at the sideways are-you-crazy look on her father's face to talk. Their father put down his beef and broccoli and said to me, "You don't talk much, do you, Chiquita?"

I put down my chopsticks and smiled. "Yeah. Some. I'm just watching you guys."

Valerie snapped her fingers. "Before you clean up anything else, videotape the damage, take some pictures. I'll need them for my attorney."

And I wanted to be like Inda and Valerie—to be able to laugh and cry and talk with my momma and have the nerve to do what I needed to do. But mostly talk to my momma. If only for five minutes.

And night before last, right after I read the note that Inda left on my car at Raymond's place, after I took Inda's faithful words from underneath my windshield, I wiped my eyes and put the bricks she left into my trunk. Then I called work to take two vacation days. I hung up and headed for the airport and came straight to Memphis. I was tired of carrying this pain with me. Tired of doing stupid bull-stuff. I knew the life I wanted, knew who I was and who I wanted to be, but I still didn't know if I'd go up to the porch if my momma invited me. I had come by late yesterday evening and left a note on the door, a note that said:

I'D HATE FOR ONE OF US TO DIE AND WE NEVER HAD A CHANCE TO AT LEAST HAVE A CONVERSATION WITH EACH OTHER. PLEASE TALK TO ME ONE TIME, JUST FOR A MINUTE OR TWO, THEN I'LL LEAVE YOU ALONE. I PROMISE. I'LL BE PARKED OUTSIDE FIRST THING IN THE MORNING.

It was three minutes before seven. I didn't know how long I'd sit out in my car and stare at the house with my heater on low and the windshield wipers fanning back and forward over the dry glass, screeching. My feet were a little cold because I'd taken off my pantsuit and wore my cross-trainers and baggy jeans. I was picking lint off my tan and gold sweater when I looked up and saw a hand come out of my momma's house. Mr. Wilson's fragile hand. Waving me to come up to the house. He waved until I turned off the engine and opened the car door.

I smelled the faint piney odors of a cleanser, burnt hair, and biscuits when I stepped into the small living room that had too much furniture. When I walked in, I tried not to look around, but I did. Faded blue walls. A brown sofa with plastic over the pillows. A black sofa that had a quilted cover over it. A big television that had a smaller television on top. A black Bible on top of that. Plastic plants. Green-gold metal peacocks were on the wall. Next to that was a picture of roses in a clear vase. A two-year-old Ford Funeral Home calendar was tacked to the wall next to an old metal file cabinet with a black clock on top.

I said a soft, "Morning."

Mr. Wilson nodded, sat down, went back to reading his paper and smoking his cigar. I stood where I was. Shaking inside and out.

He said, "Them darn Fords always in trouble 'bout something. Always in the darn paper 'bout something."

I didn't know what he was talking about.

He asked, "Why you come back here to Memphis?"

My eyes widened. My mouth opened wide. I looked deep into the paper where I thought his eyes might be. "Excuse me?"

"I didn't stutter and I know you ain't harda hearing."

"Mr. Wilson, you mind moving the paper so I can see your face?"

"You talk to grown folks any kinna way, don'tcha?"

I pulled at my ear and then patted my hands. I thought about walking out again. But I couldn't keep doing that. "No, sir. I just like to see who's talking to me."

"Respect yo' elders," he said. "I'm listening."

"I wanted to see my momma."

"Uh huh."

"And I wanted to find out about my father."

"Uh huh."

"At least what my momma could tell me about them. I mean, I'm who they created. So I want to know who they are."

"Uh huh."

"I'm a grown woman and I still don't know anything about my parents. I wanted to ask some questions. I figured if I got to know her I'd know me better."

"Uh huh."

"Actually, I had written down a list of things I wanted to talk to her about."

"Why you have'ta write 'em down?"

"So I wouldn't forget. So I wouldn't take up too much of her time if she decided to talk to me."

"Uh huh."

"Thought maybe she'd be happy to see me this time."

"Uh huh. Was you happy to see her last time?"

I didn't answer.

He said, "Uh huh."

He put the paper down, folded it real neat like it was going to be delivered to somebody else. At first I thought his face looked different because of the glasses, then I realized it was because he had his dentures in and they made his face longer.

"You different from Bae-Bae. I pose you been here and there, done did this and that. She been living right here in Memphis all her life."

"I didn't know where she was."

"She always knowed where you was."

"How?"

"She knowed." He looked at me with those magnified eyes. I didn't look away. Today they couldn't make me leave if they tried.

I broke the silence with, "I think I'm missing the point."

Another minute later he asked, "Why you crying?"

I shrugged and wiped my eyes.

"I want yawl to let the past be. If you can't, I want yawl to move on and find your own peace. Just 'cause her momma turned her back on her don't mean she gotta do the same with you."

"What did Big Momma do?"

"Your momma cried after you left that time. Wasn't a damn thang I could do to ease her pain. Upset me because I ain't seen her cry in years."

I asked, "You got any more questions for me?"

He looked at the tulips in my hand, then looked me in my eyes for a few seconds. Mr. Wilson's face softened. He shook his head then hollered, "Bae-Bae. Somebody here to see you."

And it felt good to be somebody.

His voice and the sounds of sudden movements in the next room behind the closed door made me want to jump out of my skin.

Mr. Wilson had on too-big pants, suspenders, and a stained white T-shirt. He waved, then motioned toward the kitchen, telling me to go that way. He said, "Bae-Bae'll be out dah'rectly. Coffee on the stove. Fix me a cup. One teaspoonful. Black. No sugar."

"Yes, sir."

The narrow halls had off-green walls and a white ceiling. A picture of Jesus with thorns on his head was next to an old picture of Martin Luther King, Jr., President Kennedy, and Robert Kennedy with birth-death dates and quotations of hope below each face. A maroon velvet picture of the Golden Gate Bridge.

A nicely framed picture was next to that. At first I thought it was a black-and-white picture of me holding somebody's baby. It was a picture of my grandmother holding my momma. I'd never seen a picture of my momma as a child, had never really thought about her ever having been a little girl with a bright smile. I'd never thought about my grandmother being a young, beautiful woman. Big Momma looked less than twenty. Momma looked all of one. I must've stared at that picture, at my grandmother's shoulder-length hair and timid smile, at the tiny plaits in my momma's hair for a while before I moved down to the next picture. It was one of those light wood frames that had different-sized holes for different-sized photos. All the pictures were in color. All were of me. In elementary school with two big pigtails and no front teeth, my high school cap-and-gown graduation picture, and pictures in between. I looked down the hall and Mr. Wilson was standing, supporting himself with his cane, watching me. We looked at each other for a second, then he turned and walked away. He groaned as he let himself down on the sofa. I put the flowers on the table and got a cup from the countertop.

"One teaspoonful. Black. No sugar."

"Yes, sir."

I made his coffee and set it on the coffee table in front of him. His shaky hand reached over for the cup. I picked it up and put it in his hands.

"One teaspoon, black, no sugar?"

"Yes, sir. One teaspoon, black, no sugar."

I stopped and looked at the pictures again before I went back into the kitchen. I made a cup of coffee and set it in front of me, right next to the ashtray and half pack of Salem. A dark roach came down the yellow wall, walked past the white gas stove, and crawled across the floor toward me. I stepped on it and the crunch made my doggone flesh crawl. I wiped my tennis shoe on the rust-colored mat by the back door. I looked out the window and saw their backyard with wire clothesline running from two rusty iron poles. Dogs were barking next door.

When I turned around, my momma was standing in front of me. She had on a too-big flowered dress, too-dark hose, and scuffed dark blue shoes. She'd hot-combed her hair, curled it, and put on some makeup. A little bit too much, not the correct tone for our skin, but what she'd done touched me. She looked pretty; I could smell her Estée Lauder. I put my hand up to my mouth just as she put her hand up to her mouth. Our eyes watered, but nobody cried.

I cleared my throat. "Morning, Momma."

"Morning, Chiquita. You eat?"

"A little. I went by McDonald's."

"Down on Third Street?"

"The one by the airport."

We had the same sad eyes. She sort of smiled and went back to her regular face. I put on my uncomfortable smile and slid my hands back inside my coat so I wouldn't start looking at them or tugging at my ears. I ended up jingling my keys for a few seconds before I realized what I was doing.

I pointed at the table. "I brought you a tulip. From California. A friend of mine gave me two, and I would like you to have one."

She almost smiled when she took it. Her face softened when she smelled it. Then we both sat down, me first. A tulip in front of each of us.

"Rest your coat."

I slipped out of my coat and folded it across the back of the chair. I didn't know what to say, so I just sat there slowly hand-combing my page boy.

She asked, "Your scalp itch?"

"A little. It gets real dry in the winter."

"You got that from Big Momma."

I tried to smile, but my lips wouldn't go up.

She said, "I bought this dress with the money you gave me."

"It's pretty."

My momma looked at her hands. "How you like it out there in California?"

"It's nice."

"Earthquake scare you?"

"Sometimes. Not really. Get used to it after a while."

"You done got married and had babies yet?"

"No, ma'am. I met somebody I like a lot, though."

"He hit you?"

"No ma'am. Why you ask that?"

"Your right cheek red."

I touched the side of my face. It still stung a little bit. "Yeah. My, uh, my ex-boyfriend hit me. Sorta. When we got into an argument."

"What you do?"

My voice lowered. "I caught him with another girl. Again."

"Uh huh."

"But that isn't the man I'd like to be with, though."

"Then why you with him?"

That made me blink because I didn't have an answer. "I sorta messed it up with a real good brotha, I mean man, when I left him to go back to the other knucklehead who hit me."

"He beat you a lot?"

"He, ah, we got into it three, four times. Maybe five."

"What you leave a good man for a pie dog?"

I shrugged and patted my lap. I wanted to say that I really cared about Brown and didn't care about Raymond anymore, but had a hard time connecting with Brown because of my abandonment issue.

Brown read me too well and that made me too vulnerable. I didn't want to fall deeply in love and then be deserted. Part of me expected everybody to leave me, so I always tried to leave first. But I couldn't keep blaming a momma I didn't know everytime I screwed up. I spoke my heart. "Scared."

"Of what?"

I shrugged. "Don't even know. Scared somebody might make me feel good for too long then take it away."

She nodded like she understood. "Johnny the only man who ain't never laid a hand on me."

I didn't know what to say.

"Never touched me but to love me." A second or two later she asked, "The one you like, he nice?"

"Yes, ma'am. Real nice."

"Never stay with a pie dog." There was an awkward pause. "You made out some questions?"

"Ma'am?"

"I heard you say you made out some questions of thangs you wanted to know about me and your daddy. Where they at?"

My hands shook a little as I took the papers out of my pocket and slid them over to her. She moved across the room and opened a small drawer next to the refrigerator. She took out some dime-store reading glasses, wiped them on a dish towel and sat back down.

Her eyes squinted. "Your writing pretty."

"Thank you."

"Real pretty. Just like the note you left."

I thought about Big Momma. She couldn't write anything but her name. I used to think Big Momma could read, because she always looked at the pictures in the newspaper. Mostly the sales stuff. Later I realized that she couldn't read the words, but she could recognize prices and could count the hell out of money.

After my momma looked over the questions twice, she made herself a cup of coffee and took some biscuits and sausage out of the oven. She'd heated up some brown gravy that tasted just like Big Momma's Sunday-morning cooking. While we sat there and ate in silence, our tulips under our noses, I thought, this was the only time I knew we'd ever sat down and ate together. The only peaceful moment.

When she finished she got her coat and we walked out to my car. Mr. Wilson was standing in the door when we pulled off. With his overcoat and glasses on, he sat down, lit a cigar, and guarded what was his.

47 / **CHIQUITA**

When we parked out in front of Big Momma's old house, cool rain drizzled from the cold gray skies. Ten minutes later it stopped almost as fast as it had started.

And while I drove, I was thinking about Brown, wondering if I'd done something that couldn't be undone.

On the way over, as we drove down Parkway across Florida and down Kansas, I tried to remember the places I passed. I knew I'd been to some of them. It looked a lot rougher than I remembered back then. Now Memphis had carjackings, gangs, and drug busts, just like the West Coast.

Nothing looked familiar except the five-room house where I grew up. Even though it was bricked over and had white awnings, it looked the same, just all dressed up. The hedges were cut down, a fence put up, the driveway paved over, the shed torn down, plum tree cut away, but it was the same house. Minus the furniture, I could probably blindfold myself and walk around from room to room.

The wrought-iron front door to 1858 opened and a little girl dressed in baggy jeans, sweatshirt, and winter shoes walked out with her coat in her hand and headed toward the Riverview schools. She wore her pants hip-hop style. A second later, a smooth-skinned woman with big yellow rollers walked out in her red-hooded housecoat holding a small paper sack.

She put her hand up to her mouth and called out, "Nancy."

The little girl ran back. The lady bent over and fussed at her. Nancy straightened out her pants and put her coat and gloves on while the lady fussed. The lady gave Nancy the sack lunch. They hugged. They kissed each other's cheek. Both waved bye-bye. The little girl skipped and ran to make up for lost time. She stopped running at the spot she would've been if her momma hadn't called her back. She opened the sack, took out an apple, and started eating it. A few feet later, three more children ran out of a house and they all walked away toward wherever. Her momma was still watching. When they got out of sight, the lady saw us. She smiled, waved at us, and went back in her house.

My momma was watching as hard as I. The tulip I'd given her was still in her hand. She looked like she had a face filled with memories. Me, too.

I asked, "When was the last time you been over this way?"

She said, "I ain't. Don't have no need to come this way."

Hurt was in her voice when she said that. Enough

hurt for me to sit still and not push the issue. I waited. She had asked me to bring her over here, but I didn't know why. She looked like she was in a different time and place.

"I want you to listen, 'cause I ain't gonna say it no more after today. You come all the way from California to ask and I owe you that much. Then I'm gonna let it rest."

"Yes, ma'am."

She said, real careful, "Listen good."

Her voice had emotion, tears in each word. I said a soft, "Yes, ma'am."

A few seconds later she cleared her throat again, then nodded her head for a while. "I got pregnant the first time when I was fourteen. Young boy named Early who used to live three houses over that way. He lived in that white house right there. It used to be a real pretty green back then. He was a little bit older than me. When he found out, Daddy had a fit. Tried to beat it out of me. Big Momma just watched. I called her to help, but she didn't move. I lost that baby. He told me if I ever got pregnant again, he was gonna put me out. Told me that while I was laid up in John Gaston with blood between my legs."

She stopped for a second and rubbed her eyes. I was about to ask her to stop because I felt my throat tightening up from all the pain and hurt inside of this car. Her eyes watered, but still no tears fell.

"I met your daddy and got pregnant again when I was seventeen. I was in twelfth grade at Booker T.

Washington. Daddy found out and when I got hom
a suitcase and twenny dollars was sitting out on th
porch. The twenny dollars was snuck in by Big
Momma.

"I shacked up with your daddy for a while. We
was rooming down off Mallory. I wanted him to
marry me so I could give you a name. Went downtown to the courthouse to meet him one Friday and
he never showed up. I sat down there and waited
all day for that man. Then I found out he was a pie
dog. Found out he was already married to a woman
down in Mississippi. She found out about me, came
up here with a butcher knife, and caused all kinds
of problems.

"When I asked your daddy to choose one of us,
told him he couldn't be with me and married to her,
he said he was gonna take care of us. Said he was
running down to Tupelo to get the rest of his stuff
and straighten out his business with her, but never
came back. Your momma ended up doing what she
had to do to feed her baby.

"Big Momma said a child didn't have no business
out on the streets. So she told me brang you and
what stuff I could over here because Daddy wouldn't
put a little baby girl out on the streets. But he
wouldn't let me come back past the front porch. He
was like that. The kinda church man that felt like
he always had to keep his words, no matter how
wrong they was. Said it was God's punishment for
the shame I brought on him and the church. Big

Momma felt the same way, but she changed when she saw you. Yep. She smiled at you like you was the best thing she'd ever laid eyes on.

"She told me she'd keep you a while till I got on my feet. Big Momma talked me into signing you over to them. Said Daddy told her to tell me to do that because I didn't have nothing to give you. He was working hard up at Slumber Products, clothing and feeding you. I hadn't gave you nothing since the milk left my breasts. I did what Daddy said to do, 'cause he was my daddy. I was young and didn't know no better, just did what felt right for my little girl. I was a little girl myself.

"Next time I saw you, they had you calling them Momma and Daddy. Called me Miss Thompson and looked at me like I was a stranger off the streets. You was all I had and they had took that away."

I wanted to say I was sorry, but I didn't know how it would sound.

She stared at the house. "Daddy was wrong. He did some bad thangs to me don't nobody know about."

I asked, "What kind of things?"

"Don't matter." She looked at her hands. "No need wishing bad on the dead."

I wanted to know, almost had to know, so I asked a soft, "Did my daddy have any more children?"

She hunched her shoulders. She fanned her dress. "After he broke his promises, I never heard from him again."

I wiped my eyes. "I'm sorry, Momma."

"You don't have'ta call me Momma. I ain't earned the right."

"Why you say that?"

She messed around her dress. She looked at my manicured nails, my trendy clothes, then looked at herself. "I ain't nobody you want for a momma."

"Don't say that."

"I ain't nothing much. Ain't never done nothing to let people know I passed this way."

Her sincerity shocked me and I didn't know what to say.

"You got any more questions you need to know?"

"Yes, ma'am."

"Go ahead."

I wiped my eyes. "When's your birthday?"

She sounded hurt when she said, "July seventeenth. Yours is April twenty-third."

"Twenty-first."

"That's right, that's right. The twenty-first. 'Cause your daddy had just turned twenty-one."

I looked at my hands and thought for a second. "What's your favorite color?"

She thought a second and sort of smiled. "I like sky blue. Johnny took some of his disability check and bought me a nice sky blue dress from Woolworth's last year, but I messed it up awhile back in the washing machine down at the laundry. He said I looked real nice in that dress. I like sky blue."

"You like flowers?"

"I like tulips. They pretty. Like the way they smell."

I think that was when I realized my momma was crying. Not tears. But it was that kind of crying you did when you didn't have any tears left. When they'd all been used up. The crying brought on by too many hard years. And I understood her obscure smile. Most of it had been taken away, but she'd held on to the corners.

"You need anything?"

She looked down at my car radio and said, "I always wanted one of those walk radios. They nice."

"Okay."

Her saying she wanted a gift was sort of strange to me, because I think I began to understand her. Like I'd used my body to get acceptance, she used gifts and money to get hers.

She went back to looking at the house and nodding her head at her deep thoughts as her face went through a rainbow of expressions. When her window clouded up, she wiped away the fog and kept on looking. I turned the heat back on so the windows would stay defrosted, so we could see the house that had different meanings.

"Momma?"

"Uh huh?"

"How did you get my pictures?"

"Big Momma. She sent me some off and on. After I got settled with Johnny, she'd sneak off next door and call every now and then. Three, four times a year. She'd write her name in the middle, then got one of the neighbors to address the envelope for her. Big Momma knew the address by heart."

"Did Big Momma do something to you?"

"What Big Momma did was worse than doing something. She did nothing."

"What about Uncle Vernon?"

"My half-brother was gone off to the army before I turned twelve. Me and Vernon ain't never had much to do with each other. Vernon could be a cold fish when he wanted to."

"I've got Uncle Vernon's phone number if you want to get in touch with him."

She paused then said a soft, "Maybe one day."

I didn't know how many of her words I believed, I didn't know if I believed any. I didn't try to judge how she believed, how she perceived what happened.

My weeping heart wanted to question all she'd said because Big Momma and Daddy were nothing but nice to me. Both were cookies and smiles. They were ice cream in the summertime and hot chocolate when it got cold. But, then again, I was a different child from my momma, and by the time I came along they were different parents. Maybe it was part of that Southern upbringing that made it all come out like that. Made her feel like the black sheep. And her being pregnant out of wedlock back then was looked at differently than now. I could get pregnant and nobody'd have a second thought. The biggest question would be if I was going to keep it, and if I was, how long would I be on maternity leave. And even if I never said who the father was, nobody'd be too judgmental.

She was still silently staring out the window, looking at the house we grew up in like she wanted something back. Like she had left something inside.

"Momma?"

"Un huh?"

"Want me to tell that lady we used to live there and ask if we can look around inside?"

She didn't answer. Then she said, "Let her be. That's her home."

From where I was sitting, from her profile, she looked so much like Big Momma.

A minute later she said, "When I was at John Gaston having you some white nurse held my hand and wiped the sweat out my eyes while I went through labor. Nice lady. Real friendly. Wish I could remember her name. Thank it was Miss Juanita. Yeah, that was it. Her name was Miss Juanita and she had a funny last name. Real nice looking. She talked funny. Thank she was from some part of New Yawk. She took real good care of me. I would've been down there by myself if it wasn't for her."

"She named me Chiquita?"

"Uh huh." Her voice softened. "She asked me if she could. I thought it was pretty."

Another minute later I said, "Momma?"

"Uh huh."

"Ready to go?"

"Few minutes. Few more minutes."

I put my hand on her hand and she clenched mine. I asked, "You okay?"

"When you fly out?"

"Couple of hours."

"You like that rap music?"

"Yeah. Some of it. I listen to it."

"I can't make out what they talking about."

I laughed a little. "You're not missing anything."

"Put the radio on WDIA. See if Rufus Thomas still play there."

"Okay."

"What kinda tennis shoes you got on?"

"Cross-trainers. Nike."

"Bet those expensive, huh?"

"Yes, ma'am."

"You like 'em?"

"They're all right."

Then we got quiet for a few seconds.

She asked, "What your degree in?"

I said, "I didn't finish my B.S. But I'm going back. Soon."

In college, with four classes to go, I had a hard time concentrating because I was beyond burned out. So before my GPA dropped, I withdrew. I needed a change and took time off. Ended up working for the airline. I had been flying, running from city to city, ever since. Keeping my feet off the ground. Money's not great, but I know how to budget to get the things I need.

I said, "I'd still rather be a physical therapist."

"That what they was learning you?"

"Yes ma'am. That's what I was learning."

"That's good. That's real good." She said that like she was so proud of me. She looked at the house.

I asked, "What you thinking about?"

She sniffed the flower, her voice was soft. "I wonder who I was named after."

Sometime later as the rain started back, she said, "Okay, baby. Momma's ready."

My voice cracked, "I'm sorry, Momma."

Her voice sounded as delicate as mine. "It ain't nun'a your fault. Nun'a your fault."

As soon as I pulled away from the curb, she looked at me with one of those Momma looks. "You the only thang I ever done that came out right."

I pulled over and cried. I took my wall all the way down and cried. While I let loose of all the tears I'd been holding back, all the tears I owed her because she never got the chance to be my momma, all my tears from never being her daughter, she patted her little girl's hand and cried her silent maternal tears until I stopped.

48 / **CHIQUITA**

Mr. Wilson was still sitting on the front porch when we pulled up. He spoke with his eyes, then went back to looking straight ahead toward West Memphis. The way he was staring, it looked like Mr. Wilson could see through Arkansas all the way to some part of Dallas.

We walked up the wet steps to the dry porch. Momma went inside because her shoes were hurting her corns.

"How you doing, Mr. Old Man?"

He shook a finger at me. "Keep on living, you'll see."

"Ain't you afraid you'll catch a cold?"

He coughed and shook his head. He asked, "Bygones be bygones?"

I thought about what he was asking, then said, "Bygones be bygones."

He gave me one of those smiles, one that showed only at the corners of his lips.

I said, "Can I ask you a question?"

He looked at me.

I lowered my voice. "What's a pie dog?"

"A mangy mutt that run round summa everywhere. Eat outta your yard, then tomorrow go over to your neighbor's. Scavenger."

"Oh. A Raymond."

When I said his name, I felt nothing but relief. I wanted to hate him, but I couldn't. He didn't know it, but he had a purpose. If I didn't meet him, I never would've met Inda. And if I hadn't met Inda, I wouldn't have had a chance to talk to my momma. And now that I knew his purpose had been fulfilled, he was history.

When I stepped inside, my momma had taken her coat off and laid it across the black sofa. She was holding my yellow sheets of paper that I wrote the questions on in front of her. Held them like they were more precious than the Bible. She raised them up. "You need these back, Chiquita?"

"No, ma'am."

"You mind if I keep 'em?"

"Why you want to keep them?"

"I like looking at your handwriting. It's so pretty. I ain't never seen nothing you wrote before and I want to keep it, if you don't need it."

I smiled my okay.

"Now I'm gonna let you know, I don't like telling folks good-bye, so I ain't gonna walk you to the car. I hate watching you leave. But you more than welcome to come back anytime you feel like it."

"I'll be back."

"Don't put yourself out. You got a job and a life

way 'cross the country. If you out this way, I'd like to see you. Maybe fix you something t'eat."

"Momma, I fly for free. I can come on one of my off days. I can fly you to see me for free."

"I ain't never been on a plane."

"Then I'll fly out and fly you back for a few days."

She shook her head and whispered, "I have to be here to make sure Johnny take his medicine."

"Bring Mr. Wilson."

"He ain't going no farther than that porch. The only time he left was when he went off last night to pay the light bill. They was gonna cut it off day after tomorrow."

I watched her look out at him. I watched the way she looked at him and understood the bond with her lover man.

"May I use your phone?"

"We don't have a phone, baby."

"How would I get in touch with you?"

Her body brightened up and she moved over to the sofa and got a chewed-up pencil from behind the cushion. Then she tore off a piece of paper and wrote. She took her time and wrote real slow. When she finished she looked it over and gave it to me. "This here's the number to the folks next door. Miss Lucille. She hard'a hearing so you gonna have to talk real loud. Ask her to run get Bae-Bae and she'll step out on her porch and holler my name. Say it to her real loud. Don't call after it get dark. She go to bed with the sun and won't answer her phone to save her life."

"Okay." I looked at her note and said the number out loud so I could make sure it was right before I left.

She looked at me and said a soft, "You all grown up."

"A little. Just on the outside."

She handed me the yellow paper. "Write down your address so I can see if I can send you something for your birthday."

I didn't argue. I wrote and gave her back her yellow paper.

She looked at my new writing. "My writing ain't as pretty as yours."

I looked at hers and smiled. "Yes it is."

She brought her tiny body over and gave me a quick hug, then walked toward the back of the house. "You be careful."

"Yes, ma'am."

When I walked out onto the porch, Mr. Wilson stood up. He was a little shorter than me, too. He stood there and looked at me. I said, "Thank you."

"You gone?"

"Yes, sir."

He opened his arm that wasn't on his cane. I gave his fragile body a hug. He coughed then said, "Don't run off 'cross the country and forget about where she at."

"I won't."

When I drove away he was sitting in his chair, sort of waving his cane in the air. My momma had tipped out and was standing beside him with one hand on his shoulder, waving. I blew the horn and waved back.

Already I was free from the pain. I had answers. And I had a mother. A load had been lifted. Not removed, just raised high enough where I could feel myself leave the numbness behind. I felt something coming through me. A real smile. One from the heart.

Now I had to try to correct my other wrongs. The ones with my pie dog. The more I thought about what I felt for him, the more I knew it wasn't over. Not all the way. I owed him a chocolate cake or two. One with my secret Chiquita recipe.

49 / **VALERIE**

Valerie went to see Walter. By herself. And didn't tell anybody where she was going. She picked the place, the only location that she would be with him alone. High noon. On the second floor of the West Covina Plaza right in front of the mall's police station outpost. Over her head the glass ceiling let sunlight pour inside. Blue uniformed officers sat at desks and behind a counter only a few feet behind her. A safe place with crowds of people walking by on two levels of concrete, glass, and steel.

Walter was dressed in dark slacks, white shirt and tie, dark blazer. Crisp work clothes. Valerie wore a short red skirt and white blouse. She stopped four feet from him. Wordless.

The first thing he said was, "You look smaller."

She nodded. Looked at her watch. "Five minutes. Go."

She put her ringless hands on the railing, in plain sight. His eyes batted. The end of small talk. The beginning of another kind of awkwardness.

Valerie listened as Walter spoke of the marriage, the unknowing about the future. His own fears. Outside of Super Bowl Sunday, she'd never seen him that expressive before. He looked as desperate as a losing team with time against them.

"I handled everything wrong," he said, head low, his tenor voice uneasy. "Years creep by and one day you wake up with a gray hair or two and realize you have this huge responsibility on your back. That you have to work so many hours a week just to keep things going smooth."

"That's called life, Walter." She gestured at the crowd walking and sitting in the mall below. "Everybody in your eyesight is going through that right now."

"It's hard. And you think about your choices, think about your failures. Think about the things you hadn't done that you thought you would've done by now. And then you don't see how it'll ever happen."

"We weren't nowhere near rich, but we weren't hurting for money," she said. "We could've talked about it and saved for some other things, if that was what you wanted. Material things ain't all that. You're the one who *had* to get a BMW. The expensive stereo. The Italian furniture. We could've sold the house and got a cheap one-bedroom condo in Moreno Valley and slept together on a futon. Even rented the place and moved to an apartment to give us some freedom to move around. A change in status would've been hard, but it wouldn't have killed us. If we had worked it together, hell it might've made us closer. I could've worked two jobs. I would've done anything to make it work."

"I wanted to do for you."

"For the uneducated bitch on minimum wage?"

He swallowed. "I'm sorry I said those things."

"Don't be sorry. Especially when you say what you feel."

"Will you accept my apology?"

She glanced at her watch.

"I want to do for you." He spoke with more intensity than he'd ever had for her. Then in his eyes, she saw something that disturbed her. Desire and yearning. "We can make it right."

"Walter, why now?" She shifted a few more inches away from his eyes. And her voice weakened with the weight of the memories from the good. "You had six years to talk about that."

"Because I admit how good a woman you were," he said. "And I look at you and wonder if I could give you your dreams."

"I never had any dreams. Just you. Never my own. Until now. And thanks for the offer, but I can fulfill my own dreams."

"I hoped you'd have cooled off by now." There was a long pause. Kindness started to leave his tone. "You're different. Hostile."

"Don't confuse hostility with honesty."

"Your voice is strange."

"Maybe. Yep. Different."

He gripped the steel railing, turned his hands up and down. "Are you making love to somebody else?"

"I haven't made love. I'm not sure if I've ever made love in my lifetime. I mean in the sense that I was making love to somebody who loved me at the same time. And I look forward to the day I do."

"So you're not—"

"I'm fucking a friend of mine."

His body jerked. Chest rose and fell. Valerie had expected him to raise his voice, maybe ask about the unknown male companion, where did she meet him, who was he, maybe not believe that she'd given herself to anybody but him, but Walter's shoulders slumped like he knew it was as inevitable as day giving way to nightfall. First he glanced around at the crowd. At the police behind him. Then he took a breath and calmly repeated, "Fucking."

"I know the difference between sexual gratification and making love. Making love involves a future and thinking about tomorrow and tomorrow's tomorrow."

He blew air. "You're having sex with somebody."

"Fucking."

"That's pretty crass."

"I don't love him. And for me it's a release. The caressing and talking. A companion to go to movies and dinner with. Somebody who respects me and makes me feel like somebody. And that's a very human thing. To need company and to release frustration. Something that you'd give yourself without invitation to me."

"I've never heard you say *fucking*." His eyes

moved away. "I don't like you talking vulgar like that. That ain't like you."

"Don't misinterpret what I said. What my friend gives comes to me with passion. That and a lot of well-deserved lust. And I know that since I've just got out of a mentally abusive relationship, and he won't be around forever, the emotions won't have the chance to get deep and out of hand like they did with you. It'll just be a transitional thing until I get settled with my other things and move on." She nodded. "Until then. Fucking."

"Will you consider stopping fucking?" He sighed like death was inside his lungs dancing around, his voice wavering slightly. "Will you stop being with him so we can work it out?"

"You mean give up something else for you? No." She shook her head, slow and remorseful. Days ago, she had written down a list of things that she'd given up for Walter. Things she had not done for herself. She stopped at two pages. Stopped when her tears made the ink bleed. Then she wrote "things to do" at the top of the list and taped it to the front of the refrigerator.

"Whoever he is, the brother is just using you."

She almost grinned. "And?"

"You say the guy don't mean shit to you. You wouldn't even try?"

"Even if I tried, I'd never forget what you did to me." Then the bitterness rose in her tone. After she swallowed, she looked at him. "Do you ever wonder how old our children would be now?"

At first he looked confused, then his face pained when he realized what she meant. Her green eyes hardened. His pleading eyes softened. Then he looked away. She held her stare.

She let out a faint tisk filled with pity for his shallowness. "I didn't think so."

"Never knew it bothered you."

"What bothers me more is that it never bothered you."

"We can get past that. We could get what we had back."

"Then if you hurt me again, I'd kill you. Plain and simple." She was surprised by the veracity of her soft words. And at that moment she knew coming to see him was the right thing. It validated what she felt. "First time shame on you, second time shame on me. And the second time won't happen. Because without thought or hesitation I'd kill you." She laughed. "And that makes me happy because I'd let myself do it."

His voice lowered. "You're crazy."

"No. I'm sane. Crazy is when you put up with bullshit day in and day out. Sane is when you eliminate the madness and get on with your life."

Valerie hiked her purse up on her shoulder, put her shades on, and walked away. Long, easy strides. The way Daniel ran. The way he'd been teaching her to run and control her breathing and measure each stride so she could go the distance. With each step, freedom echoed in the clicks of her heels, moved with the arousing sway in her hips.

Still, his voice followed her. "Where are you going?"

She tapped her watch twice. "Five minutes are over. See you in divorce court."

50 / **INDA**

Michael and I had owned the perfect evening. For real this time.

We ate dinner at Chin-Chin's in Marina del Rey, then took in a movie at the AMC. Later we found a nice place to hold hands and walk and talk, like we always did on most Sunday nights, this time down on the beach in Playa del Rey. A nice not-too-crowded, not-too-cool midnight stroll that started on the beach and moved to my flitting my feet in and out of the water while I threw bread crumbs to sea-gulls, chased the waves, then had Michael piggy-backing me, and then him chasing and tickling me, and, you know, stuff like that.

Then we got out our multicolored Mexican blanket we picked up last weekend in Cabo and found a nice secluded spot, one of those dark cozy corners where nobody could sneak up on you and catch you doing what you shouldn't be doing, and did what we shouldn't've been doing. And all I can do is raise my hand and go, umph, umPH, UMPH! And it was nice to be getting some much deserved and very sincere affection, under the stars, where you can smell the ocean, where you can see the waves breaking in, where you can see the half-moon shining and bouncing on the water, with a slow-handed brotha who knows how to do what needs to be done to get it done, a brotha who makes you feel comfortable and knows how to take suggestions, and realizes lovemaking is more than just his erection wrapped in protection aimed in my direction, is definitely a perfect selection for—

"Oooo oooh babeee, it's yours, take it all, go babybee go, yes baby, yes ahhhhh yesss."

Sorry about that. I guess what he just did broke my train of thought and sent me into a hand waving Lawd-haf-murcy Inda-moment.

I guess I was too deep into our second groove, had gotten way too bold for my own good, pulled my gold sundress over my head and stripped bootynaked so I could get the full effect of the ocean breeze molesting and caressing my sweaty body while Michael molested and caressed me, when just as I started walking up the sweet road to a nice, healthy orgasm, just when I started to get to that point where I started soft-sucking his neck, had tensed my buttocks and was swiveling my hips and pushing upwards while I kept on massaging his buttocks and murmuring his name over and over, because he loved it when I said his name to signal my orgasm because it made him work it like an Ethiopian at a last-chance buffet, somebody shined a damn flashlight in my face, dead between my eyes. But, hell, it was too late to stop then because I wasn't just on my way, I was there, bucking like a rodeo queen, hoping Michael could hold on for another eight seconds. I screamed and climaxed, Michael screamed and climaxed, and whoever it was with the flashlight just plain old screamed. We scared the shit out of whoever scared the shit out of us.

Blinded, we tried to find our coordination, bumbled around and fumbled the covers back over us the best we could so we could try to find out what nosey-ass was throwing a monkey wrench into my long overdue fantasy.

"Uh, police," the sistuh officer said. "The beach is closed. Closes at ten."

Sistuh-Police shined the light on that *oh-shit* expression in my face. I was so ashamed of myself I couldn't think of a damn thing to say. Even though she was younger than me, I swallowed, dropped my eyes and said, "Yes, ma'am."

The way she was scowling at us, I knew we were on the way to somebody's correctional facility. In my mind I was ready to make that phone call from Sybil Brand or wherever and have Red come rescue my ass one more time. Sistuh-Police shined the flashlight across our cups and bottle of wine.

"No alcohol permitted on the beach."

I said a too-stupid, "Oh."

"Signs are posted."

"It's my fault," Michael said. "I brought it for me. She doesn't drink."

"But I see two cups."

Couldn't deny that, so I didn't even try.

The light ran across our blanket and stopped on the new and the used condom. Now we'd be in trouble for littering too. She cleared her throat and made an irritated tisk noise that scared the shit out of me.

Her partner called out, "Clear?"

She hesitated, then yelled back, "Clear!"

She clicked off her flashlight. "Could you step over here for a minute, ma'am."

I felt around for my sand-filled sundress, finally got it on, wiped it down, and walked over. "I'm so embarrassed," I said.

She looked at me and shook her head. My makeup had melted, hair was every which-a-way, half of it stuck to the sweat on my face. And to top it off, she just saw me at one of my most personal Inda-moments. I looked down at my feet because I had a too-nervous, all-right-I'm-busted grin. "We're going to jail?"

She sorta grinned. "I'll be back in an hour. Be gone."

"An hour?"

Sistuh-Cop winked. "Maybe an hour and a half. And make sure to clear this area of the, uh, birth-control devices."

I blushed like a sixteen-year-old. "Okay."

"And keep it down." She giggled. "The noise. It carries."

"Okay."

She shook her head and waved one hand side to

side as she walked away. "You go, girl. *Damn* you, go."

I think I turned purple. A beautiful, happy shade.

As Sistuh-Cop disappeared over the sands and into the darkness, we lay our blanket back out and let the noises carry and mix with the sounds of the breaking waves.

And while we stole a few quiet moments and cuddled without a word, let me tell you what I thought. What I felt. OooOooo. Sistuh, my sistuh. Now, you're going to think this sounds a tad bit silly, but lean in close, put the book up to your ear and listen with your seat of passion anyway. Now this is what I call a somewhat of a sensitive-butt-naked-with-the-gentle-ocean-breeze-blowing-over-my-body-while-a-man-ran-his-hands-up-and-down-my-sweaty-skin kinda Inda-moment, so I know if I hear it again, it came from you. Between us, understand?

Have you ever been in one of those cold, dark storms, like one of the ones they have down South where it's hailing the size of golf balls, and it seems to just go on and on? One that swells and gets worse by the second and, before you know it, starts to twist and turn into a growing hurricane that you thought would never end? You know, the storm that had oh-too-strong twister winds that kept banging against your too-thin window, and made it seem like your walls were just about to give in on you? And maybe your shutters kept slamming against the walls, almost being ripped off the hinges, and you wished they did get torn off because the constant creaking and slamming was both irritating and scaring you to death at the same time? And I mean it's louder than hell be damned and you can't get away from it because it seems like the roar of the thunder and the constant streaks of lightning will never end so you can have a moment's peace? One of those horrific whirlwinds that sends mile-high tornadoes from hell and it seems like your house is about to be ripped off its foundation? One of those seasons where you just wanna close your damn eyes and either sleep through it or just lay down and die?

Then gradually, just as you'd made up your mind that that was the way it was going to be the rest of your days, just as you were ready to give up, just as you got ready to scream out your surrenders, the winds start to ease off, and the storm gradually changes into a hard rain. Then some of that old fear that was clogging your exhausted heart starts to ease up. Then the hail that was about to crush your panes stops and slows to a light rain. When you take your hands from over your eyes and come out of the corner you scrunched up in, you peep and see it's slowed to a bearable drizzle. You wipe the fear from your brow, remember how to breathe, then step outside. And you see that the storm washed away everything that had an awful odor, anything that smelled like Chino, and left a crisp fresh smell in the air. But most of all, the sky turns blue, birds start to sing, and you notice the sun. You stand back and watch the sun you thought had abandoned you come back. You smile as it returns and shoves dark cloud after dark cloud aside and comes out to smile down on you. You raise your hands to the sun and can't help but smile as it takes away the cold. You feel the warmth.

But even as it shines on you and gives back what the storm had tried to take away, you realize that without the storm and cloudy days, you'd never really grow to appreciate the calm and the oh-so-nice feeling of peace. Without the darkness you'd never appreciate the warm sun on your face.

I guess what I'm trying to say is, well, just that.

Michael has been my sunshine after the storm.

Sistuh-girlfriend, he's been all that and a rainbow.

51 / **INDA**

I let my windows down and let my hair bounce with the Sunday sunrise. I jammed my radio on a station playing hits from yesterday, cranked it up as loud as I could stand it when I left Michael's town house down by Cal State Long Beach. Rejuvenated with hope. I drove up 7th Street with pretty-boy El DeBarge telling me he couldn't get enough and Michael Jackson telling me I was not alone, got on the 605 with R. Kelly calling my body right before Tevin wanted to talk to me for a minute, broke the speed limit by a good twenty with Bloodstone taking me on a Natural High, then Jon B. and Babyface told me I was someone to love, merged to the 60 with Johnny Gill trying to rub me the right way, whizzed up the 71 and helped Toni Braxton breathe again, crossed Pipeline and headed for the crib, pointing my finger, doing the neck and trying to outsing Aretha Franklin, letting her man know she was willing to forgive—but she can't forget.

I screeched my brakes and screamed my best scream of joy when I saw my fat cat Carlton was sitting in the driveway, looking like he'd never left and was waiting for me to come home and feed him.

But when I jumped out and bounced up and down and called his name, as usual, he slowly turned his head and looked at me like I was crazy. He had been so evil since I got him neutered. I hugged him anyway. He should learn to appreciate the concerned woman I am. Not every sistuh cares about you enough to cut your balls off.

I said a babyish, "Where you been, huh? You run off from your momma?"

He yawned and turned his head. I think he extended the middle finger on his left paw.

"And I'm happy to see you, too."

Just then the front door opened. I heard Red yell my name and ask me what was my problem. My little sister was barefoot in coochie cutter shorts over black stretch pants and a ragged T-shirt. Looking like a hooch in training.

I asked, "Running today?"

"Already ran with Daniel. Did three. Nonstop."

"Congratulations." I grinned. "What'cha doing now?"

"Studying."

I pointed. "Carlton came back."

She smiled. "He's been there all morning."

"How'd he get over here?"

"I went over and looked around your old complex. He had moved in with one of your neighbors. One with female cats."

"Figures."

She took off her reading glasses and bent over

laughing when she saw me on the concrete in my baggy jean shorts and T-shirt, rolling around like a five-year-old and teasing Carlton.

Red said, "Got another surprise for you."

"What?"

"Be open-minded."

"Walter's here?"

"Don't mess up my morning."

"What?"

"Just be open-minded. Promise?"

I tisked. "Promise."

Red walked back in and a second later Chiquita walked out. I let my Carlton go, got up and straightened my clothes.

She finger-waved, exhaled, and said a shaky, "Hi."

"Well, hi yourself. Long time no see."

She had a nice lip-quivering smile on her reluctant face and a fresh tulip in her hand. She walked over and gave it to me. I could've asked her a million and one questions, I could've gotten indignant and cursed her out for dogging my friendship, I could've slapped the shit out of her for leading my brother on then leaving him hanging, but I didn't. Because I knew where her head was at and knew how it worked. Sometimes even when you know it ain't right, you have to go back until you're strong enough to leave. It ain't fair, but that's real. We all have our own methods of dealing with the madness. So I took the tulip that smelled of love and friendship and gave her my friendliest smile and a loving girl-to-girl hug. And it was all sincere, because me, Red, and Brown had spent a lot of long moments wondering about her. And Brown's never said a nasty word about her.

"I saw my momma."

That took my breath away and made my heart race. "And?"

"We're friends."

Talk about four eyes sprouting tears from nowhere. Her Mexican-brown skin looked fresher. Had a subtle glow. And a damn good tan. Those little stress bumps around her cheekbones were gone.

She said, "Sorry about, you know."

"That's okay. Got your freedom?"

"Think so. Yeah. Got my strength. I can deal. I've been on my own for over a month. Almost two."

"You sure you're back, or just stopping by?"

"I'm back. For good. Got room for another sister in your big fat heart?"

I nodded and looked into her eyes and saw the truth. She looked like a sistuh set free from a lot of pain and confusion. "Yep. Plenty of room for a sister like you in my heart. We got room in the house too if you ever want to move up this way and help two sistuhs pay the cost to be the boss."

"I might surprise you." She smiled. "Love you, Inda."

"Love you, too."

She bit her lip. "Brown hate me?"

"That ain't my business. Ask him."

"Same doggone thing Red said. *After* she sat me down and cussed me out. She cusses more than you now. Then Red made me call your mother and apologize for being an asshole to your mother's only son."

"When Red's mad, she gets to tripping." I laughed. "You call Brown?"

"Grrrl, any-who. Brown didn't swear, but he went off on me too. I mean off-off. I almost hung up." She laughed a nervous laugh. "Then he told me to stay here. He's coming by after church so we can talk. Grrrl, I'm scared. But I'm not running away. Y'all are gonna have to call the sheriff to make me leave."

"Good."

"Still my friend?"

"Yep. My notes don't lie."

After we hugged and rocked a while she said, "You know what?"

"What sistuh-girlfriend?"

"I used your bricks."

I stopped walking, my eyes bugged out and I did one of those Erica Kane, *All My Children,* damn-near-choke-to-death gasps. Only mine was good enough to win an Emmy.

"I put them in the trunk of my car until the right moment. I didn't know a doggone brick could fly so far."

All I could visualize was my girl in a riot mood, slinging bricks, breaking glass, and running like a cheetah. Then I saw a bat screeching out of a cave.

Chiquita said, "But that was after the superglue."

I didn't even want to know the hows or whens or whys, I just let my imagination keep on a-rolling and started laughing. "Chiquita, we too good-a sistuhs and too damn old to be tripping out like that. You're going to be twenty-nine next week."

"Don't remind me."

"Leave the stupid stuff for the teeny-boppers."

"Know why I did it?"

"Why?"

"I *hate* my hair."

I laughed and held her close to me. "You could stand to lighten it a bit. That color makes your face look sad."

"Now you tell me."

As we walked toward the house, she started fanning her blouse and singing the blues. I waved my hand side to side and joined in on the part I remembered: "The way I use'ta luv ya' bay-baaaay, That's the way I hate'cha now."

Carlton looked up at us and rolled his sleepy eyes.

52 / **VALERIE**

Valerie was dressed in purple sweats, sitting bare-foot on her kitchen floor next to Carlton. Hair lightened. Toe and fingernails clear. All the curtains in the house were open, so the sun's brilliance gave light to the variety of blossoming houseplants that filled the kitchen and the living room. Her house had become a home turned into a flourishing forest with glossy white walls. Few pictures. Little furniture. Lots of space. KLON jazz on the radio to keep the atmosphere serene.

She loved it.

Earlier, she was in the backyard by the pool stretching and trying to do the splits while she listened to the old Poetic Justice soundtrack on her Walkman. She could easily get all the way down on her right side, but her left hamstring was still a little tight. When side one ended, she flipped the tape over and started doing thirty minutes of intense sit-ups—abdominal crunches, obliques, and leg raises. Then push-ups for the biceps and dips for the triceps.

When she finished working out, she showered, grabbed her notebook and textbooks, then sat on the new carpet with her legs folded under her as she studied. While she read, she half watched the local news on the television that Daniel had begged her to keep as a present. That was on the day she took him to the airport. The last time she saw him. The school had made a mistake on his paperwork, so the three months he was supposed to be in her life ended up being close to six beautiful months of therapeutic pleasure.

A few minutes later, the mailman rang with two certified packages for her. One was her two-week-late alimony check. The other made her smile. Daniel had sent her another big postcard and a small gift from North Carolina. This one wished her good luck on her finals and encouraged her to start preparing for the CPA exam. Even though she had a little over a year, he thought she should get a jump-start on it, especially since she'd been out so long. He said he was glad to hear she was still running three times a week, up to almost four miles each time, and that she was taking a weight-training class at Cal Poly Pomona. He missed jogging with her. He missed her. He wanted to know how she liked working out so much, if she'd gotten used to it.

She fingered her shoulder-length hair and smiled. "I'm down to one-eighteen and a size eight. So, hey. Whatever works, works."

Daniel still wanted to send for her when she had a free weekend, or on break, maybe for her birthday, but only if it didn't interfere with her part-time internship at the accounting firm. He also said he'd send the information she had asked for on applying for fellowships within the next couple of weeks. She hadn't told him but she had already checked on being an MBA graduate exchange student and wanted to spend at least a year by herself in Europe, maybe France or Italy.

When Inda walked downstairs from her bedroom, she was dressed in a T-shirt with a picture of a frustrated Elmer Fudd chasing a jovial Bugs Bunny into a "Wabbit-hole" on the front. Big sister had almost finished unpacking her boxes and had arranged most of her furniture to her liking. When Inda had moved in, Valerie kept her promise and gave her the master bedroom and decorator rights. Valerie took the smallest of the two remaining rooms. Yesterday, she put an ad in the local newspaper to rent out the third.

But before the ink in the advertisement dried, Chiquita had said she'd move in if her transfer went through. She wasn't coming up because of Brown, but because she'd been accepted to college at CSUF, in Fullerton, which was not far from Chino Hills. She was trying to figure out how she'd adjust her work schedule to be able to take a class or two. She'd talk more about it as soon as she and Brown got back from the week they were spending in Memphis and Atlanta.

Most of the morning Inda had been going from room to room, half-ass cleaning up. It was Inda's weekend to do the major cleaning—vacuum upstairs, the mopping, laundry, and dusting. It was Valerie's week to do the cooking and vacuum downstairs. Inda watered and fed her own plants.

Inda was in big frazzled socks, boxers, and a white ribbed T-shirt, walking around reading *Waiting to Exhale* as she laughed and cursed out whatever or whoever she read about. After seven more months, the book marker was still only three-quarters of the way through.

Valerie said, "You might as well go rent the video with your fiancé. Check out Whitney Houston and Angela Bassett and—"

"Shut up with the roll call, Red." Inda gnarled her face then muttered, "I hope Robin gets her shit together before she pisses me off. *Damn*, she's stupid."

"She's not. She's human. I liked her the best." Valerie waved the postcard up in the air. "Finish the book so I can read it again. I want to see how close the movie stayed to the story line in the book."

Inda took the postcard and read Daniel's handwritten romance. "Hummm. Juicy, juicy. Sounds good. Smells good."

"That's the Giorgio I sent him for his birthday."

"You going?"

Valerie smiled, then got up and sat at the dining-room table. "Nope. He's getting too serious."

"He's been good to you."

"He's been a good *friend*. I've only been officially single a few weeks. And I'm happy. I told him to keep in touch, study hard, and let me know if he ever comes back this way after he graduates. If I'm free, and he's free, then *maybe* we'll get together. If it's convenient and we aren't seeing anybody, and we're both healed, you know. But in the meantime, I'm dating, so don't wait for me. One thing at a time. I got shit to do and that's not on my five-year plan."

"He's paying for the whole ticket, right?"

"So?"

"Whatever, Red."

"Whatever, Black."

If you loved SISTER, SISTER,
you won't want to miss
Eric Jerome Dickey's hot and sassy,
cool and wise new novel—

FRIENDS AND LOVERS

Turn the page for an exciting
special preview!

A Dutton hardcover on sale now
at your favorite bookstore.

Tyrel

If all I knew about how to treat a woman was based on what I learned from watching my daddy and the way he mistreated women, then I wouldn't know a damn thing worth knowing.

My father owned a little grocery store in South Central. He went there from sunup to sundown, every day of the week, took money, and made more money with money he took. That was where I got my business sense from. He provided for his family.

And others.

I'd see all of my daddy's girlfriends-of-the-week come and stand around and flirt and eat for free. He'd even take money out of the register and give them a scrap or two. I wouldn't speak to any of them. Neither would my twin sister, Mye. We call each other Twin. Moms never came over to the store from our house. Never. Not even the time one of the stores caught on fire. She had a look in the corner of her eye that said she wished the whole store had burned to the ground. I guess she knew what was going on before Mye told all. Momma had to know. No way a man could carry on like that for years and she wouldn't know.

Me and Twin used to work the store. Only I worked at McDonald's too. Me and Pops were at odds because I couldn't really handle the situation, but Mye knew how to put the women in check. Gave them all a hard time when they came by expecting something free. What I learned about women being good and strong, I learned from watching my own mother. She had serious resilience. Character and integrity. If it wasn't for the respect I have for my own sister, the way she put me in check whenever I did something disrespectful, I'd be just like my daddy.

When me and Twin got into college and got an apartment in Leimert Park—I went to CSLA with Leonard and Twin went to UCLA—I guess Moms and Dad figured we were grown, on our own, could handle the rent and the truth that we, the neighborhood, and the church already knew. After being married on paper for thirty years, they moved out of their separate bedrooms, packed up separate U-Hauls, and went their separate ways. Without a quarrel or a kiss good-bye. He sold the stores, the house, pretty much sold out of our lives. Pops went to Arizona. Moms bought a condo in Diamond Bar, but went to Chicago for a weekend and didn't come back. Twin fell in love with one of her law school professors—an older brother—and jumped the broom.

I'm still in Los Angeles. Wondering when I'll start my own family. When I'll do it right, like my twin has done.

That's what I was thinking about this morning when my financial planner said she could finally meet me for lunch. Only today she wasn't my financial planner. Lisa Nichols was the sister who had been avoiding me for the last two weeks. Which was fine. Because that two weeks had given me enough time to cool off. Enough time to play the message she'd left on my machine over and over. Gave reality a chance to waft in and thicken.

Hi, Tyrel. This is Lisa giving you a call. It's 12:38, Tuesday afternoon. Awkward moment last night, yes. Ahem. Wanted to tell you, wanted to tell you, ahem, I wanted to tell you in person, that I was seeing Rick again and, ahem, didn't get the opportunity to because you didn't—well, I guess I didn't get to page you because I had to go to a possible meeting and, well, plan a briefing, so, didn't get to talk to you and didn't think I was going to hear from you last night, so, kind of awkward with, ah, huh, my husband right beside me, so, anyway I did want to tell you and let you know and, you know, because you'e a friend and sorry you had to find out that way, so, didn't mean to hang up on you. I dunno. I dunno what this does to our friendship. I mean not intimacy, but like friendship-friendship. So; I dunno. If you don't want me to call you let me know. Just talk to you later. Bye.

I was at a Mandarin fast-food restaurant on Fairfax and Slauson. The place was crowded with blue-collar Mexicans and blacks and Asians ordering the three-dollar lunch special. Most people got their food in a bag and left. The booth I was in gave me a view of Home Depot, LA Hot Wings, and a 76 gas station. I had been waiting since eleven-fifteen. Lisa pulled up in her Volvo wagon a few minutes after twelve. Her first time being late. She parked facing me. We were eye to eye. I nodded. She nodded. She opened her door, sat there a moment like she was contemplating coming inside; then at last she got out. Took a hard breath, shivered despite the heat, had a let's-get-this-over-with attitude under her hard expression.

She stood next to her car like she was some sort of diva de jour, her back to the fire station and oil fields, dark shades hiding what I could already see. Uneasiness in her breathing. Mahogany skin, slender, pageboy haircut, blue pinstripe pant suit, dark Ferragamos, diamond earrings, wedding ring.

I nodded. No smile. Just a nod.

She adjusted her jacket, moved hair from her face, adjusted her purse on her shoulder, took a fidget step in my direction.

Inside my head I heard her voice, echoes from the message she had left on my machine the morning after the incident. She didn't have the nerve to call me at home. And I've never missed a day of work since I was old enough to work.

She had chopped her hair off since last we freaked and fled, had traded the Miata and bought a family Volvo wagon, changed her hair and the color of her nails. Lisa sat down at the table and smiled at me like I was a customer at the DMV. The smell of her perfume sweetened the bitter taste in my mouth.

She said, "You order?"

"Yeah. Broccoli and chicken. I ordered you the usual."

"I'm not really hungry enough to eat a combo."

"Take it with you."

She opened her purse and slid me a five-dollar bill. I opened my wallet and handed her a dollar.

Her eyes darted left to right. "Would you mind if we moved to a table not facing Slauson?"

"Why?"

"Because."

"Where?"

"Back over in the corner."

We moved where we couldn't be seen from the streets. When we got settled I said, "How are the kids?"

She cleared her throat. "Malik and Jasmine are fine."

I didn't know why I asked about her children, especially since I'd never met them. I knew that question, that dose of realness, would make her uneasy. She acted like her children were her shame. They were with her husband. When she left him six months ago, he got the kids and the house in View Park. Their place was right next to the Ray Charles mansion. She got the condo overlooking the Pacific in Hermosa Beach.

The Chinese man who ran the business brought our trays to us.

He gave a brief bow and said, "How are you, Tyrel and Lisa? Nice to see you."

We spoke. He left. Smiling, rushing to the next customer.

Like me, the food was silently steaming. Lisa

grabbed her chopsticks and started eating at a hundred miles an hour. Head down, shoulders square and forward. Kept her eyes on her place.

I said, "Thought you weren't hungry."

"Nerves."

Neither one of us said anything for a while. Ate and thought. Made me wonder if everything to say had already been said. Or if what needed to be said wasn't really worth saying.

The first thing Lisa said when she finished was, "It's best for my children."

I nodded. That was a tired line. Damn tired.

She said, "I hate it when you shut down like that."

"Hard to talk in a fucked-up situation."

"How do you feel about it? Don't shut me out, Tyrel."

"Oh, now you want to be a therapist?"

"I've never been in a situation like this."

"Ball's in your court. What do you feel?"

She shifted. "Lonely. I have to make this decision myself."

I said, "Actually, since you've got your husband in your bed, you're already out the door. I just want to know what happened so I don't make the same mistake twice."

Her tone was lean when she repeated, "Mistake."

"What would you call it? Or was I just Mr. T?"

"Mr. T?"

"Mr. Transitional. The transitional man."

"No. It wasn't like that. Everything was going fine

until we had that scary incident two weeks ago last Monday.''

''When I left work early and met you at the Hilton?''

''Yeah, when I got the room. When your damn condom came off.''

''And you freaked out.''

''I didn't freak out. Reality of what I was doing hit home.''

''You screamed, fell on the floor, kicked the wall, ran around the room, locked yourself in the bathroom, and cried 'why me' for a while.''

''Okay, I freaked out. I was upset. I mean, you're nice and I care about you, but I could've gotten pregnant.''

''Would that have been so bad? You know I want to have kids.''

''And I don't want to have any more kids.''

''You're only twenty-nine.''

''Twenty-nine, with two children, and I'm done having babies. And I don't want to have a house filled with babies by different daddies. That's ghetto. I don't want to have to explain to my five- and seven-year-old why their mother is having another child by a man other than their father, a man I'm not married to. Shit, I've got a daughter. That could change her value system.''

''What about your son's value system?''

She blinked. Mouth was halfway open. She swallowed. Tapped the table with the tip of her nails. A don't-do-this-to-me gaze was in her eyes. She said, "It's already hard enough explaining to them why their father and I aren't together."

"How did you end up back with your husband?"

"It wasn't planned."

"But it wasn't as out of the question as you made it sound."

"I was mad then."

"Uh-huh."

"He'd fucked me over with seeing the kids. He'd tell me I could see them on the weekend, and when I got there, he'd be gone all day, then say he forgot I was coming to get them."

"I'm talking about you and him re-consummating the night after you were consummating with me."

"You know how I feel about him. I don't need a man who feels threatened every time I do a little bit better for myself."

"But you're going back."

"You know how it is."

"Wouldn't know. Monday you're telling me how you despise him because of custody. Tuesday you're hanging up on me."

"That moment the condom came off put things in perspective. I have a family and I don't think it's right for me to not give it a second try."

"A third try."

"Okay, a third try."

"Do you love your husband?"

"He's my husband. I don't have to love him."

I laughed.

Lisa asked, "What's funny?"

"That put things in perspective for me."

All I needed was closure. And this relationship that never was a relationship was closed. If she never wanted to have any more kids, then this was a dead end from the get-go. Now I needed to move on to single, sane, and stable sisters.

If all she knew about how to treat a man was based on what she had learned from watching her mother and the way she mistreated men, then she didn't know a damn thing worth knowing.

She said, "How's your friend Leonard doing?"

"He's fine."

"I think I heard his name on KJLH. He's supposed to be at the Color of Comedy or something."

I shrugged. "Haven't talked to him in a couple of weeks."

"I saw him on some sitcom. He's still on the road?"

"Yeah. Comedy is keeping him busy. He's coming back from D.C. tonight and doing a show on Sunset this weekend." I paused. "You know, I had already bought tickets for me and you to go to the Playboy Jazz Festival this week."

"I know."

"And I had bought us box seats. One hundred a ticket."

She rubbed her neck and let out a weak, nervous

laugh. "This means we won't be going. Not together anyway."

"You're going?"

"Yeah. Me and my husband are going."

"Oh. You two have tickets already?"

"Uh, yeah. We're taking the children. You still going?"

I shrugged. "If I can hook up with Leonard. Maybe I'll get him to go so I won't be throwing my money away."

"I could reimburse you."

"You've done enough already."

Before she could adjust her tense mood, or reach for her tan-colored Coach handbag, I flipped to a business tone and talked about who was going to handle my portfolio. I dropped the Playboy issue with the play-girl at my table because I knew she hated to part with her money. I let it go and asked which financial planner was going to plan my finances.

She said, "I can still handle your portfolio. I have no problem dealing on a professional level. That's how we started out. It could work. We wouldn't have that much contact."

"I'm not comfortable with trusting you right now."

"Business is business."

"And the rest is bullshit."

"Right. I handle my business. I've never mishandled yours."

I took the trays to the dumpster, emptied them.

We headed for the door. When we got outside into the heat and blended with the sound of traffic and the smell of smog, she put her shades on. I put mine on too. L.A. felt small today.

I said, "I want you to know, I don't have a problem with your being responsible and putting your children's welfare in front of your social life. I just don't like being the last to know what's going on. I don't like decisions being made without me."

"What you're saying is you like to maintain your control."

I didn't answer. The underlying accusation pierced and stung. Looking at my watch gave me a moment to ease my mood.

She touched my hand and asked, "You want to get a room?"

"One for the road?"

"No. I mean we can go on seeing each other off and on. When it's convenient for both of us. When we can get away."

"Sounds like you're trying to maintain your control."

"Not control. I'm not controlling. Just me missing you."

"Asking for a sperm donation?"

"That a yes or a no? We're good together like that."

"Jury's still out on the booty call."

She licked her upper lip, glanced at her shoes. Looked like she was about to go into a *PleaseBaby-*

PleaseBabyPleaseBabyBabyPlease routine. She said, "You seeing somebody already?"

"Not your business."

"Are you?"

I didn't answer. I just said, "What about your kids?"

She shifted, pursed her lips. "Can I have an hour today?"

"I've got to get back to work."

"Meeting?"

"Yeah. Another corporate tryst."

"Think about my offer. I'm free after six."

I moved my hand from her life. "Thanks for the offer."

"You're right. I don't know why I did that."

The pissed-off mood I had held back the entire lunch meeting seeped out as soon as I left. Coolness changed to fire. All around me were carloads of women. I drove like a demon, top down, shades on, necktie swinging in the wind. My charge to some kind of resented freedom was slowed by a red light by Pepperdine University and the 90 expressway.

A Range Rover stopped next to me. I peeped and saw a buck-toothed sister with a crooked weave, smiling like she was in nirvana. I pushed a button and let my convertible top up.

It was almost one. Leonard should be up. I flipped open my cellular and called my buddy.

The first thing Leonard said was, "How did it go?"

We've been ace-coon since elementary. Outside of Twin, Leonard was the only person who knew me so well he could pick up my true mood from the first tone. I gave him the details.

He said, "You should've known that shit when she didn't call you back. How do you feel about it?"

"I'm cool."

"Ty."

"Serious." I chuckled. "I'm cool."

"You know I'll snatch that weave out of her head and break both of her knees for you. She'll come crawling back."

We laughed. His phone beeped. It was the brother who books the Color of Comedy calling him about a show next Friday.

I said, "What are you doing later?"

"Speaking for a few minutes at one of those survivor of drug-abuse programs, hitting the Comedy store and try to get on. The usual. Got time for the gym this eve?"

"Cool. Handle your business. See you at six."

Leonard said, "I'll check back with you in a couple of hours to make sure you ain't gone postal and hurt nobody."

"Do that."

"Learn to vent."

"I'm cool."

"See ya later, alligator."

"After while, crocodile."

I hung up. My smile dropped; brotherly laughter faded in the winds the way smog did after a sweet summer rain.